Also by Catherine Cookson

and published by Corgi Books

The 'Mary Ann' Series

The 'Mallen' Series

By Catherine Cookson as Catherine Marchant

House of Men

Catherine Marchant

CORGI BOOKS
A DIVISION OF TRANSWORLD PUBLISHERS LTD

HOUSE OF MEN
A CORGI BOOK 0 552 11372 7

Originally published in Great Britain
by Macdonald and Jane's

PRINTING HISTORY
Macdonald and Jane's edition published 1963
Corgi edition published 1975
Corgi edition reprinted 1975
Corgi edition reprinted 1977
Corgi edition reissued 1980

Corgi Books are published by Transworld Publishers Ltd.,
Century House, 61–63 Uxbridge Road,
Ealing, London W5 5SA.
Made and printed in Great Britain by
Hunt Barnard Printing Ltd., Aylesbury, Bucks.

House of Men

1

As I dressed, my hands shook slightly, as they always did when I was excited, but it was a long while since I had felt excitement over anything—two years, in fact. The excitement then had ended in pain, humiliating pain. I had wanted no more excitement; all I wanted was to live my life out quietly in this cottage high up on the wild fells, with my dear parents for companionship. At twenty-seven years of age that is all I wanted. Sometimes I had to tell myself that I was only twenty-seven and was young enough to forget and to snap out of it. Still young enough to like people and want to be among them as I once had. But all the telling in the world didn't alter the fact that I was now half afraid of people—at least, of the impersonal horde of the town, of even the less impersonal group in the office. Perhaps the latter moreso because of their curiosity. "Why," they would ask, "don't you ever go to a dance?" "Why don't you stay and do a show?" "Why don't you take up something at night school?" To all this I had one answer. We lived too far out of Alnwick. We were miles even from Shilbottle or Newton. In any case, it took me nearly two hours to get home, for whichever way I went I had a mile and a half to walk over the fells to my home. "But why," they would probe, "did your people want to go and live out in the wilds? It isn't fair to you." Sometimes I had replied angrily, "Nor were the pits fair to my father; he didn't deserve silicosis." I never went on to tell them that the other reason we lived in the outlandish spot was because the cottage, owing to its isolation, had been selling at a gift price, and my mother, who had had a longing all her life to own the four walls that surrounded her and the land they stood on, had taken a plunge and mortgaged three hundred pounds. She would not at the time take the money I had saved, for she said I would be needing it for my wedding. But, as it turned out, I didn't need it. And so I paid off the mortgage on the cottage, and with my wage and my parents' double pension—they were both over sixty-five —we lived a comfortable existence. That is, when I reached home, for the journey over the past few winters had told on me. But if the journey I was about to take this morning proved successful it might mean the end of that long tramp to and from the bus each day.

It was Rodney Stringer, the baker in Rothcorn, who had said to me some weeks ago, "Bill Arnold is looking for a part-time bookkeeper and typist and such. His building business is growing and he can't see to the books himself, not with his wife being ill and that. Now if you could get another part-time job near at hand it would save you this trek every day."

Rodney had been giving me a lift in the bread van when he said this, and I had smiled at him and said, "Yes, if I could get another part-time job, but you know yourself they're as rare around here as gold mines."

I had always been able to talk to Rodney, even on occasions to laugh with him, but never at him, as some of the villagers did. Too soft to clag holes with. That was their opinion of Rodney. This I knew was because he had allowed himself to be pursued, was even on the point of being bullied into a promise of marriage by Hazel Osborne. Hazel had been born and bred in the village; she had married the village carpenter and odd-job man. Unfortunately, after two years he had died. Some folks put it unkindly and said he had escaped, but, whichever it was, it left Hazel with a young baby and an ardent nature, and with a reputation of hot temper and peevishness. Hazel, at thirty-two, realized that her chances of remarriage were few and far between, so fastened on the most pliable male in the small community, who happened to be Rodney Stringer, the baker. I don't think there was anyone in the village who didn't warn Rodney that Hazel was after his blood.

But Rodney was one of these kind men who couldn't bear to say no or hurt anyone's feelings. And he had almost become Hazel's property when we came to live on the fells above the village of Rothcorn. But after he was seen giving me a lift for the third time in a week, the men in *The Fox and Hounds* began laying bets on Hazel getting her nose put out. Mrs. Bailey in the post office gave me this information. I didn't tell her that they would lose their bets, nor, on being given this information, did I shun Rodney, because I had no fear of any overtures from him. I recognized him as a natural, kindly soul, and not so soft and pliable as he allowed the villagers to imagine.

· But that he had a deep interest in me and my welfare at heart I had proof of, and only yesterday at the latest, for, meeting me, supposedly by off-chance, at the foot of the fell, he showed me an advert in the *Northumberland Times,* which read: "Wanted: part-time secretary to writer. Apply Maurice Rossiter, Tor-Fret House, near Long Framlington, Northumberland."

"But, Rodney," I had said, "it's only part-time; I must have a full-time job."

"Bill Arnold'll take you on. I asked him afore I came up. Only too glad, he said; he's up to the eyes."

"You are kind, Rodney."

I had touched his hand, but only for a second, for the colour had risen in his face and he had said quickly, "It's nowt. It's nowt at all." And then he added, "Why don't you phone them and ask for an appointment? I'll take you down to the call-box at Biddys Cross and you can do it from there, eh?"

I became smitten with his enthusiasm and so I let him take me to Biddys Cross, where I phoned the advertiser, Maurice Rossiter, with the result that at ten o'clock on this Saturday morning I was to go to Tor-Fret and see this man.

My mother's voice came from the foot of the stairs at this moment, calling quietly, "It's ready, lass."

"I won't be a minute," I called back. I was washed and dressed, but I decided against putting my make-up on until I had had my breakfast, and so it was actually only a minute or so later when I went down the narrow stairs which led directly into the living-room. A room bright with china and brass, and sunshine; made comfortable with a couple of good rugs and three easy chairs, and made interesting with a piano and one wall completely lined with books.

My father was already seated at the breakfast table, which was set under the window, and, his face turning towards me, he pointed outwards, saying, "What do you bet I can't see Coquet Island and the lighthouse? The air's as clear as glass. Look. Look there." He was bending towards the window now.

I sat down opposite to him, and I, too, bent forward and looked out on to the scene that was both majestic and beautiful, for now the sun was softening the fells where they rose one behind the other, mighty shelves of rock, driving for ever onwards, touched here and there with grass and heather, and defying anyone at this moment to imagine them blotted out by wet fret or mist so thick that its weight lay on you; or wind-driven snow that blinded your eyes and sealed your lips with ice. And this could happen in a few short weeks from now, for we were at the end of September.

My father was saying, "Look . . . that speck out there against the blue. . . . Down there . . . look."

"Don't be daft," put in my mother as she placed the teapot on its stand on the table. "You'll be thinking next you're seeing Alnwick Castle."

"That's the Head, or if it isn't it's the Island. I bet you what you like an' I bet I could see Alnwick Castle a morning as clear as this, but I'd have to look t'other way," he laughed.

"Get your breakfast now and don't be silly." My mother sat down and began to pour out the tea.

My mother's voice always held a sharp note that would have made a stranger imagine there was no softness in her, and there they would have been gravely mistaken. She was generous-hearted was my mother, and gentle and kind. But she put on a brusque front like the front that lots of women put on when their men are hale and hearty, and working. She kept this front for my father to give him the idea that he was no less a man than he had always been, and it worked well, for my father did not pity himself. Although he couldn't walk far and could never go down into the village unless he was sure of the help of a strong arm to bring him back up the fell, he occupied himself in a thousand and one ways in his "miner's mansion", as he sometimes referred to our five-roomed cottage.

My father looked at me now and said, "You're going to have as far to walk if you get it. Have you thought of that?"

"Oh, I won't have as far," I said. "Not half as far. In the summer, or even on good days in the winter, I could go upwards"—I pointed out of the window to the right—"over Neete Fell. I could get down to the valley that way. I could do it in half an hour, too. And in bad weather I could get a bus from the village to either Long Framlington or Swarland, whichever road is best. I'll have to find out, anyway."

My mother nodded at me and said, "Well, when you see him don't let him beat you down. Some of these writers are as mean as muck, I'm told."

"Oh, Mother." I laughed at her but said nothing more, for I couldn't see myself haggling with this unknown writer. And, anyway, I was quite prepared to have my wages reduced in order to save myself the wearing journey in the coming months.

11

A short while later, they both came to the door to see me off, and my mother put out her hands and picked an imaginary thread from the lapel of my suit as she said, "I'm glad to see you put on your grey. It's a nice cut."

"Shows off your figure," said my father. "An' you've got a grand figure."

"Be quiet," said my mother. "She knows what kind of a figure she's got. Go on now."

As she pushed me gently forward she bent and kissed me swiftly on the cheek; at the same time my father's hand came on my arm with a gentle pat, and I left them and walked down the rough road between the sloping banks of grass and heather. And when I came to the steep incline that would take me from their sight, I turned and waved to them. They were standing outside the door close together, and they waved as vigorously as if I was leaving them for ever. And I might have been. Little did I know that morning that I might have been doing just that.

There were two paths leading down from our house. The one I was on now brought me just outside the village on the south side, and I always used this one because it was easier to get the bus this way. The other one was slightly longer and met up with the main road on the north side of the village—about a mile, I should say, from the village proper.

Some time later, when I reached Rothcorn, I stood in the little main street among the irregular grey-stoned houses waiting for the bus. And as I waited I was hailed by first one, and then another. Mrs. Bailey came to the post office door, which was also her front door, and shouted, "Grand morning, isn't it?" And I called back across the road, "Yes. Yes, it's a grand morning." And Bill Arnold from his yard farther along the street, hearing her voice, put his head around the gate and, seeing me, said, "Hello there." And then he added, "I hope you get it."

And I called back, "Yes, yes, so do I."

And Mrs. Bailey, picking up his words, repeated them

as she looked towards me again, calling, "Yes, an' I hope you get it an' all."

This brought Mr. Shennel, the butcher, to the front of his window, even though he was in the process of serving a customer, and he raised his hand. As I answered the salute I was well awar that before I returned to the village the whole of Rothcorn would know that I had been for an interview with the younger Rossiter of Tor-Fret.

It was strange, but up till yesterday I had never heard the name of Rossiter, and only once had I seen the name Tor-Fret. That was one Sunday last year when I had gone over the top of Neete Fell and crossed down into the other valley, where, after passing some dense woodland, I came abruptly upon a pair of rusty iron gates hanging from high pillars, on which, at one time, had stood two stone birds. One now lay on its side, its legs dangling over the edge of a pillar, while the other lay some distance away on the grass. At either side the land stretched away flat except for the woodland on the left, and there was no evidence of a road beyond the gates. One could be forgiven for imagining that they were the last remains of an old estate. Bitten into the stone of each pillar was a word—"Tor" on the one, "Fret" on the other. I found out, on enquiry, that these gates had at one time been guardian to the main drive to the house, but they hadn't been used for years now.

The voice on the phone last night had said, "Take the bus towards Long Framlington, and ask to be put down at Peter's Well. The road from there leads straight up to the house."

Half an hour later I was walking up this road. The sun was shining brightly, I was slightly warm and very nervous. The road wound steeply upwards around the brow of a hill, and from one point I could make out the dark blur of the wood where it covered the fell far away to the left of me. That would be where the iron gates were. And then I was walking between outcrops of rock, hedge-high for quite some distance, but still there was no sign of a house. Then, turning another sharp bend in the road, I almost fell over a pair of legs stretched out across my path. I let out a stifled squeal. It was hard to say who was the most surprised, the man sitting with his back to the rock wall or myself. After regarding each other with different degrees of amazement for some seconds, it was he who spoke first. "You lost ya way?" he said.

"No, I don't think so. This is the way to Tor-Fret, isn't it?"

"Aye, it is an' all. But what be you doin' on the road to Tor-Fret . . . eh?"

I was inclined to say, "That's my business," when he swung himself over on to his two hands and with his corduroy dusty buttocks sticking upwards he slowly straightened himself and confronted me. He was a good head taller than myself—and I was five feet seven—with a thin face covered with a ragged beard, two small bright eyes, and clothes in which he had evidently spent the night.

"Who are ya? Who ya goin' ta see? . . . The Big Fella . . . Logan?"

I was about to answer when again he interrupted, stating, "You'll get no change out of 'im. You on a begging spree, or somethin' . . . charity like?"

"I'm going on business."

"Aal reet, aal reet. Divn't get cocky. I was just askin'. I knaw a lot aboot them up there. Could put you reet if you hadn't been near the hoose afore. Aa'll tell ya now for nothin' though: you'd better keep away from the back door or Hollings'll give ya his boot in your backside."

I bestowed on my informant a look that I hoped would put him in his place and moved briskly on. It didn't, because his rumbling laugh came at my back. I was, although I tried to pretend otherwise, more than a little frightened. He was a queer creature. The fells bred characters, I knew, but he was definitely odd.

It was a good fifteen minutes since I had left the main road; and I was just thinking that I was jumping out of the frying-pan into the fire by imagining this new post would shorten my trek, when I saw the house. It was made of local stone and was long and flat-faced. Lying somewhat back from the front façade at each end was a wing that broke the austerity of the whole. The house stood on a natural plateau of rock, smooth and flat enough to have been converted into an enormous terrace. I had come upon the house from the right-hand side, and edging this terrace at the far side was what appeared to be gardens, but from this distance they looked a tangle of shrubs and weeds.

Remembering the warning of the odd man back on the road I made my way towards the front door, but in doing so I had to pass two sets of long windows. It was as I passed the second two nearest the front door that the voices came to me. Two men's voices talking rapidly, apparently trying to talk each other down. When I stood under the pillared porch, the voices were still distinct. Then one voice alone was speaking and it said, "Julian was an excellent secretary, and he didn't mind the conditions."

Naturally these words caught my attention and they were followed immediately by the other voice. This voice was deep and cold sounding. It said, "No, but I did. He was costing much more than we can afford and you know it."

"I told you I'd square up when this one comes out. Becker says it's nearly bound to go."

The other voice was even colder now, and deeper, the tone scathing. "Nearly. . . . If I remember rightly, he said that about the last two. I told you before that your work won't have any appeal until you forget yourself and widen your scope. You're not the only one in the world that's handicapped."

In the blank silence that followed this, I looked about me for a bell. All I saw was a long iron rod going through a ring. The top end of the rod disappeared into the stone roof of the porch. As I pulled on this ancient contraption, what I thought of as "the nice" voice came again, saying, "I liked Julian, that's why you made it impossible for him."

"Different species are housed in different ways." The cold voice was speaking in an ordinary tone now. "You put a dog in a kennel, and if you must keep a tiger you get a cage. We have no boudoir in the house—not as yet, anyway—and when we do acquire such a room there will, I hope, be the right specimen in it."

"I hate you when you're being clever." There was the sound of rage in the nice voice now.

"And at other times."

"Yes, by God! And at other times, too!"

I pulled on the bell again, twice now, sharply. I could hear no distant jangle, but what I did hear was a door banging, and then almost instantly the front door was pulled wide and I was confronted by . . . The Big Fellow. The odd man's description sprang to my mind as I looked up into the dark countenance glaring at me.

"Good . . . good morning. I'm . . ." My nervous voice did not finish before the man said, "Oh yes. Yes. Come in. You're early." He looked at his watch. Ten o'clock it was. . . . "Come in." His voice seemed to jerk me through the door and into the hall. "In here." He pushed open a door and stood aside to allow me to enter, and when he had closed the door behind me he stood looking at me for a moment very much in the way I had seen farmers look at penned cattle in Alnwick Market. His eyes moved from my feet upwards to the crown of my head. Then they came down again to hold, penetratingly, my wide-eyed stare. For staring I was; I couldn't help but stare at this man. He was tall, say six feet one or two, and broad with it, yet his bigness did not emanate from his size alone. Perhaps the impression of largeness came from his deep voice, or was it from his face? He had an outsize of a nose—my father would have called it a neb. His eyes were dark brown and deep-set. His mouth was thin and long, and I noticed the upper lip had been slit at one time, for from the left corner to about an inch up the cheek was a white seared mark which, strangely enough, gave the lip the illusion of an ever present smile, not a sneer as one would expect. But a sneer, I thought, would have gone better with his voice and manner than a smile.

"What is your name? I didn't quite catch it last night on the phone."

"Mitchell. Kate Mitchell."

"Oh . . . Kate." There was even a wrinkle of distaste to his nose. "He won't like that. I mean my brother. It is my brother who is the writer."

I felt my chin moving upwards. For a second my indignation at his rudeness took away my nervousness. I, too, wasn't struck on my name, but it was my mother's name and if for nothing else was worth defending.

I said with a touch of what I hoped was quite hauteur, "I have never known anyone else object to my name. And it doesn't interfere with my typing."

He had lowered his eyes, but they lifted quickly to mine now and he stared at me fixedly for some seconds before he said, and quietly now, "I'm sorry. But my brother is . . . well, he's a little temperamental. I had better explain. He had polio some years ago and it left him crippled down the left side. Because of his handicap he has been humoured a great deal, you understand?"

No, I didn't, and when I made no answer he went on, "What wage are you expecting?"

"Well, say four pounds. I could do three hours a morning for five mornings. . . . That would cover part of my bus fare, too."

"I don't suppose he'd want you in the mornings, it would be mostly in the afternoons. He's not too good in the mornings. Well, four pounds, that would be all right."

Not only because it would be a much better arrangement for me if I could come here in the morning and work for Bill Arnold in the afternoon, but also because I had an unaccountably strong desire to stand up to this man that I spoke now as I did. This alone was surprising,

2

for I was not of an aggressive nature. There was only one man in my life who had made me feel I wanted to hit back, and that was over. But I now said, "This house is a long way out, and if I came in the afternoons it would mean going home in the dark in the winter. It wouldn't be very pleasant. I don't think I can see my way clear to. . ."

His voice cut me off sharply, when with raised hands he said, "All right, all right, we'll go into that later. You had better see him first." Abruptly he turned his back on me only to turn and face me as quickly again, and the side of the lip with the cut in it was uptilted further as he said, "And don't look so much like a frightened rabbit. That show of defiance was too thin. If you hope to survive with my brother you've got to have a mind of your own and show it to him."

Again his back was towards me, again he was holding the door open for me, and I stepped into the hall without looking at him and followed him across it.

If I took in the conditions of my surroundings it was unconsciously, for, to put it mildly, I was almost overwhelmed with apprehension, and then The Big Fellow— it was strange, but right from the first I thought of him in my mind by this title—ushered me into a large light room which I saw immediately faced the great expanse of rocked terrace and was the room from which I had earlier heard the argument. And there, his face half turned from me, I saw Maurice Rossiter for the first time.

"Well, there you are." It was a brusque introduction and farewell at the same time, and before I had time to turn and say a stiff thank you, the man had left the room and I was staring across the wide space towards the most beautiful face I had ever seen in my life. The eyes that looked at me were blue and wide apart. The nose was straight, the mouth thin, but the lips had shape to them. The skin was not pale, like that of an invalid, but cream-tinted, like a delicate shade of sun-tan you see on some women. But it was the shape of the face that gave it its beauty—the bone formation. Years ago, when we had lived in Durham, I went to art classes and I remember being told to copy in detail the light and shade of a skull, and I remember marvelling at what was under our skin. The uncanny thing about this face was that it showed itself to be akin to that of The Big Fellow. The features in both cases were strangely alike, but here they were filed down, melted as it were into softness. The only flaw in the beauty of this man was in his mouth, for it drooped noticeably at the corners.

"Please come over here and sit down."

I walked towards him and sat down and felt, quite suddenly, at my ease.

"You must excuse me not getting up; I don't move unless I've got to. It's very bad for me. I should keep on the move, they tell me, but I'm naturally lazy." He smiled at me and I smiled back, a wide friendly smile. Because that is how I felt . . . friendly towards this man.

"What is your name?"

I hesitated, then said quietly, "Kate Mitchell."

His blue eyes were looking into mine, and the corners of his mouth came up and he repeated as his brother had done, "Kate?" but in what a different way could not be imagined. Again he said, "Kate?" And then he smiled as he said, "You know, you look like a Kate. . . . But please——" He put out his hand which, unlike his face, was not beautiful, being short and thick, even podgy, and he went on, "But please, I don't mean to be rude. The Kate I mean is . . . well, sensible, shrewd and . . . rather beautiful in a way. . . . Am I being really offensive?"

I found myself saying quite glibly, "No woman is offended when she is told she is beautiful, but in this case I know it is a very kind exaggeration."

And I did know it was such. I knew I was sensible; I did not think I was shrewd. I would not have been taken in so easily if I had been shrewd. As for being beautiful . . . no, I had what is called a nice face—a kind face you could say. My best feature was my grey eyes, and yet they were my weakness, for I could not control their expression. Whatever I felt I showed in my eyes. And at this moment I was showing that I wasn't offended or displeased, and the man opposite to me let his head rest against the high back of the chair and gave a sigh before saying, "You know, I'm glad you came. I must be quite truthful and tell you that I wasn't anticipating your visit. Even now you are an unknown quantity. Like the renowned Kate you may have the temper of a shrew, who knows? And I may experience it when I work you too hard. Yet I have the feeling we will work well together . . . that is if." He pulled himself from the back of the chair and bent his head towards me, smiling quizzically as he repeated, "That is if you can type from my scribble, and take shorthand from my speedy orations."

"I have a pad in my bag. Would you . . . would you like to give me a test now?"

"Yes, Yes. Go ahead."

I wasn't prepared for the speed at which he spoke, and I was sure he was doing it to test me. Twice I had to stop and ask him to repeat a word. After about three minutes he stopped and said, "That will do. Read it." After I had read the letter through he nodded his head slowly twice, saying, "Very good, very good. Julian couldn't have done that. . . . Julian was my last secretary. He lived here for a time. . . . Now I'll get you to type one of my usual sheets." As he made to rise I asked hastily, "Can I get it for you?" And he paused in a twisted position as he gripped the arm of the chair, and, turning his head towards me, he said, "If you are to work for me you will have to get used to my shuffling, so I had better give you a demonstration of it now."

I did not speak but watched him pull himself up and then move towards the desk. With each step the straight right half of him was dragged over sideways to accommodate the shrunken left side of his body. And the effect was weird; it was as if he was doing a step of a grotesque dance, and when the action was repeated again and

20

again it sent a chill through me, and the feeling did not ease until, at the desk, he turned and faced me, saying, "Come and try this."

The thin spidery writing not only filled the quartosized sheet of paper but went down the margin on the right-hand side, along the bottom and up the other side. As I looked at it he said, "I haven't picked you a bad sheet."

I sat down at the side table where the typewriter was, and I thought as I put the paper into the machine: If this wasn't a bad sheet, then I wouldn't like to see one that is. It took me a long time to do the sheet, nearly fifteen minutes, during which time he did not speak but sat watching me. This brought back the feeling of nervousness. But when at last I handed him the page and a half of clean script he merely glanced at it, but smiled at me and said, "I don't think we need worry, need we?" Then, turning from me, he added, "I suppose my brother has dealt with the matter of fees?" He did not term it wages.

"Yes. We agreed on four pounds."

"Four pounds!" His face came round to me, one eyebrow raised. The whole face had a cynical look now which marred its beauty, but I did not blame him for feeling like this towards his brother, for the man had got my back up immediately.

"Ah, well." The smile was once again on his face, and his head went back as he said, "You must have a drink of something before you go, you've had a long trek. Coffee or tea? Which is it to be?"

"Thank you. I'd like a cup of coffee."

He took a hand bell off the table, the handle of which I noticed was made from the hoof of some animal, and, hobbling with his weird gait the full length of the room, he opened a door and rang the bell. I could hear the noise jangling through the house. By the time he had returned and placed the bell on the table there came through the door he had left open a wizened-looking man with white hair. He could have been anything from fifty to eighty years old. Even before Maurice Rossiter said,

"Would you bring two cups of coffee, Hollings?" I knew this was the man whom the queer person on the road had warned me against disturbing. The man was looking at me much in the same way as had Logan Rossiter, in a scrutinizing, weighing-up sort of way. And he did not turn on the order he had been given, but continued to look at me until my future employer said, "I'd better introduce you. This is Hollings. He keeps the house and everybody in order; don't you, Hollings?" The man did not reply, and Maurice Rossiter said with a slight edge to his voice, "This is Miss Mitchell. She'll be coming here some part of every day to do my work."

The man moved his eyes and looked at Maurice Rossiter, one long penetrating look, then turned away. He had not spoken, and when the door closed on him, Mr. Rossiter smiled and said, "You'll get used to Hollings. I had better warn you though: he has the idea that Tor-Fret and all it holds is his property. You see . . ." He took a long breath and motioned me to sit down opposite to him again before he continued. "You see, like all of us he was born in this house. His father served my grandfather, and he and my father ran the moors together as boys. They fished the Coquet, vying with each other for the biggest salmon catch. They rode and shot together. I understand they were more like brothers than if they had been real brothers—for my father had three brothers of his own, but he seemed to prefer Hollings. Well, my father is dead, but his brothers are still with us, and so of course is Hollings. He would, I fancy, like to think he has taken my father's place. In the old days you know this house was known as . . . 'The House of Men'. I sometimes wonder what my mother felt like when she first came here. But she did not stay long, she died when I was five." He now abruptly turned his eyes towards the window and changed the conversation by saying, "Isn't that a beautiful view!"

I followed his gaze and looked across the wide terrace, down the sloping valley. There was nothing finicky about the view. The fields were large. The patches of dying heather covered great expanses of land, and in the far, far distance I could see the gleam of rivulets running down the hillside. And below, far below, away to the right, the ribbon of the river Coquet twisting and turning, tumbling its way towards Amble and the sea. And beyond the river, blurred by distance, the massive hill of Simonside.

"It's beautiful," I said, "very beautiful, and much softer than our valley."

"I have never asked you where you come from?"

"We live above Rothcorn, quite a way above, in a little cottage. I understand it was at one time an inn. Although I don't know why anyone would go that far for a drink or a bed."

"Above Rothcorn? That's a wild stretch."

"Yes, it is rather."

"Why . . .?" He was about to ask me the usual question, why we lived in such an out-of-the-way place, when the door opened abruptly and in came two old men, for the sole purpose, I knew, of having a look at me, and like Hollings, but in a different way, they stared at me without speaking.

I saw immediately that their appearance had annoyed Mr. Rossiter, and he showed it by saying curtly, "Can't you see I'm busy!" and followed this immediately with, "These are my uncles: Mr. Stanley Rossiter," he pointed to the taller and more pleasant-looking of the two small men, and then to the shorter, adding, "and Mr. Bernard."

They both inclined their heads towards me and said quietly, "How do you do?"

"How do you do?" I said in reply. Except for their expressions they were so much alike I knew immediately they were twins.

"Well, what is it?" Mr. Maurice still sounded annoyed.

"Nothing, nothing." Mr. Stanley smiled widely, and then continued, "It's a beautiful morning."

Mr. Bernard did not speak, and after one last look at

23

me he turned abruptly about and went out of the room.

Maurice Rossiter, looking now at Mr. Stanley, said pointedly, "Would you mind closing the door as you go out, Uncle?"

This elicited a high laugh from the old man, and before he did as he was ordered he bowed slightly towards me. I had the impression that the two old men would prove rather amusing.

"Well now." Maurice Rossiter's eyebrows were raised as he looked at me with a half smile and said, "You have seen five of us, there are only three more. Bennett, who cooks for us, is very old, and so his cooking suffers, and, consequently, so do we. And then there's Patterson, who does outside jobs; and my third uncle, Stephen, who is bedridden.

At this moment, from a far door Hollings entered carrying a tray, and at the same instant my eyes were distracted from him by the sight of The Big Fellow running past the window and across the plateau towards the pathway by which I had come up to the house. He was running at great speed as if he was chasing someone, but as far as I could see there was no one in sight.

Maurice Rossiter's attention, too, was caught by his brother's action. And I watched him pull himself forward in his seat to catch a last glimpse of the flying figure. Then he sat back and took the coffee from Hollings. I, too, took a cup from Hollings's hand and said, "Thank you," but the man did not speak.

It would seem that the sight of his brother had disturbed Maurice Rossiter, for he gulped at his coffee and did not speak to me as I drank mine; and then quite abruptly he dismissed me by pulling himself once again on to his feet and saying, "When can you start?"

I, too, was on my feet now. "I'll have to give a week's notice. I could begin a week come Monday."

"Very well. You'll come in the afternoons?" Before I could state my preference for the mornings he put in, "Do so for the first week, anyway. You will help me considerably if you comply in this." It was as if we had discussed the matter, but we hadn't. He spoke as if he had been present at the conversation I'd had with his brother, moreover his words were now stilted. They had what I call an office politeness about them that took away the friendliness of the interview. "Very well," I said. "Goodbye."

But he had turned to the window now and was craning his neck forward, and it was a full minute before he brought his face round to me and said, "Oh, goodbye, Goodbye."

I went into the hall. There was no one about so I let myself out of the front door and walked across the terrace; as I passed the first long windows I knew that Maurice Rossiter was still standing there, but I did not look towards him.

I reached the road, and when I was once out of sight of the house I stopped and, as it were, asked myself what I thought. And I got no answer. I did not know whether I was glad or sorry that I had got the job.

I had passed around the second deep bend of the road when I saw Logan Rossiter again. The sight of him brought me to a dead stop, and with my mouth agape. Then I let out a cry and ran on to the heathered slope, shouting, "No, no, don't! Stop it! Don't!" The Big Fellow was kneeling in the heather, one knee on the chest of the odd man I had met earlier on the road, and his hands were tight around his throat.

I have always been afraid of men fighting, but in this moment I seemed to have lost all sense of fear. The one thought in my mind was to stop him strangling the man beneath him. I clutched the collar of his coat and pulled. I don't think my strength had anything to do with his loosening his hold; it was more surprise that made him relax his grip. As if my action had brought him to his right senses again, he heaved himself backwards on to his hunkers, and his hands falling to his sides, he dropped his head for a moment. I stood looking down at him, my breathing as heavy as if I myself had been in the conflict, and my voice cracked as I said, "Do you want to kill him? He looks dead."

As he pulled himself slowly to his feet he growled, "Yes, I want to kill him, but it's hard to kill trash. . . . Get up!" He raised his foot and kicked at the man's leg.

"Don't . . . don't be so cruel." There was anger now in both my voice and face and I glared at him for a moment before turning from him. But as I went to bend over the man The Big Fellow's hand on my arm almost jerked me from the ground, and his lips left his teeth bare as he cried, "Don't touch him!" Then, thrusting me aside, he stood over the prostrate figure again and said, "Get up." And to my amazement the man, using the same action as he had done on the road, turned on to his face and with the aid of his hands and thrusting his buttocks once again skywards levered himself upwards. When he stood straight he swayed a little and put his hand to his throat. And then in a whining voice he said, "Aa was only after some grapes from the 'othouse. That was aall. Aa never went near the hoose an' aa didn't see nebody. An' aa never spoke ta nebody."

"I've warned you what would happen if I caught you about here again. Now this is the last time, you understand? There'll be nobody to save your bacon next time. Get going."

The man retreated a few steps, went to turn away, then, turning back, said, "Ya might 've killed me that time, an' then ya would 've hung, ya would."

"The next time there'll be no doubt about it. As to the hanging, your neck will be worth paying that price for." The tone now was the caustic one I had heard him use to his brother.

I stood dividing my gaze between the swaying gait of the departing figure and this man with the polished, cutting, sarcastic way of speaking, but whom I had just witnessed acting like a savage. He said now, still without taking his eyes from the man, "If ever you come across

26

that character—his name is Weaver—give him a wide berth."

"I have already come across him. I spoke to him on my way up."

Slowly he turned his eyes towards me. "And I suppose you took him for a gentle eccentric figure. A bit of a dolt, but harmless."

In answer to this I replied, "You can't murder a man because you dislike him."

"No? . . . You have a lot to learn. Well"—he began dusting himself down, still looking at me—"I suppose you feel very heroic?"

"I feel nothing of the sort." I was looking him straight in the eye. "But on the other hand, nor do I feel like a frightened rabbit."

The white line on his lip moved upwards as his head moved down and he glanced at me from under his eyebrows for a moment, then laughed softly. It wasn't an unpleasant laugh. "Did you find favour in my brother's eyes?" he said.

"I don't like the way you phrase that, Mr. Rossiter. But I have satisfied your brother that I can both type and take down shorthand, and he feels that I would suit him."

"Doubtless . . . doubtless. . . . Where do you live?"

"Above Rothcorn, at the bottom of Neete Fell."

"That's a long way to come." His voice had even a considerate note to it now, but I ignored it and said quickly, "Goodbye, Mr. Rossiter."

He did not say goodbye, but instead, "You're going down the road, so am I. We can hardly walk one behind the other, can we?" And with this he took up a position by my side and in the most embarrassed silence I have ever experienced we went down the fell road together.

Not until the main road came in sight did he speak again and then he said, "I garage my car just beyond Peter's Well, near the cottages there. If you've got a mind to walk along the road with me I will give you a lift to the village."

"The bus is due now." I looked at my wrist-watch. "Thank you all the same."

"Very well."

Where the path came in to the main road he stopped, and looking at me, a smile squarely on his face now, a smile that softened his big features, he said, "I don't suppose you and I are likely to meet much in the future; I am away a good part of the week, so I'll say now I hope that you enjoy your work."

"I'm sure I will."

"Yes, so am I." His head moved in small nods and I could see that he was amused, for he repeated, "So am I." Then, "Goodbye, Miss Mitchell." Even his tone of farewell had a touch of amusement to it.

"Goodbye, Mr. Rossiter."

When he left me I stood waiting for the bus and looking straight ahead across the road to the far fells. I felt indignant, annoyed, "worked-up" as my mother would say. I didn't like the man, and I, too, hoped that we wouldn't see much of each other.

2

"Do you mean to say the boss of the house was strangling the tramp fellow?"

"Yes, I do," I answered my father.

"He couldn't have been badly hurt if he got up so quick and walked away," put in my mother in her matter-of-fact way. "And he must have been up to something for the man to have done that; there are always two sides to everything. But look, lass, you have never told us a thing about the house. What does it look like? What is it like inside?"

I looked towards the fire in the high grate, and I blinked for a moment trying to recall the inside of the house. It was odd, but I hadn't taken much notice of my surroundings; I had been too taken up with the inhabitants of the house. Yet now it seemed I was back there, standing in the hall, and I said slowly, "There is a large hall but it's dull looking. I would say the whole place could do with one of your . . . groundings." I smiled at her. "The stairs go up from the far end of the hall, and I remember now, they were quite bare. I think they were oak. The first room I was shown into was small and overfull with books, and old furniture in great need of a polish; but Mr. Rossiter's room, the one that looked out on to the terrace with the beautiful view, that wasn't crowded at all. But it wasn't any cleaner than the rest. The place wasn't dirty, if you know what I mean, but it wasn't . . ." I spread my hands wide. "It wasn't like our kind of cleanness."

"No spit and polish?" said my father. "Well, that's to be expected if there isn't a woman about nagging all the time." He cast a swift smiling glance towards my mother. "There'll be nobody to stop them puttin' their feet on the chairs if they want to. Although in me time I've known some dirty housewives, and some men that were more finicky than women about the place. . . . How many men did you say were there?"

"Five in the family, I think, and three servants, two in and one out."

My mother at this point narrowed her eyes and looked at me as she said slowly, "You won't mind working among them?"

I took my eyes from her face as I replied, "No . . . no, I won't mind working among them." My mother, I knew, was thinking back to the time when I had judged all men's actions on those of one man. Of men in general I was still distrustful, but here and there I was finding the odd one I could trust and like. Such a man was Rodney Stringer. Another, I felt, could be my future employer,

Maurice Rossiter, but I wasn't quite sure. It was early days yet and I had learned not to judge on short acquaintance.

My mother said now, "Oh, I'm glad that you're not going to have those long winter treks. You'll be able to get there and back in half the time." And so I thought.

I worked my notice the following week, and I was surprised and not a little touched at the genuine regret the girls in the office showed at my coming departure. And I laughed when they expressed their envy at my going to work for an author—so romantic, so different from invoices on cattle feed. I myself did not look upon my future employment as bordering on the romantic, but I remember I laughed a lot that week. I felt much lighter, even gay in myself.

And so the Monday morning came when I went down into the village and started work with Bill Arnold. This work was not unlike that which I had just left in the office in Alnwick, the only difference being it was much more casual, less organized and with many, many more teabreaks. And when I finished at twelve-thirty Bill showed himself to be very pleased with my efforts.

It was impossible for me to get home for lunch if I was to get to Tor-Fret by two o'clock, so I had brought some sandwiches with me. Even then I had not realized until I actually experienced it what a rush it was, getting from one job to another. And later that week I decided to cut my time short at Bill's and make it up on a Saturday morning. This I eventually did. But now, after gulping my sandwiches, I caught the bus and was off to my first session at Tor-Fret.

I arrived at the house at ten minutes to two, hot and not a little nervous. I need not have worried. My first afternoon was as pleasant as anyone could have wished for. Maurice Rossiter was courtesy itself. I was to start typing a book he had done, and he assured me that if I was stumped in any way I was just to come in to him, he would be in the adjoining room.

Around three o'clock the uncles looked in. They stood one at each side of me and watched me type, much to my embarrassment. It was as if they had not seen anyone type before. But I knew it wasn't the typewriter they were looking at—it was me. And through them I began to realize how strange it was for Tor-Fret to have a woman within its walls. These old twins looked to me to be in the late sixties, and I learned that afternoon that it was Mr. Stanley who did most of the talking. Mr. Bernard sounded rather grumpy. He looked a bit grumpy, too. They both had round faces, small round eyes and thick eyebrows, and they both smelt the same. I was a bit embarrassed by the smell at first, because neither of them appeared to be in any way under the influence of drink, yet they reeked of something approaching the smell of whisky. I was to learn a lot about that smell.

"Do you think you'll stay?" said Mr. Stanley.

I stopped my typing. "I hope so," I said.

"What about the winter?" This was about the only thing Mr. Bernard said that afternoon. I turned and smiled up into his crumpled face.

"I'll manage. Our side . . . I mean where my home is, is much rougher than here."

"Tut!" was all the comment he made to this.

And then there was Hollings. About half-past three he entered the room without knocking. He was carrying a very neatly set tray, on which there was a small silver teapot with milk jug to match, a thin cup and saucer, and a plate holding three cakes. The cakes turned out to be very nice indeed and I wondered if the old cook had made them, for Mr. Maurice had suggested that his cooking left a great deal to be desired. At five o'clock I took my leave with a sense of achievement, sent on my way by the pleased smile of my employer.

Before the week was up I had a good insight into Mr. Maurice's make-up, and this came about through the book I was typing for him. The book was entitled *The Nightmare of the Body*, and it began with a man waking up in hospital and realizing that he was crippled with polio. The man had been handsome and attractive and, by the sound of it, very virile. There had been women in his life, and, among other things, he lamented the future lack of this pleasure. Part of the story I realized could be fictitious, but before I had worked five days on it I became just a little critical, even a little tired of the whine that ran through it. The "I" was very prominent in every line, as also was the self-pity. Regretfully, very regretfully, I knew that Logan Rossiter had been right when he had said to his brother, "You will never write well until you forget yourself." Yet in spite of this I knew that my employer was a writer, he could tell a story. I had done a lot of reading; I had my father to thank for this, for he was a great reader. I remember the first book he told me to get from the library. It was a book on Northumberland. "Know your own county, lass, know your own ground and the world will fall into place around it." He was right, too. He was right in most things, was my father.

That week-end I arranged with Bill about the alterations in my working hours and he only too readily allowed me to make any change I liked so long as I did the work for him. And so it was that on the Monday of the second week I left the village early and came up the long fell, home to have a good dinner before starting out for Tor-Fret, this time by the top road over Neete Fell. It was a beautiful day, like summer. I thought, whimsically, it was as if the weather god had mislaid this day and had pushed it in while there was yet time.

It had been my intention to ask Mr. Maurice if there was a way to the house approaching it from over Neete Fell, but it had slipped my mind. So my father and I had pored over a local map on Sunday and came to the conclusion that I had only to skirt the top of the wood that lay beyond the other valley and I would actually be in the grounds of of the house. We did not know if the wood belonged to the Rossiter estate or not.

From the top of Neete Fell I could see for miles on every side. The scene was both elating and awe-inspiring. I could see the river Coquet twisting and turning like a silver snake. I could see groups of dots on its flower-strewn banks which I knew to be cattle. I thought I could see the river Alwin where it frothed down the hillside to join the Coquet, but perhaps that was my heightened imagination. As I gazed through the glorious white light of that bright day it wasn't my imagination that the mottled moving patches away up on the steep face of a fell were the massed bodies of sheep, black-faced, long-haired, moorland sheep. And as I looked over and down to my left I knew that the thin column of blue smoke, spiralling upwards, came from the chimneys of Tor-Fret. And I thought: Dad was right. It did not strike me for a moment that I would not be able to get on to the Rossiter land. There were no railings around here. Stone walls yes, but you could climb those. On each side of the Ros-siter land lay two large farms and these were bounded by rough stone walls.

I actually ran down the winding path between the banks of heather, and for a moment I heard myself humming a tune. I skirted the wood. I walked along by the side of a low stone wall until I saw an opening in the undergrowth, and then I climbed the wall and found myself on a sort of pathway. It had once been a broad path but was now almost covered with bramble, and I had to stop a number of times and disentangle my coat from the briars. I had not gone very far when I came to a crossroad of paths and with the choice of three before me. As the house lay to the left of me I took the left-hand one, and within a few minutes found myself walking up a steep rise which I knew to be an outcrop of rock—the moors and fells were studded with these obstructions. The path had disappeared now, but I realized that it would be easier to climb this comparatively small rock than push my way through the undergrowth. And I was glad that I had decided to do this, when a few steps further on I reached the top and there saw down below me to my right a surprising scene. A lake, an inland lake. Lakes large and small are not unusual in this county, but I had not known that one was so near at hand, and in the grounds of the Rossiter estate. I could see from where I stood that if I had gone straight on I would have come to the shore of this lake. I looked at my watch, it was just turned half-past one. I looked to my left again. There in the distance lay the house, I could see the entire stretch of roofs. I decided on the spur of the moment to retrace my steps and spend a few minutes by the water.

It is not big issues that decide our destiny but little ones. The pampering of little wishes, little desires. I had the desire to go and stand by the water for a few minutes, and I gave way to this desire and it set the seal on my future life.

Having reached the crossroads again, I walked along the middle path. It was narrow and carpet-soft with pine needles, which I felt had not been disturbed for a long time. The path turned twice, und then I came abruptly upon an obstacle, surprising and yet not so surprising. It was the back of a summer-house, and I saw immediately that I could not make my way around it, for growing tightly up to its sides was a dense mass of undergrowth. I was disappointed; I had so wanted to see that little lake. I looked at the black weathered wood and saw just above my eye level, to the right, a knot hole. I raised myself on tiptoe, leaned over the bramble and, placing my hands against the wood, looked through the hole. Then there wasn't a part of my body that wasn't hot and burning with embarrassment. I brought my face quickly from the wood and found that I had put my hand tightly across my mouth. It was at this moment that the girl's voice came to me. It was a refined easy sort of voice and it said, "Stop it a moment, darling . . . listen. What was that?"

"What was what? Don't be silly . . . nothing. Come here."

"No, no, listen. I'm sure I heard someone."

"You couldn't have heard anyone, my sweet darling. Isn't Weaver on the lookout? And nothing or no one escapes Weaver. He will warn me if anyone comes up— anyone, that is, except our earnest Kate. Our prim, industrious, and delightfully earnest Kate."

My hand slipped slowly from my mouth. The voice was the voice of my employer, and it was full of ridicule, hurtful ridicule. Yet he had been so charming, so kind, so thoughtful.

The girl's voice said now, "But are you sure he's gone?"

"My dearest dear, Patterson drove him to the station en route for London town, then returned the car to the garage. I told you, we had one hell of a row, my dear brother and I, concerning that very journey. . . . Oh, come here. I want to forget it for this afternoon, at any rate. . . ." There came a pause. I was too afraid to move in case they heard me and when the voice came again it had lost its bantering tone. "I say I want to forget it but I can't. If he doesn't sell that land I think I'll kill him. Keeping us all on the bread line when he could get a hundred and fifty thousand for that strip. What does it matter if there's a few rows of houses at the bottom of the hill? We won't see them."

"Listen, darling, listen." It was the girl's voice. "I am serious now, really, I'm serious. . . . Let's go away. Look . . . I'll get work of some kind."

Maurice Rossiter's laugh came to me. He was choking with it. And then he said, "Oh, you darling . . . you darling . . . darling . . . darling." Each darling was punctuated by the sound of a kiss. "You'll get work of some kind? Oh, that's funny. The hardest work you've ever done in your life is throw your leg over a horse. You're lazy; beautiful and lazy." There was another pause.

"But I could try, Maurice. We could take a chance. . . ."

"Be quiet, don't be silly." The tone of my employer's voice had changed with such suddenness that it didn't seem to belong to the same man, and now he said bitterly, "You know full well I haven't got a farthing. I'm as dependent on him for what I eat as a baby at its mother's breast. Moreover, for years now I've been used to being looked after. I need to be looked after, I must be looked after; I can't manage on my own, you know I can't. I need a man there." It was like the voice from the novel, the character in *The Nightmare of the Flesh* speaking in person. "Things are bad enough as they are now, skimping and scraping, everything being cut down. But at least I have my rooms and attention, and I have my work. Could I work if I was in, say, a maisonette or some basement flat?"

"But if he does sell the land would he give you anything?"

There was a long pause before I heard Maurice Rossiter's voice again, and then he said, "He mightn't give me anything, but he'd give it to you, darling. You've only got to say the word, and you're going to say it, aren't you?"

"But after . . . What about us after, Maurice?"

"Leave that to Maurice. I've told you, just you leave everything to me. I may not be able to use my limbs to the full, but thank God I can use my brain . . . and my good side. . . . But now, come on to the water with you, come on. I want to come alive."

I heard swift movements and a scuffling sound and laughter, and under its protection I lifted one foot slowly after the other and made my retreat.

The day was still bright, but nothing was shining any more. There was one word running through my mind: it was . . . duplicity. It repeated itself again and again . . . duplicity, duplicity. And it wasn't because of what Maurice Rossiter thought of me, but because of the underlying meaning to the conversation I had overheard, that it stayed with me.

Without thinking of where I was going, I had automatically taken the path towards the outcrop of rock again, and had almost reached the top when I stopped. If they were on the shores of the lake they would see me from here. I turned my eyes slowly towards the water. My view was obstructed by a spreading branch of a fir tree, but as I moved my head to the side, there, as in a framed picture, was a section of the lake, and standing poised, quite naked, on its shore was the girl I had seen through the knot hole in the summer-house. Her body was merged into the white light, and from this distance she looked like a young girl in her early teens, but the face I had glimpsed in that hot blushing moment was of someone as old as myself. Perhaps a year or two older or a year or two younger. Then into the picture came the loping contorted figure of Maurice Rossiter. Before he reached the girl she had turned her white body from him and dived into the water. In the next instant he was with her, and then even from this distance it seemed as if I was witnessing a miracle, for I saw, not one arm but both his arms cutting the water like the fins of a fish as he pursued the girl. And not only his arms but both his legs were in action. He had said, "let me come alive," and undoubtedly only in the water could he know full life. I had heard how water gave agility to some polio-afflicted people, and now it seemed, as I said, that I was watching a miracle. And I could have been happy for him if it hadn't been for that one word . . . duplicity.

I was hesitating whether to risk crossing the top of the small rock when my whole attention was caught by the flash of moving sunlight, like the sun reflected from glass, and after blinking I looked to my left in the direction of the house. The trees were high here, as also were more outcrops of rock, and I saw lying along the top of a flat shelf, and skilfully hidden, at least from anyone down below on the lake side, a man. He was almost hidden from me but for the top of a bald head and the dark blur of his body. I did not attempt to go forward over the mound of the rock, but stepped backwards, and, kneeling down so as not to be seen myself, I looked upwards. The man was lying flat on his stomach. His clothes were not rough country clothes; he was wearing a black suit. And I noticed that his feet, which were hanging over the end of the sloping shelf of rock, were fitted with shining black boots. The flash that had blinded me was the glass of his binoculars as he brought them to his face, and there he was now looking through these binoculars down on to the lake, on to Maurice Rossiter and the girl, whoever she was. I felt sick. I turned about, and within a few minutes I had crossed over the stone wall again.

It was now a quarter to two and I would be late. But this could not be helped. I would have to walk the length of the wood . . . on its outside, go along the road that led to the stone gates, then cut across the fell until I came out on the path near St. Peter's Well, for I must take this path to the house. The Man Weaver must see me. If he didn't how would I explain my arrival? Could I say I came in by the path which skirted the lake?

I arrived twenty minutes late, hot, tired and still feeling nauseated inside. At what point on the road Weaver spied me I don't know. I heard no strange bird calls, no signals; the only sound on this hot September day was the persistent cooing of a wood pigeon.

It was quite usual for me not to see my employer for anything up to an hour after my arrival. The last page which I had transcribed would be left on my desk and I would go on from there. If I was unable to make out some word, or the sense of an over-written sentence, I would knock on the third door which led out of this room. This door led into the other large terrace-framed room which was furnished like a drawing-room, but which was actually his bedroom. I'd only had to trouble him three times within the past week, and each time I had found him propped up on a couch busily writing, but today I determined that no matter how bad the script was I would not go near him. . . . Prime Kate, earnest Kate. . . . Yet I knew it wasn't his private opinion of me that was colouring my thoughts but the two-facedness of the man. Yes, that was an ordinary way of putting it, the way my father or mother would have described him, and it was accurate. I did not like Logan Rossiter, he was rude and overbearing, but I found that equally I did not like the idea of his charming-mannered and handsome-faced brother making a fool of him . . . "making a monkey" out of him. Again my father's expression was most adequate, because that apparently was what was happening. Maurice Rossiter was "making a monkey" out of his brother and in a most detestable way. I had no way of telling what the actual relationship was between the dark-haired, white-bodied nymph by the lake and Logan Rossiter, but I hoped, in this moment, that it wasn't deep. I had been hurt, and although, as I said, my disposition towards the man was not kindly, I felt I should hate to see him humiliated . . . "made a monkey out of". I had been made a monkey out of . . .

"Here's a day for you." It was nearly four o'clock when Maurice Rossiter greeted me in this airy fashion. His eyes were bright; his hair, I noticed, was still damp; and although the dragging of his left side was very much in evidence, it appeared to me now like a crippled leech clinging to the side of a giant. For today my employer looked as big as his brother, and I realized that if he had been whole he would have been even larger than Logan Rossiter, and together with his beauty he would, like the character in his book before he was struck with illness, have mown all women down.

"Have you had your tea?"

"Yes, thank you."

"What is it?" He had stopped opposite my desk. "Aren't you well?" His head was bent towards me, his expression sympathetic. I would have melted under it last week, but now I looked back at him and lied, "I have a slight touch of migraine. I'm sometimes subject to head-aches."

"Oh, bad luck." He spoke now with the indifference of a very healthy person for a sickly creature. It was rather absurd, but perhaps, I reminded myself, he might be feeling very healthy at this moment; certainly he'd had an

39

unusual afternoon. Unusual to me, I reminded myself, perhaps not unusual to him. That was not the first time, by many a score, he had swum that lake, and never, I should imagine, without company.

"Mr. Rossiter . . ." He was moving towards the window as I spoke and he lumbered round and looked at me, his face smiling. "Would it be in order if I took the manuscript home and did it there? I have a typewriter. I could easily, and bring it back when it's . . ."

"No, no. It would not be in order." His words were spaced and cool. "I want the manuscript done here. Apart from having only the one copy, anything could happen to it once it left this house. I want to work on the finished script every morning. I find it much easier to correct in type. You understand that?"

"Yes, yes, I do, but I just thought . . ."

"Are you getting tired of it?" Here spoke a vain man, here was the hero of the novel.

"No, no," I said. "I'm not getting tired of it. I am very interested in the book. It was merely a suggestion."

"Well, it won't do. I am sorry. You understand that? I am sorry, but I have to have the work on the spot. I thought you understood that when you came."

"It wasn't discussed as far as I remember."

"Kate." His eyes narrowed and he hobbled towards me again. "What is it? Don't tell me there's nothing wrong. I can tell by your eyes. I've learnt that much about you already—they give you away. . . . Has someone upset you? Or . . . Oh, Kate. . . ." He pointed his finger at me, wagging it about an inch from my face as he said with mock severity, "It's the shrew in you coming out. I told you you'd give me a sample of it. Someone's upset you and you're taking it out on me. Now that's it, isn't it? . . . Have you a boy friend?"

The abrupt and surprising question brought the colour flushing into my cheeks. I felt my face go scarlet. Characteristically now, his head went back and his laugh rang out. "It's years since I saw a woman blush. Oh, Kate, you're delightful."

I felt gauche, stupid, and was suddenly on the point of tears. I think it was only the door opening which saved me from this humiliation. It was the twins, and Maurice Rossiter greeted them with, "Come in, come in. Our industrious Kate has a cross between a headache, a temper and a dose of the blues. What do you suggest for it?"

"Headache?" Bernard Rossiter nodded his white head at me, and said in his terse clipped way, "Have the very thing to cure headache. Early in the day for it though. Should never be touched before six o'clock, 'cept on special occasions . . . Eh, Maurice?" He turned his head quickly and looked at his nephew. And Maurice Rossiter answered gaily, "Except on special occasions! You're right there, Uncle, and this is a special occasion. We can't have Kate with a headache, can we?"

Mr. Stanley now leant towards me and said quietly, "Is it bad, my dear?"

"Yes, yes, it is rather." And it was true, my head was now thumping.

"Go and bring her a glass." Maurice Rossiter was speaking now to his Uncle Bernard. And then he cried, "Better still, she's never seen the cellars. That's it, take her down. Come on, come on, leave that toil and sweat." He put out his hand and gripped my elbow, and I was amazed at the strength and power behind his hold because it brought me to my feet. "Go on, go on with the old 'uns. I'll give you half an hour. I'm being generous, mind you, very generous. Half an hour from my work." He moved his head slowly from side to side.

"Come along, my dear." Mr. Stanley had hold of my arm now as if he were escorting an invalid, and Mr. Bernard, opening the door, preceded us into the hall.

Again I felt like crying, for now the phrase "Being made a monkey of" seemed more appropriate still. Maurice Rossiter was enjoying himself. I realized that this man could create situations for his employment.

Good or bad, if he created them they would give him enjoyment.

When, after crossing the hall and going down a long passage, Mr. Bernard opened a door from which dropped a flight of stairs, Mr. Stanley, seeming to sense my feelings, said, "My nephew's in a merry mood today, you must take advantage of it. It isn't often that he will sacrifice his work for anything, or even anyone. Come along, my dear. You go first, Bernard."

"Well, isn't that what I'm doing?"

The somewhat querulous reply came up from the dark well of the staircase. And then a light was switched on and a strange, and for me unusual, scene was illuminated.

Following Mr. Stanley, I went cautiously down the narrow wooden stairs and gazed over an enormous cellar, which was, I could see, split into sections by low frameworks, frameworks holding bottles, apparently hundreds and hundreds of bottles, and against a side wall I saw the round contours of a row of barrels. Then I reached the floor, which I recognized immediately was rough rock. Mr. Stanley, following the direction of my eyes, remarked, "That surprises you, doesn't it? They built in those days. Tor-Fret is built on rock. The foundations were hewn out of rock." His voice was full of pride.

"Never mind the foundations." Bernard's voice was still querulous. "It's a foundation she wants inside, not under her feet."

I was now standing in a sort of room, made so by partitions full of bottles on two sides and a long rough oak table on the third side. I sniffed at the air—it was dry, not warm, and yet not cold—and gazed about me. This evidently pleased the old man, and, catching at my interest, Mr. Stanley began to point out various things to me, such as one complete frame holding perhaps a hundred bottles all lying on their sides and having red sealing wax on the corks. "Pretty they look," he said, patting a bottle affectionately. "Wax keeps out the rot. Corks rot,

42

you know; a nasty little pest gets in. Won't be drunk for many a day, these. But . . . come now, sit down here." He pulled a chair forward with the air of a host, then, turning to his brother, he said, "What shall we give her first?"

As they both looked contemplatingly at each other, I put in quickly, "Oh, please, I must tell you I'm not used to wines, except for a sherry now and again."

"Oh, my God!" Mr. Bernard raised his hands above his head and cast his eyes ceilingwards. "Don't mention that word. Bottles'll hear and wine'll ferment."

I laughed up at the old man. Already I felt better. This then was what caused the peculiar smell that hung around them. They made wine . . . wines, I should say, for there must have been dozens of different kinds in the racks.

"The nineteen thirty-four?"

Mr. Bernard looked at his brother, and, inclining his head slowly like a doctor giving a verdict, said, "Nineteen thirty-four it is."

As Mr. Bernard disappeared around the partition, Mr. Stanley drew up a high wooden stool to the table and, sitting down, looked at me, his face straight, and said quietly, almost in a whisper, "Have you really got a headache, or has my nephew upset you?"

I was startled and must have shown it, for he said quickly, but still softly, "Don't worry, but you must try not to let him upset you. He is used to having his own way and cannot stand being balked. But you be firm, my dear, you be firm." He touched my hand quickly. The action was more in the nature of a nervous spasm than a gesture of sympathy, and when the clink of glasses came from somewhere beyond the partition he rose abruptly and went to the opening and said, "Are you draining the bottle?"

Mr. Bernard's answer was merely a grunt, and then he appeared round the framework carrying a pewter tray on which stood three plain wine glasses half-filled with a red wine, a deep rich red, yet clear, you could almost say transparent. And when, with a courtesy that did not belong to this generation, Mr. Bernard presented me with a glass of wine, I knew that an honour was being bestowed on me, and that these two dear old men did not take the matter lightly. They were standing one at each side of me now and silently we raised our glasses to each other, and then I sipped the wine.

As I have already said, I know nothing at all about wine, having tasted only sherry and on one special occasion, which I don't want to remember, champagne. But from this glass I recognized that I was drinking something rare. I let the liquid rest on my tongue before gently sliding into my throat. I have no words to describe the taste; I can only say that the sensation of warmth was almost immediate. And I remember thinking quaintly: It's like drinking joy.

"What is it made of?" I asked Mr. Stanley.

"Oh, well now . . . Grapes for one thing. Our own grapes, too, mind, and a little brandy added. But it isn't only what goes in, it's how you treat it after. . . . Give it rest and it will repay you. Don't you think this tastes beautiful?"

"Beautiful," I repeated.

"Do you know"——he leant towards me——"wine has been made in this cellar for over three hundred years. And not only wine"——his bushy brows came low over his eyes——"whisky. . . . In the bad old days, when they wanted to warm the blood before a local fight, they would gather in here." He embraced the whole cellar with the sweep of one arm. "I remember my grandfather telling me that as a boy he saw thirty to forty men roaring drunk in this very place. They were celebrating a raid."

"A raid? On the Scots?"

"On the Scots!" The laughter choked in Mr. Stanley's throat. "Nothing so heroic, my dear. Another farmer's sheep. They'd bring them down here and slaughter them by the dozen. There'd be meat for all through the winter. And in the spring our sheep would go to market and there'd be money for everybody who worked for 'The Rossiter'. Up till this last generation, you know, every owner of Tor-Fret was referred to as 'The Rossiter'." Mr. Stanley shook his head. "Ah, things happened in those days; they lived in those days."

"Aye, and they died in those days," put in his brother in a way that sounded to me, for the monent, very like my father. "And if such things happened today you'd be scared to death, you know you would. So be quiet, be quiet."

Strangely enough, Mr. Stanley obeyed his taciturn brother. I had finished my wine and I rose to my feet now, saying, "I had better be getting back, but thank you very much. I have never in my life tasted anything so wonderful."

I held the empty glass towards Mr. Bernard, and as he took it from me he said in his sawn-off way of speaking, 'Makin' blackberry next. Come down, watch us . . . at it."

"Thank you, I'd love to."

They did not lead me back to the staircase along the way I had come, but without remarking on it they both walked slowly between the different partitions, very much like two ardent gardeners quietly showing off prize blooms. And as they went they made such remarks as, "That's equal to your Vin de Tete," and, "There's race for you"—this latter remark being accompanied by a pat on the neck of a bottle, one of about thirty in a rack separate from others. They now led me round the back of the cellar. It was a place apart, and here evidently was where the wine was made. There was a bench holding boxes of corks, labels, and wooden mallets. There was a long wooden trough with a tap above it, then a contraption of pipes, which were connected to the trough and also to what looked like an old-fashioned boiler. There was also an out-of-date stove in a recess, but it appeared not to have been used for years, and right next to it was a door. This too looked ancient and out of use. Mr. Bernard now said with a little grin, "Make you a Trabhalbodor in the summer."

I did not know what a Trabhalbodor was, and when I said so Mr. Stanley explained, "He means he'll get you to help tread the grapes."

"Oh." I laughed, and Mr. Bernard laughed with me, as pleased as a child at his joke.

Mr. Bernard did not come out of the cellar with us but bade me farewell from the bottom of the steps, and when I had reached the hall and Mr. Stanley had closed the cellar door he stood facing me, and without any preamble he said, "Our elder brother Stephen's an invalid, bedridden this last six years. Not senile or anything. Quite all right, quite all right. Sometime—when you've a minute—after Maurice's work's done, would you look in on him? He'd like that very much—very much."

"Yes, yes, certainly. Just tell me when it is convenient."

"All right, I will. Goodbye. And . . . and may I say I've enjoyed your company."

He turned away from me as he finished speaking, and I looked after him and thought: Oh, they are nice. Unreservedly I liked the old men.

I now went along the corridor and across the hall and into the big room, and thankfully I found it empty. Nor did I see Maurice Rossiter again that afternoon.

The effect of the wine stayed with me for quite a time. At one period of the afternoon I could have put my head down on the desk and fallen asleep. But by the time I had finished for the day my mind was clear and I was once again viewing Maurice Rossiter from the same viewpoint as I had done earlier.

Before I reached home I had made up my mind that I would not tell my parents of the scene I had witnessed that afternoon. But had I decided to tell them I would have been prevented from doing so by the atmosphere that pervaded the house and which I sensed as soon as I entered. It was an atmosphere of apprehension, and I knew immediately I looked at their faces that something was wrong, and I hadn't long to wait to find out what it was.

"Tired, lass?" It was my father's greeting.

"Yes, a little. It was warm walking up the hill."

"Did you find the way to the house?"

"Yes, yes, I found it all right." This undescriptive statement seemed to satisfy him. At any other time he would have wanted to know every turn I had taken in the path, but now he just nodded and looked towards my mother. She had her back towards me and was standing at the table arranging and rearranging the crockery. The fact that she hadn't spoken to me was proof in itself that something was amiss. Had she had a row with my father? But no; whatever words she had with father never coloured the atmosphere. I went into the back kitchen and washed my hands, and when I returned to the table she handed me a cup of tea and gave me a smile, a smile having in it traces of nervousness and apprehension and, I thought, pity. And then I knew why. Sitting down at my side, she said, "You'd better know right away, we've had a visitor." My eyes did not move from her face until she said, "Arthur's been here."

"And he nearly got me toe in his . . ."

"Be quiet!" said my mother. My father's descriptive phrase, like that of the man Weaver, was very expressive and conveyed the kind of reception Arthur Boyne had received. I did not say to my mother, "What did he want?" I said nothing, for my heart was beginning to race as it hadn't done for a long time. My mother said now, "I'll give it to you straight, lass . . . condensed. He's parted from her and going to get a divorce."

I got slowly to my feet and looked down on her and said in a voice that sounded strangely calm, even indifferent, "That won't make the slightest difference to me. What gave him the idea it would?"

"He's had a hell of a time. He's sorry for himself. He wants sympathy." My father's tone was caustic.

"Well, I'm afraid he'll have to look elsewhere."

47

"I told him that." It was my father again speaking. "An' I told him that if he showed his nose in this door again . . ."

"Be quiet, Tom!" my mother put in impatiently, then went on, "He said, when he left her she took the child and plonked it on his mother."

I rose and walked towards the stairs as my mother said, "Have this cup of tea, lass." But I shook my head.

Upstairs I sat on the end of my bed, my arm leaning on the wooden rail, and I looked with unseeing eyes into the purple light that was spreading over the fells, for in this moment my vision was filled with a picture of a plump face, a plump face above a plump body . . . the plumpness of adolescence. I had seen that face only once. It was on a Sunday afternoon. We had just washed up after having dinner. My mother and father were sitting in deckchairs on the strip of green at the back of the house. I answered the knock at the front door and there she stood. This young self-assured, loud-mouthed girl. And she told me almost immediately that she was carrying Arthur Boyne's child. "What are you going to do about it?" she asked.

I learnt that she and Arthur had met on a number of Sunday evenings on the train from Alnwick to Durham. Arthur was returning after visiting me. Her people lived in Alnwick, but she stayed with an aunt in Durham, where she worked, and came up to Alnwick for the weekends.

My wedding was set for two months ahead. I had everything ready. The girl was seventeen, I was twenty-five, and seemed old to her, and with the cruelty of extreme youth she did not hesitate to let me feel this. The reason for Arthur's sudden desire to emigrate had been made clear. Also a number of things which had puzzled me during the past months.

Arthur had written to me this particular week-end to say he couldn't get over because his father was not very well and his mother was worried. The reason for the excuse was only too plain now. He was leaving it to the girl to "spill the beans" as she had threatened. She told me this herself as she stood with a stance that exaggerated the swelling curve of her stomach.

And now it was over for him and he thought that all he had to do was to make his plight known to me and things would link up from where they had broken off. Kind Kate, generous Kate, big-hearted Kate, would understand. "You know, Kate, one of the reasons why I love you is because you're kind, you've got a big heart. Oh, aye, and you're bonny an' all." I remember the actual day he had said those words. It was as we lay in the heather just down there below this cottage window. We had taken the bus for a day out and it had deposited us in the village, and from there we had walked right up to this fell. It was that day we had seen the empty cottage and gone home to my parents full of it. . . .

I stood up. My heart was racing less wildly now. It was over and done with, dead. It had been dead from the moment that girl had knocked on the front door and we had faced each other. It could never be revived. But, oh, I didn't want to endure any more scenes, any more pleas. My life was settled now; emotionally it was stagnant, and that was how I wanted it to remain.

After a time I went downstairs again and I said to my mother, "You didn't tell him where I worked."

"Of course not. What do you take me for? But mind, there's one thing I can tell you—he'll be back."

For the remainder of that week I was filled with apprehension, but nothing unusual occurred, either concerning my own private life, which included my work for Bill, or my life when I was within the four walls of Tor-Fret, except perhaps one thing, which was, in its own way, very pleasant. It happened on the Friday when Mr. Stanley came into the room as I was putting on my coat and said to me, "Could you spare a minute? He'd like to

4

see you." He jerked his chin upwards. And I realized he was referring to the brother he had spoken about earlier.

"Yes, yes, of course."

"You have time?"

"Oh yes. Plenty of time."

He looked towards the far door, and then he said quietly, "You . . . you have seen Maurice?"

It was his way of asking if I had told my employer I was going. I shook my head. "I haven't seen him all afternoon. I think he's out somewhere."

"Ah, yes, yes. He'll be gone to the pool." The old man's voice sank lower still. "He never says when he's going. Let's no one go with him either." He nodded his head quickly at this point. "It's understandable. He won't be helped. . . . Doesn't like people viewing him. Understandable, understandable."

Doesn't like people viewing him! He had made his retreat very safe, had Mr. Maurice. The members of the household respected his wishes and left him to himself at the lake. The word duplicity grew larger before my eyes. And I asked myself if I was such a gullible type that I had not seen some evidence of this trait when I first met him. Yet why decry my lack of perception, for wasn't he deceiving, and successfully, other members of his family? But that, I told myself once again as I went out of the room with Mr. Stanley, had nothing to do with me, nothing. It wasn't my business.

I went up the broad bare oak stairs on to a wide landing, then from this down a narrow corridor which opened up into a square hallway, the walls of which were covered with pictures, mostly portraits. I guessed I was in the south wing of the house which was to the right of the terraced rooms. It struck me that the invalid's room was a long way from the centre of the house, until I learned that it was almost above the kitchens and easily accessible by a back stairway.

Mr. Stanley turned yet another corner, and then he opened a door and across his shoulder I saw Logan Rossiter carrying an old man in his arms towards a bed. They both turned their heads sharply in our direction, and it was the old man who spoke, and with a voice so strong that it denied all connection with his frail, night-shirted body. "You beardless old goat! Why couldn't you knock, or wait?"

By this time Logan Rossiter had deposited the old man in the bed and covered him up; and as he arranged the pillows and with strange gentleness pressed him back among them, he said, "Now, old 'un, behave yourself; you have a visitor."

"That's what I mean, that's what I mean."

"Now, now. Let me put your two hairs straight," went on Logan, and I watched him wet the end of his finger in his mouth and take the long wisp of white hair upwards from the brow, before turning to me and saying with studied politeness, "Good afternoon, Miss Mitchell."

"Good afternoon."

"Didn't know you were in, Logan," said Mr. Stanley now. "When did you arrive?"

"Oh, about half an hour since."

"You've been up here all the time?"

"Yes. His nibs here"—he gave the old man in the bed a gentle punch with his fist—"was yelling blue murder for company."

"Well, not a soul, not a soul near me since dinner-time. You two!" He pointed at Mr. Stanley as if his twin was standing by his side. "You two, never out of the cellar, slopping about. . . . A man could die."

"You don't turn your nose up at the slop." Mr. Stanley nodded towards his brother.

But now the old man did not answer him; he was looking at me as if he was just becoming aware of my presence. And I watched his face soften. He raised his hand and said, "Come here. Come over here and sit down beside me." He patted the counterpane.

And when I hesitated to sit on the bed, Logan Rossiter said, "Go on, sit down. He likes ladies sitting on his bed,

51

the old reprobate." Again he gently punched the old man, and this elicited a chuckle from him, but he did not take his eyes from me, and when I sat down he took hold of my hand and did not speak for a long time but just stared at me. And then he said a strange thing. "I felt you. I felt you the first day you came into the house. You were down there." He pointed over towards the floor at the far end of the room which I thought must be the beginning of the drawing-room. "Nobody told me you had come, but I felt it. I said to myself, 'There's a woman down there, and she's nice.' "

"Don't believe a word he's saying," Logan Rossiter put in.

"It's true, it's true, Logan; I did have that feeling. And it's true that she's nice." He brought his eyes from his nephew and looked at me full in the face again as he repeated the compliment. "And you are nice, you are nice, my dear."

Logan Rossiter seemed to be amused and this brought embarrassment to me. If he hadn't been in the room I am sure I would have felt perfectly at ease with the old man, for, like his two younger brothers, he had a charm that was captivating. My thoughts at this point went off at a tangent. All the Rossiters apparently had charm, except perhaps the eldest . . . and yet . . .

As if he was divining my thoughts and determined to make me see him in a new light, in the light of the Rossiters being a charming family as a whole, he said now to his uncle, "I think you are right. I think Maurice is very fortunate in his choice of a new secretary." There was no sarcasm underlying the words, the tone was ordinary; even so, I felt more embarrassed than ever.

I was saved from replying by Hollings entering the room carrying a tray on which there was a meal set. He had come in by the door which led down into the kitchens, and he showed no surprise at seeing me. There was a general movement. I had risen from the bed and was near Hollings as, balancing the tray on one hand, he went to pull a small table towards him. Instinctively my hands went out to assist him, and when he had placed the tray on the table he looked at me and said, "Thank you, madam."

It had a strange sound, a nice sound, although by omitting to address me as . . . miss, he had placed me in a category beyond youth. I found I was very pleased by it—"Thank you, madam." I had never been called "madam" before, except in a shop I had once visited in Newcastle, but Hollings' way of saying "madam" was different altogether; moreover, it was the first time the man had opened his mouth to me.

"Come along, we must all get going and let him have his supper. Say goodbye now." Logan Rossiter bent towards the old man. "Say goodbye now, Uncle."

The old man's interest was riveted on his tray now and he seemed to bring his eyes reluctantly on to me again, but his tone still held the ring of sincerity when he said, "Goodbye, my dear; goodbye. But promise me, promise me, you'll come up again. Any time, any time. . . . But not when I'm out of bed." He laughed and flapped his hand at Mr. Stanley. "Dolt, that's what you are, dolt."

After assuring him that I would come and see him again I said goodbye. As I went out of the room with Mr. Stanley, we were followed by Logan Rossiter, and when we were crossing the gallery he said, "My uncle is a character, but he never says what he doesn't mean . . . except"—he put his hand on Mr. Stanley's shoulder—"to his brothers. But that is brotherly licence, isn't it, Uncle?" Without waiting for a reply he turned to me and continued, "He would, I know, very much like you to visit him now and then."

"I'll be pleased to."

"Thank you."

When we reached the main hall Mr. Stanley mumbled a goodbye and left us, and Logan Rossiter, turning to me, said, "You're leaving now?"

"Yes, I've finished."

"I'm going down the hill, I'll walk with you." There was no "May I?" It was a definite statement. He lifted his hat from the hallstand which was made of upturned antlers, an ugly thing but somehow not out of place in its surroundings, and then we were walking across the terrace and down the fell, and silence surrounded us again. I couldn't speak, and he didn't until we were halfway down the road, and then he said, "You're finding my brother amenable?"

"Yes. Yes, quite." I was looking ahead as I spoke.

"You like the work?"

"Yes, it's very interesting."

"But what do you really think of it?" I knew that he was looking at me, but I kept my eyes on the road ahead as I answered, "It's . . . it's a little too personal."

He stopped abruptly and this action brought my eyes towards him, and I stopped, too. "You're right; you're absolutely, utterly right. I've been telling him that for years. But please . . . I'd better warn you. If he asks your opinion, don't tell him what you've just told me. For, you know, a writer is as susceptible to hurt with regard to his work as a mother is about her child. You criticize a writer's work, and even if he knows you're right he will hate you. It's strange, but no matter how old a writer is he never grows up in this respect. Other men have to, but not writers. I'm a solicitor, and if I hated all the people who criticize me, then my life would become unbearable."

As I looked at him I endorsed in my mind what he was saying. Yes, life for him would become unbearable, for he could arouse dislike very easily, whether it was warranted or not. And now, and not for the first time during the last few days, I was wondering if I had misjudged this man as I had, in the opposite way, judged his brother.

We moved forward again and the silence descended on us once more, until, on reaching the main road, a car swept past us to pull up on the grass verge. And I saw Logan Rossiter's face light up as he lifted his hand to hail the driver. The driver was a girl. As Logan Rossiter helped her out of the car she stood just below his shoulder. Her hair was dark, not black, nor yet dark chestnut, but something of the sheen that you see on the dark feathers of a mallard when it is flying against the light. Her eyes were deep brown, the eye sockets long, and the brows curbing them took their hue from the hair. The mouth was full and wide, the skin of her face a warm peach—not like her body, which I knew to be pure white. Here was the girl I'd seen standing naked before Maurice Rossiter on the shore of the lake, and now Logan Rossiter, taking her hand, brought her the few steps towards me, saying, "Let me introduce my fiancée, Miss Noreen Badcliff." Then, turning his head, he said, "Miss Kate Mitchell. Maurice's secretary, you know."

The girl and I stared at each other for a long second. She looked straight into my eyes, and I into hers, and I knew that had I not known her real nature I would have found her attractive, fascinatingly attractive. She was small, petite; her figure even in her plain suit was perfect. She was like a miniature Venus—and The Big Fellow was in love with her.

"I'm very pleased to meet you."

Not the usual greeting of "How-do-you-do?" but the more sincere "I'm very pleased to meet you." I would have been captivated by her had I not known her real nature. Birds of a feather. You could hardly pass a thread between her and my employer. I inclined my head but found that I couldn't speak. To my surprise—for really it was no business of mine—I found myself consumed with anger against her for making a fool of . . . The Big Fellow. It didn't seem right somehow that he should be taken for a ride by his brother and this girl.

What I would have answered her by way of introduction I do not know, for I was saved by the bus coming round the bend of the main road, and I turned my head quickly towards it and then back, saying, "Excuse me, I must catch the bus. Some of them, they . . . they won't wait." I darted from them and ran towards the oncoming vehicle. I had been unjust to the drivers of the buses; they would stop anywhere for you on this lonely road.

My anger against the girl persisted all the way home and blotted out the personal matters in my life, and I wondered, among other things, and not for the first time since it had happened, who the man was who had lain on the rock above the lake. The fact that he was spying did not say much for his own character, but I had a feeling of relief engendered by the thought that this unknown man might be the means of exposing the underhand game of Maurice Rossiter and this girl. Unless he meant to use his knowledge to blackmail the pair of them. Of one thing I was certain: the man was not a member of the household. I had by now met them all—Patterson the outside man, and Bennett the old cook—but none of them was as bald as the man I had seen lying on the rock. Nor did any of them wear fine highly polished black boots. Hollings wore a black suit and black shoes, but Hollings had thick white hair.

A little way out of the village I saw Rodney with the van waiting by the roadside near the path that went up behind the village and up to the cottage. It was a path broad and even enough to take the van for quite some way, so I alighted and went back to him. "I waited for the bus," he said. "I thought you'd like a lift up."

"That's kind of you, Rodney." I smiled my thanks, and at the same time I was wishing he hadn't, for I was wanting to be alone. Yet I was grateful for the lift up the steep hill. He had hardly started the motor before he said, "That fellow you used to knock around with when you first came here, he was in *The Fox* last night, and I heard him ask Ossie where you were working now and I tipped him the wink to keep mum—I mean Ossie. I thought perhaps you wouldn't want him to know."

"Thanks, Rodney. You did right." I closed my eyes wearily. Villages were rather like enlarged homes, they knew all about you. It was no use trying to hide anything

56

from them. Like the members of a family, they either liked you or disliked you. Yet whatever touched you, touched them. Rodney drove the van straight over a hillock and for a moment we were thrown together, and then he said as he still kept his eyes ahead, "If you want him dealt with at any time you've just got to say."

"Thanks, Rodney," I said. "I'll remember, but I don't think it will come to that."

"I'm popping over to Amble," he said.

"Are you?" I didn't ask why and somehow I thought he was disappointed by my lack of interest. Then when he had stopped the van at the nearest point it could get to the house he suddenly turned to me and said, "You haven't any time for me as a fellow . . . I mean . . . You know?"

"Oh, Rodney. . . ."

"That's O.K." He touched my sleeve. "Just wanted to make sure. . . . It's O.K. It's O.K. Don't worry." His voice was high and rushed. "You and me's good friends. Appreciate it an' all, I do. . . . It's O.K. Good night, Kate. Good night. Be seeing you."

"Good night, Rodney."

My voice sounded sad, and I felt sad. What a pity I couldn't like Rodney. But I did like him, you couldn't help but like him. . . . But marry him? Oh! And live a life of platitudes? As this thought came to me I realized with almost a shock how temperamentally alike Rodney and Arthur were, and for the first time since Arthur and I had parted I felt a surging sense of relief at what I had escaped from.

3

It was raining as I crossed the terrace towards the front door on that Monday afternoon, but before I reached the porch there came towards me a strange man carrying a leather bag. And on each side of him were the twins. The man glanced at me casually as I passed, but the two old men nodded quickly at me, and then I heard Mr. Stanley's voice saying "Goodbye, doctor. Goodbye, and thank you for all you've done."

I hesitated in the hall for a moment, thinking: It's Mr. Stephen who must be worse, poor old soul. Yet on Friday he had seemed so alive and well in spite of his fragile look. And then the old men were facing me, both their faces perturbed. It was Mr. Stanley who said, "Oh, my dear, it's been a weekend. What a lot has happened since you were here last."

"Is it Mr. Stephen?" I asked.

They both shook their heads vigorously. "No, no. Young Logan." It was Mr. Bernard speaking now. "Fell over the drop. . . . Wonder didn't break his neck."

I found that I was cupping my cheek with one hand as I repeated, "Mr. Logan? Is he badly hurt?"

"His ankle's broken and his shoulder's out," Mr. Stanley said. "But there's hardly a part of him that's not black and blue. We can't understand it." He moved his head slowly from side to side, and, looking at his brother, he said, "Can we?"

Mr. Bernard's head jerked quickly and he brought out, "Knows every rock like back of his hand. Every nook 'n' cranny. Can't make it out."

"What did he say about it?" My voice was a whisper.

"Not much, not much." It was Mr. Bernard still going on. "Says he must have slipped. Slipped, be damned, I say. It's funny. It's funny, I tell you, Stanley, it's funny." He was nodding at his brother now, and Mr. Stanley, putting his hand on his twin's shoulder, said, "All right, all right, don't get worked up." Then he turned his face towards me, saying, "We'll be seeing you later."

When I entered my room I stopped just within the door, because there, sitting at the desk, was Maurice Rossiter, and his eyes seemed to be waiting for me. His face looked white and rather drawn, and he did not give me

58

the usual greeting but said right away, "I heard the uncles telling you. As they said, we've had a weekend of it."

I walked towards the desk and looked intently into this man's face. If he was putting on a show of concern, then he was doing it admirably. Even being able to turn pale on command, for pale he was, much paler than I had ever seen him. I felt as I stared at him that his concern was genuine—at least at the moment.

"When did it happen?" I asked.

"Saturday afternoon. Broad daylight. We . . . we can't understand it." He looked down at the desk, adding, "I was just gathering up some papers, although I don't feel a bit like writing. In fact, I feel very much off colour today."

He looked up at me expecting some word of sympathy, but I couldn't respond; and as I turned from him to go and hang up my coat I felt his eyes on my back. When I returned to the desk he was at the other side but still looking at his papers, his hand fumbling among them, and he said, "We had such a good time, too, on Friday night. He celebrated his engagement, you know. We were all together at supper. It was like old times. I understand you've met Miss Badcliff."

I raised my head and looked across the space into his waiting eyes and said in a flat voice, "Yes, I've met Miss Badcliff." Perhaps it was the tone of my voice that made his eyes narrow, and as he looked at me I warned myself to be careful, for I was very near to throwing my knowledge at him.

He was staring at me with a puzzled, penetrating look now; then he jerked his chin upwards. I had learned that this characteristic action meant that he was dismissing something from his mind . . . putting it aside. Following this, he left me to my work.

The next hour I worked mechanically because I was thinking . . . thinking of Logan Rossiter falling over a cliff in broad daylight. A man, moreover, who knew the fells like the back of his hand, as had been said. When Hollings brought my tea in I spoke to him. It was the first time I had done this except to thank him for the service. I said, "How is Mr. Logan, Hollings?"

"He's in pretty bad shape, madam. But lucky, very lucky he's alive."

I ventured further. "It's odd that he should have slipped in the daylight."

"Very odd, if he had slipped, madam." Now the old man looked at me for a moment in silence, penetrating silence. And then he said, "You use the road to the bottom more than anybody except Mr. Logan himself. Have you seen any strangers about lately?"

"No, Hollings." I shook my head. "The first day I came I saw a man—I think his name is Weaver. I saw him twice in the one day."

"And you haven't seen him since?"

I paused. Somehow I felt inclined to tell Hollings that, although I hadn't seen the man again, yet I knew he was about the place watching from some point above the path that led down to the road, but all I said was, "No. No, I haven't seen him since."

He leant further across the table towards me now and I could just hear his voice as he said, "Should you see him at any time would you be good enough to tell me . . . on the quiet, that is, madam. Do you understand?"

I nodded once, then said, "Yes, Hollings, I understand. I'll tell you if I see him."

"Thank you, madam." He straightened up, and with his measured step he walked out of the room. . . . I liked Hollings. . . . But then I mustn't forget I had liked Maurice Rossiter. Who in this house was honest, and who wasn't? Could you tell?

"What was Hollings on about?" I was surprised to see my employer standing within the door of his room, his appearance had been so abrupt.

"On about?" I screwed up my face. "I asked him if Mr. Logan was any better and he said not much. He was

60

telling me about . . . about his injuries." My lie was fumbled, but it apparently satisfied him and I watched him come shuffling across the room with his weird dancing step. He passed my desk and went out of the door, and I looked down at my typewriter and drew in a deep breath.

It was almost at this moment that a wood pigeon flew over the house. At least I heard its call. Coo-oo! Coo. Coo-oo! Coo. You don't usually hear a wood pigeon call in flight but I didn't think of this at the time, though I was to remember it later that day.

I had been sitting typing for about perhaps fifteen minutes when, to my utter amazement, I heard the voice of my employer together with that of another man coming from his room. Startled, I looked towards the door through which he had just recently passed, and then over the wide space towards his room. He could, of course, have re-entered his room by the door at the end of the hall, yet he rarely used this way because of two steps that led down to it. But it wasn't my employer's voice that startled me as much as that of the other man, for I recognized it. It was the whine of the odd man, Weaver. I would have recognized it from out of a hundred voices. I found myself on my feet compelled to go towards the door. I had a sheet of typescript in my hand. Necessity was making me wily. Should Maurice Rossiter open the door I was on my way to ask a question. But as I stood outside, my head bent forward, I felt my face crinkling with bewilderment. Their voices were behind the door yet seemed distant. I can't explain it; as if the voices were echoes, and too far away for me to make out what they were saying. I did not think about what I was going to do or I wouldn't have had the courage to do it, but as I tapped on the door I opened it, not waiting to be bidden to enter. And there I stood with the door in my hand gaping at the empty room. Empty but for the voices, still like echoes but nearer now and coming from the far corner of the room. Coming—I realized in blank amazement

—from a corner cupboard, an old weathered oak cupboard that had not seen polish for years. It was impossible for any one person to be in the cupboard, let alone two. But the sound drew me towards it, and as if I were touching something hot I turned the brass handle. And then the voices were no longer an echo. Although they still appeared to be coming from a distance, what they were saying was clearly intelligible. But for the moment I couldn't take in the words I was hearing because I was looking at the back of the cupboard. The inside did not lead to a point as would be expected from a corner cupboard, but was cut off short by a slat of wood, about—I should imagine—nine inches wide. And in this panel of wood right on my eye level was a door of about twelve inches high. It was not wide open, but wide enough for me to see from the edge of it that on its inside it was padded with some grey material about twice as thick as the wood itself. And now my attention was jerked from the little door by the sound of Maurice Rossiter's voice, saying, "You blasted fool!" followed immediately by the voice of Weaver. "How was Aa t'know, Mr. Maurice? There he was goin' down the hill, and when he was near the bottom what did he do but turn his backside 'round an' come back. An' you gone t' the lake, an' when I calls ya don't answer."

"There was no need, you imbecile. I was alone."

"But how the hell was Aa to work that oot, I ask ya, when I saw her along the road a while afore, makin' this way?"

"But not to meet me." The words were a low hiss now.

"But how was Aa to know, I ask ya? An' then he goes in the hoose an' comes oot as if the devil was after him an' makes along by the greenhouses t' the lake. What was Aa to think, I ask ya?"

"I don't expect you to think. I expect you to do as you're told. Do you realize you might have killed him?"

"How was Aa ta know he would topple over? Him as is

as steady on his pins as the rocks themsels. An' it wasn't a big stone, an' Aa just toppled it ower as if it was fallin' like."

"Toppled it over as if it was falling!" The voice was scathing. "You might as well have put your name and address on it. Don't you know he's on to you? And may God help you if he gets any proof. He'll send you along the line for life. I'm telling you."

"He'll send me along no line." Weaver's voice was suddenly no longer whining but heavy with threat. "If it's me or him, Aa know who it'll be."

"Be quiet, listen." There came a pause, and then Maurice Rossiter's voice hissing, "Get going. There's someone coming."

The someone I recognized as Mr. Stanley, for his voice came in a high echo of surprise, exclaiming, "Why, Maurice! What are you doing here? It's a long time since you managed . . ." The voice broke off and I heard the sound of quick footsteps, and then Mr. Stanley speaking again in hushed tones, saying, and sternly this time, "Now, Maurice. . . ."

"It's all right, it's all right, Uncle. I only came down for a drink. I fancied it, I'm a bit het up."

There was another pause before Mr. Stanley spoke, and then he said, "It was agreed that we have wine at meal times only. Now wasn't it? No more high jinks, or low jinks. Anyway, if you wanted a glass why didn't you ask me? I would have got it for you. . . . Maurice, you didn't come down here for wine. You . . ."

At this point I almost let out a high scream. Only the action of clapping my hands tightly over my mouth prevented the sound escaping, for there were fingers touching my shoulder. I felt I had been caught in the act of stealing, or something equally dishonest. It was some seconds before I turned my body from the cupboard and looked to see who had found me out. And perhaps the gulp I gave was in relief when I saw Hollings looking at me, and raising his fingers to warn me to silence. Then he, too, was listening. I could not concentrate on what was being said any more and only snatches of the voices came to me. The shock of Hollings finding me had turned my legs to water and I had some difficulty in standing. I turned away from the corner cupboard, and as I did so I heard Mr. Stanley's voice, the tone angry, now, saying, "Don't lie, Maurice. The drain door is unlocked. Look, you can't get over that."

I sat down on the couch where Maurice Rossiter usually rested in the afternoon and watched Hollings shutting out the voices by closing the little door. He followed this by closing the cupboard door. Then, coming towards me, he said, "How did you find that out?"

"I . . . I didn't. I just heard the voices from the other room. I recognized the man Weaver speaking. I came in here, and when I opened the cupboard door, well . . ." I spread my hands out to him.

"The trap-door was open?"

"Yes."

Hollings, putting his hand out towards my elbow, said, "We'd better go into the other room."

When I was seated at my desk, Hollings, standing opposite to me, said, "That ingenious contraption is simply an air vent leading down into the cellar. My late master's grandfather had a number constructed in several rooms in the house all leading down to the cellar. You see, right up to the beginning of the last century this was a very wild stretch of country." I nodded. I had read quite a bit about the lawlessness that had gone on in the last century, in some parts of the county. "But my late master had all the vents sealed up. I wasn't aware that the one in Mr. Maurice's room had been opened." He paused now, and, leaning towards me, he said slowly, "No doubt you are already aware that there are two opposing camps in this house. May I ask which one you are likely to support, madam?"

The question actually made me tremble. I certainly wasn't on Maurice Rossiter's side, althought I was working for him, but could I say I was on the side of . . . The Big Fellow? I was sorry that he had been hurt, but I didn't really like the man any better now than when I had first met him. I said, "I don't wish to take sides. It is really no business of mine, is it?"

"You cannot live in this house, even for a short time each day as you do, and not take sides, madam. You are either for my master or against him."

"Which master?" I asked, looking him straight in the eye.

"Mr. Logan," he said.

"I would be on the side of right," I said, still evading a direct answer.

"That's good enough for me." He nodded his head. "And now can you tell me what you heard between Weaver and Mr. Maurice? And I would ask you to hurry, madam. Mr. Maurice might be back at any moment."

"I understand that Weaver threw a boulder which toppled Mr. Logan over the cliff."

"We know that, madam." The "we" referred to himself and Logan Rossiter. "But did he say why he did it, at that time, and at that particular place?"

I stared across into the thin wrinkled face, and not for the life of me could I say, "Because he thought that Mr. Logan's fiancée would be at the lakeside with Mr. Maurice." And Hollings was prevented from repeating his question by the sound of a shuffling step in the hall coming towards my door. On this, with just a quick nod towards me, he went swiftly towards Mr. Maurice's room, and a second after he had closed the door behind him Maurice Rossiter entered by the hall door. He passed me as if I wasn't there. And for this I was thankful.

4

It rained heavily all day on the Sunday, and as I stood peeling the potatoes for the Sunday dinner at the little kitchen window that looked almost directly up towards Neete Fell, my mother, coming behind me, said for at least the fifth time since I had come downstairs this morning, "Don't worry now; come on, buck up." She put her hand on my shoulder.

I stopped my work and turned round to her, a potato in one hand, a knife in the other, and, shaking my head, I said, "I'm not worrying about him; I've told you it was over two years ago. I couldn't alter myself now even if I wanted to."

She did not move back from me, but she drew her head into her shoulders as if to view me from a different angle. "If it isn't him, then what is it?" she said. "For something's worrying you."

I placed the potato back in the bowl, and resting my hands on the little draining-board, looked at the sheets of drifting rain, like waves following one another across the brow of the fell, and I made up my mind to tell her and my father what was worrying me, for I was in a state of uncertainty as to the right thing to do. And so I said to her, "Come into the room and I'll tell you. . . ."

Because of my father's frequent interruptions the telling took some time, for he demanded to know the ins and outs of every incident, asking questions that I could not answer, as I did not know the answers. My mother hadn't spoken at all during the telling, and not until I had quite finished did she say quietly, "I would leave there, lass."

"No, no, I wouldn't advise that, Kate." My father was shaking his head at her sombrely. "This is really none of her business that I can see. She is just worrying herself about something that doesn't concern her." He turned to me again. "You go up there to type that fellow's work. Well, then, type his work and keep yourself to yourself and let them get on with it."

"It's easier said than done."

"Yes," quickly endorsed my mother, "it's easier said than done. And I say to you again, lass: you leave that place."

I looked at her for a moment and then turned my eyes away, "No," I said quietly. "No, I won't leave until I've got to." As I made this decision—and it was a decision, for I had been wavering in my mind since Friday night whether I would give up the job or not—and voiced it, I experienced the most odd sensation. I could only explain it by saying that if Hollings had been standing before me at that moment and had asked, "Which side are you on?" I would, without any hesitation, have answered, "Mr. Logan's."

My father said at this point, "It seems that this fellow's mind's twisted as well as his body."

He was right there, I thought, for if Maurice Rossiter had not been stricken by polio he would have led a gay life, even a wild one. His novel gave me glimpses of the kind of life he would have chosen. This being denied him, he was holding a grudge, not against all mankind but against his brother, and the question I was asking myself now was, why? I recalled the conversation I had overheard in the summer-house and I couldn't see him venting such destructive spleen and bitterness on his brother just because he kept a tight hold on the purse-strings. It seemed too small a reason to evoke so much malice.

My father, smiling broadly at me now, patted my knee as he said, "You go on about your own business and take no heed of anybody. Take all in and say nowt. . . . At least you can't grumble about it being a dull job, now can you?"

My mother rose from the chair, repeating my father's

words as she looked at him, "Say nowt . . . except keep you informed of everything that's going on."

"Aye . . . eye." He laughed up at her. "It will be like a story, having a chapter read to me every night. But mind"—he dug his finger towards me—"you'll have to make it exciting. Aye, aye, I want some thrills. Real or make-believe, I want some thrills." Now his hand came and clasped my arm firmly as he continued quickly in a soft serious tone, "I'm only funnin', don't lass; don't look so glum. Everything will turn out all right, you'll see."

In the kitchen again and behind the closed door, my mother said once more to me, "I would leave there, lass. You take my advice and leave there."

Real or fancy, I could report to thrills the following week. Tor-Fret was quiet. I did my work; Maurice Rossiter's manner towards me was ordinary, business-like and ordinary. I enquired every day how Mr. Logan was and was told he was improving. The twins asked me to go up and see Mr. Stephen but warned me that, should he refer to Mr. Logan's illness, I was to speak of it as 'flu. No, there was no exciting episode to relate to my father. And in my private life only one thing happened out of the ordinary. I was in the bus coming back to Rothcorn. It was almost full and I had to take the last empty seat and sit next to Hazel Osborne, who, after keeping a steady silence the whole of the journey, turned towards me just before I was about to alight, and with primmed lips said, "You thought you were putting me nose out, didn't you? Well, yours is out now. Mr. Rodney's after somebody in Amble. . . . How d'you like it?"

As I stood up I smiled at her and whispered back, "I like it very much," and left her with that to chew on.

In the kitchen that night we laughed over this. It was the first real laugh I'd had for some time. . . .

But the following week at Tor-Fret was not so quiet. The change started almost before I had settled down to my work on the Monday afternoon. After a very cursory greeting Maurice Rossiter said, "You'll have to do all Friday's work over again, the script is a mess."

"How do you make that out?" I said after staring at him blankly for a moment.

"How do I make that out? . . . How do you spell incredulous?"

"i . . n . . c . . r . . e . . d . . u . . l . . o . . u . . s."

"Oh, you do? Well, look at that."

I took the sheet from his hand and there underscored in red ink was the word incredible.

My father, and many of those with whom I had been brought up in the mining village, would often make the statement, "It's hardly credible." In consequence I had always found myself using incredible rather than incredulous. And last Friday I had been so disturbed with one thing and another I hadn't paid attention, with the result that I had used the familiar term.

"I'm sorry," I said. "It's my mistake."

"And there's hardly a page where you haven't forgotten your spacing. Look at that . . . and that." He pointed pages out to me where joined words were scored heavily through with the red pencil.

Again I said I was sorry. I told him I had been in a hurry and hadn't checked the work.

"But you're supposed to. That's what I engage you for." He stared at me fixedly for a moment, then, dragging himself round, said, "All right, all right, get on with it."

On this, something flared up in me and I only stopped myself from crying at his back, "No, you get on with it," and walking out.

At three o'clock, when Hollings brought my tea, I was still fuming. He also brought me a message from Logan Rossiter. It was to the effect that he would like to see me after I had finished my work. I had as yet no inkling that this message was the reason for Maurice Rossiter's bad mood. I paid particular attention to my work all afternoon and checked it thoroughly before leaving it in a neat pile at the side of my desk. I hadn't seen anything more of my employer and didn't want to. I picked up my hat and coat and went out into the hall in search of Hollings, and almost immediately he appeared from the far passage-way. He beckoned me and we mounted the stairs, and neither of us spoke. He crossed the broad landing and knocked on a door, and when a voice from within the room bade him enter he opened the door and stood aside, allowing me to pass him, then closed the door again. And I was in the room looking towards the window, where sat Logan Rossiter. Discounting the plastered foot and the arm in a sling, I was startled at the change in him. Sitting there he no longer appeared to me like . . . The Big Fellow. He seemed to have shrunk. Perhaps this illusion was helped by the outsize winged leather chair in which he was sitting.

His eyes were on me as I went towards him and I spoke first. "Are you feeling better, Mr. Rossiter?" I asked quietly.

"Yes. Yes, I'm much better. Please sit down." He pointed, and then added, "You will be thinking by now that Tor-Fret is full of doddering invalids."

"No. No, I don't think that." I could find nothing original to say but kept looking at his face where one side was mottled with bruise marks from the chin to the brow. One eye looked swollen still, and was yellow tinged. And as I stared at him, pity rose in me. Yet I wasn't thinking so much of him at this moment as of the man Weaver. I could see him as I had done that first morning on the road, and there sprang into being a hatred for that rascally individual.

Logan Rossiter was saying now, "I wonder if you will do me a favour?"

"Certainly, I will if I can." My voice was low, and, as Maurice Rossiter would say, earnest sounding.

"It's a busy time. I have a lot of work piling up. My clerk was here at the week-end and he suggested sending one of the girls out to take down my letters. But it's such a long way from Alnwick and I wondered . . . I wondered if it wouldn't be too much for you—that is, whether you could give me an hour after you have finished with Maurice? I would get Patterson to run you home later."

I did not stop to think, or even hesitate, but said, "Yes, yes, of course. It won't be any trouble. And as long as I can get away before dark I can easily get the bus."

"Thank you. It will be only for a week or so—a fortnight I should say at the most." He now turned his head and looked out of the window. The view, I noticed, took in a number of greenhouses, some of them in a sad state of repair. Beyond these I knew lay the lake, but it was shut from view by the trees and the outcrops of rock. Quite abruptly he said, "How are you going to manage in the winter? We're often cut off up here. A few years ago I wasn't able to get up to the house for a week; I had to stay down in the town." Then before I could make any answer he turned to me and added, "You could quite easily do Maurice's typing at home, couldn't you? Have you a typewriter?"

I dropped my eyes away from his and said, "Yes. Yes, I have a typewriter. And I have put that to Mr. Maurice, but . . . but he wants his work done on the spot."

"Oh, we'll see about that." For the first time since coming into the room he sounded like the Logan Rossiter I had come to know. The tone sharp, the words clipped. And then, his tone changing abruptly again, he said, "But should you not come up here Uncle Stepehen would miss you . . . he's quite taken to you." His eyes were hard on me, yet the whole expression on his face had softened. He looked different altogether when he was speaking kindly and I felt a warmth spreading over me. "I like Mr. Stephen," I said.

We were looking at each other, and strangely now it was not my eyes that dropped away but his, and, changing the subject yet again, he said, "Do you like your other work? You do work down in the village, don't you?"

"Yes. And I like it in a way," I said, "but it's routine. There's nothing exciting about it, although you do a bit of everything, costing and wages, all things connected with a builder's business."

"Have you any brothers or sisters?"

"No, I'm the only one."

"What is your father?"

"He was a miner. But he got silicosis."

"Oh dear, dear." His brows drew together and I felt the stretching of his skin to be painful.

"Is he bedridden?"

"Oh no, not at all."

"What does he do with himself to pass the time?"

As I looked at this man whom I had thoroughly disliked—let there be no mistake about that—I got the strange idea he was merely asking questions to keep me with him because he was lonely. Disregard this feeling as I would, it persisted, and so, after a little hesitation, I found myself relating my father's activities. I told him that he was very handy about the house, that he read a great deal. I told him the names of some of his books and how he had introduced me to selective reading. I told him also that he played the piano, being quite an accomplished pianist, although self-taught, mostly through Star Folio albums. And all the while he sat looking at me, his eyes on my face, his big-framed body relaxed in the leather chair, until a voice broke in. The voice came from outside the door and it said, "All right, darling?" It was a question, and Logan Rossiter, turning his eyes sharply from my face, looked across the room and called, "Yes, yes. All right, my dear," and in came the girl.

I was on my feet before she reached the chair, and as their hands joined I turned away, saying, "I'll come up tomorrow night, Mr. Rossiter."

"Oh, stay, don't go."

"No, please don't go." It was the girl speaking now. She was looking straight at me, a smile on her face. "Please don't go because of me."

"I'll miss my bus if I don't hurry." I looked at my watch, and as I did so I thought that this was becoming a lame excuse. This was the second time that I had almost dived out of this girl's presence under the excuse of catching a bus. I glanced towards Logan Rossiter and asked, "It will be all right for tomorrow night?"

"Yes, thank you. . . . Thank you, Kate. . . . Goodnight."

"Goodnight, sir."

"Goodnight." I looked towards the girl, then went out, and as I crossed the landing I wasn't thinking of her but that Logan Rossiter had called me by my name . . . the name he had turned his nose up at on our first meeting. And I liked the way he had said it. . . . Kate.

When I reached home I gave my father another episode, but I didn't stress the fact that I had found Logan Rossiter vastly changed . . . at least, in his manner towards me.

The following morning Rodney Stringer put his head round the door of the cubby-hole of my office in the yard, and after saying, "Hello there," added, "I'm going to Shirston this afternoon; I could give you a lift as far as the well. . . . O.K.?"

"O.K., Rodney," I said. "Thanks."

As he went to withdraw, one of the workmen, stacking slates just outside the main door, shouted, "You be careful of him, miss. Proper Casanova he's turnin' out to be."

Rodney looked back at me rather sheepishly as he said, "You can't move in this village. I've sworn afore I'll get meself into the town. . . . See you later then."

"All right, Rodney." I smiled on hearing him doing verbal battle with the man outside. . . .

Later that morning, when I came down the hill after having my dinner, there he was, and I had hardly got into the cab beside him before he said, "Well, I'd better tell you right away before that lot"—he jerked his head back towards the village—"get one in. I've taken up seriously with a girl in Amble."

"Oh, I am glad, Rodney."

"Yes, I thought you'd be." He swung round the bend before going on, "Well, as there was no look-in with you —oh, I realized that almost from the beginning—I had to do something."

"But I like you very much, Rodney, you know that."

"Yes, but likin' and the other thing are poles apart, you know that too."

"Yes . . . yes." I looked straight before me. And now he took his eyes for a second from the road and, glancing at me, with a twinkle commented dryly, "I had to do something or Hazel would have had me pinned for life. . . . Oh, I couldn't have stood that. No." Then, looking ahead again, he added, "You'll like her."

"I'm sure I shall, Rodney.

He sighed and, after a short silence, asked, "How you getting on up there?"

"Oh, all right."

"What they like?"

"Like men. There's eight of them."

"No women?"

"No. No women." I did not add, "Not yet."

"My hat?" We laughed again.

"I heard something funny the other day," he said. "But you can't believe anything they say, it's so stretched. But I heard they had big drinking bouts, went as mad as hatters."

"They might have done years ago, last century, but not now," I said.

"Oh, but this was only recently. Or at least that's what was inferred."

"I think they're mistaken."

"Aye; as I said, everything's stretched. It always is in a village. Oh, aye, more so in a village . . . don't I know." He laughed again. He was still laughing when he dropped me at the end of the road. . . .

Fifteen minutes later I entered Tor-Fret. I crossed the hall, opened the door of the room and came to a dead stop. There, with his back to me, stood a strange man. He was dressed in black, he had a completely bald head and was wearing black shiny boots, and when he turned from Maurice Rossiter towards me I saw, to my gaping amazement, that the stranger was a minister. He was well into his sixties, perhaps older than he looked, for his portly figure and round red face gave the impression of vibrant health. I had been wrong in summing up character before, and this warned me against the instant recoil I had from this man. This recoil was not only caused by my sure knowledge that here was the person I had seen spying from the top of the rock, but by something behind the geniality in the pale-blue eyes.

"Ah . . . Kate." Maurice Rossiter seemed in one of his happy moods today, and he introduced the minister on a light note, saying, "This is the Reverend Fallenbor . . . Retired. And this, Reverend, is Miss Kate Mitchell, my . . . my very efficient secretary." What a different diagnosis of my capabilities from yesterday.

"How do you do, Miss Mitchell?" The minister was shaking my hand, holding it firmly—I could almost say gripping it hard, as some men do when they try to impress you with their hand-shake by bruising your bones. "Very pleased to make your acquaintance, Miss Mitchell. . . . My, my, you don't know what a phenomenon you are. For to my knowledge you're the first female to be on the staff of Tor-Fret for many, many years. In fact, Maurice"—he turned his head towards my employer—"I can't remember one, can you?"

"Yes, oh yes." Maurice Rossiter's voice was sober. Then he added, "But Kate is only the forerunner. There are new times coming to the house. There'll be a permanent lady shortly, and some of us will have to pull our socks up then, I'm afraid."

"Yes, indeed, indeed. Pull your socks up. Definitely you'll have to pull your socks up." The minister was laughing now, his stomach thrust out, his hand squarely placed across it as if to stop its shaking. And it seemed as if his hand had accomplished this, for quite suddenly his laughter ceased and I could see no reason for its abrupt ending except that my employer, who was standing somewhere to the side of me, had made some gesture which had cautioned the minister to check his gaiety. And this could have been so, because on looking at my employer I was surprised at the complete change in him also, for his face at the moment was stiff. But he quickly assumed his expression of charm and gaiety of manner as my eyes rested on him, and he heckled the minister playfully now, saying, "Come on, I'm going to throw you out. I want some work out of Kate, because one of these days she's going to tell me politely—Kate is always polite, Vicar . . ." He cast his eyes sideways at me before going on, "She's going to tell me that I must take a week's notice, for she is going into Alnwick to work for Logan."

"Never, never, not after she's worked for you." The minister was holding his hand palm upwards towards Maurice, and for the moment I felt my stomach heave a little at the smarminess of this individual. Evidently this man was someone whom my employer knew and trusted, someone who was in the know. Yet I had seen him spying on them, watching their every move through binoculars. My stomach heaved again. And I felt my lip curling. There was something in my make-up, some quality bred of my parents, that jibbed at this kind of nastiness. I turned from the two men and sat down at my desk and lowered my eyes to the typewriter.

"Goodbye, Miss Mitchell."

I inclined my head without raising my eyes and said, "Goodbye, sir."

They went out and the door closed after them, and I had a strong desire to open all the windows wide.

I did not start typing but sat with my hands clasped tightly on my lap, staring towards the broard terrace, and asking myself if I should tell Hollings what I knew about this minister. I couldn't tell Logan Rossiter, but Hollings was different. Hollings, I felt, would sift and sort out information and pass on only that which would help his master. Yet as I sat there I knew that I was afraid to divulge my knowledge of this man's actions to anyone, even my parents, and in the episode I would give my father tonight there would be no mention of the man who had been lying on the top of the rock. . . .

At five minutes past five I went up the stairs and across the landing to Logan Rossiter's door, and when I knocked I was bidden immediately to enter. He looked a little brighter tonight, more impatient, more himself, but his voice held no impatience when he spoke to me. It was unusually quiet, but his first words surprised me. "You're late. I thought for a moment you weren't coming. It's just on twenty past."

"Is it? I'm sorry. I thought it was only turned five past."

He turned a little travelling clock round on the table at his side. "It says twenty past, I must be fast." He smiled, and as I looked at his stretching skin I felt again rising in me an unusual surge of pity. His face looked so sore, so stiff and sore. I said to him, "How are you feeling today?"

"Oh . . . oh, much better. I'm better if I can work. . . . Look"—he held out some sheets to me—"I've been writing with my left hand. Can you make it out?"

I took the papers and began to read, then said, "Yes, yes, I can."

"They're just notes but they'll give me a lead. Oh, but before we start I must tell you, I've started on Borrow's *Lavengro*. Your telling me last night of some of the books that your father had read rather whetted my appetite. Look, I've got almost a third of the way through."

He had leant towards the window where some books were placed on a low table and his hand was on one of them when he stopped speaking, and, pulling himself up sharply with the aid of his one good arm and his stick, he almost overbalanced in his effort to look further out of the window. In fact, for a moment I saw his cheek pressed against the glass as he strained his eyes downwards. This room, as I have said, looked towards the

77

greenhouses and the lake. There was also a path which led round the side to the back of the house and the stables, and it seemed to be towards this that his straining eyes were directed. When with an exhausted sigh he flopped back in the chair he drew in a number of sharp breaths before saying to me, and in a tone that belonged definitely to The Big Fellow, "Are there any visitors downstairs?"

"There was earlier on this afternoon, a minister, the Reverend Fallenbor."

The reaction that my answer to his question evoked was startling. It was as if I was seeing him on the hillside again, trying to choke the life out of Weaver. His one good hand gripped the arm of his chair until the knuckles strained white through the flesh, and his painfully stretched skin moved across the bones of his face as he ground his teeth together.

I was standing up now, quite close to his chair, and I bent towards him and said, "Don't agitate yourself. You'll only make yourself ill . . . please."

He looked up at me, right into my eyes, and I watched the tenseness fall from his face, to be replaced by an expression of weariness. I could almost say disillusionment. And as he stared at me I had the odd feeling that he was in need of help. And there came back to my mind a fairy story that my father used to read to me. It was about a giant, so big that no one could go near him, and so he was left lonely in his castle on a hilltop, until one day a little girl came to the gates and talked to him through the bars. And when he opened the gates she did not run away like the rest of them but went in because she knew he was lonely. And then a miracle happened, for the giant decreased in size until he became a boy, just a little older than herself. And of course they married and lived happily ever after. . . . Here was the giant then, and he was lonely, but the girl at the gate was not me, it was Noreen Badcliff. Didn't she know that her giant was lonely? My thoughts were pulled from such fey thinking as he said, "Fallenbor's a reprobate, a real reprobate."

"But he's a minister." My voice was soft.

"Minister? Psst! . . . Minister who's lucky not to be defrocked. The valley got too hot for him years ago and he was moved, but after he retired he came back. I . . . I've forbidden him this house."

"I'm sorry. I'm sorry, I shouldn't have told you."

"You shouldn't have told me? . . . You should have joined the conspiracy of lies and deceit? . . . Oh!" He moved his head from side to side. "You don't want to hear all that. But you know——" He stopped abruptly, and, looking up at me again with the same intent look, he moved his big head slowly before going on: "But you know, Kate, if there was anyone I could talk to I think it could be you." His head was still moving when, after another pause, he added, "This might seem strange, for I'm not deluding myself that you like me; in fact I would, at a rough guess, say you disliked me. . . . At least . . ."

"No! Oh no!" My eyes were blinking and my face scarlet as I gave him this denial, and then, turning my glance away, I said, "Not now. I did at first, but not now. Your manner . . ."

"Yes, my manner, to say the least, is unfortunate. Overbearing, arrogant. Oh, I know. Oh, I know. . . . Sit down, Kate."

I sat down and watched him lean towards me, putting his weight on the arm of the chair as he said, "Can I talk to you?"

"Yes, if it will help." I was breathing rather quickly as if I had been running.

"The person I should talk to, I know, should be Noreen, but I can't; she's too closely linked with Maurice."

My eyes, giving me away again, brought from him now the explanation. "You see," he said, "we were all brought up together, more or less, and at one time she was very fond of Maurice, so much as that . . . well, I thought . . . I thought it was Maurice she loved, not me. Even after his illness I still imagined things hadn't changed . . . but they had, unfortunately for him. Added to this, my brother and I don't see eye to eye on a number of things. I could never countenance his type of friends, for one thing. He was rather cosmopolitan in his tastes. We had numbers of queer people staying here at one time, among them the Reverend Fallenbor. He . . . Maurice even palled up with men like Weaver. You see, he was of an irresponsible romantic turn of mind and tried, in his way, to push Tor-Fret back a century. . . . I cannot go into all those happenings, but I had to put my foot down and this caused bad feeling between us. And then he was struck with polio and somehow things never righted themselves. Anyway, because Noreen is still in sympathy with him I cannot talk with her, at least about what is troubling me most at present." He paused here for a long moment before he said, "Three times in the last year someone has tried to polish me off." He pointed to the white line of the slit running down his lip. "That was a knife. It was aimed at my temple, but the point just grazed my lip."

Just grazed, I thought. Just grazed was definitely an understatement.

"Then one night last winter I was knocked senseless on the terrace there, below. It was snowing and I could have frozen to death, or at least been finished off by loss of blood from a scalp wound." He put his hand to the crown of his head where the hair was combed sideways away from the natural parting, then went on, "Now this . . . and I'm quite well aware who the culprit is."

"The man Weaver." My voice was a whisper.

"Yes, the man Weaver, Kate. Yes, I know who wants to finish me. But what I don't actually know is why. There could be any one of a number of reasons. I couldn't, for instance, think he wants to kill me just because I cut him off from free drinks. Of course, men have been killed for less, yet I can't think that's the reason for these attacks, or any of the other things that come to mind; he would have attempted them earlier, and not waited until this last year. And the odd thing is that they've always happened after I've left the house and have returned unexpectedly."

I could not meet his eyes now, and I said, "But why don't you call in the police?"

"No. Not yet, at any rate. I feel there's something behind all this, something personal, something connected...."

He stopped, and now it was his turn to shift his gaze, and he was silent for a moment before looking at me. And then he smiled and said, "Anyway, it's done me good to talk. I feel better, lighter somehow. You know, Kate"— his head drooped forward—"I think you would make a very good friend."

My face was hot again, but I could look at him and say, "I hope so." I could look at him because my eyes had nothing to betray as yet ... as yet I did not know what was to happen to me. His hand came towards me and I put mine in it. It was a quiet grasp, and then he said, "Well, now shall we get down to work?"

"Yes," I said with a laugh to cover the confusion that was creeping over me, "or else it will pay you to get someone out from Alnwick."

And so we worked in a harmony that is impossible to describe; and later, when I went down the hill, part of me was worried about Logan Rossiter, but the greater part was happy because of him.

I had almost reached the main road when I saw Noreen Badcliff coming towards me, and as we came abreast she stopped and said, "Hello."

"Hello," I answered, and self-consciously made to move on when her hand touched my arm, and after compelling my gaze for some moments she said quickly, "Why do you dislike me?"

The forthright question, so much the reverse of her nature as I saw it, nonplussed me, to say the least, and it was natural in such circumstances that I should deny my feeling towards her, saying, "What makes you think I dislike you?"

6

She put her head on one side and smiled, a quiet smile that heightened her beauty still further, as she answered, "Your manner, the look in your eyes the first time we met. I can't remember anyone looking at me like that before, at least not without some good reason." She moved her head slowly.

It was on the tip of my tongue to say I had a very good reason, but I told myself yet once again it wasn't my business, and so rather inanely I reverted to the old excuse, "If I don't hurry," I said, "I'll miss my . . ."

She cut off my words by closing her eyes and exclaiming, "Oh, don't tell me you're going to miss your bus again—that will be the third time. This only proves you've something against me, and for the life of me I can't think what it can be."

"No?" The question was out before I could stop it, and the inflection I gave to the word proved to her conclusively that she was right in her surmise. I had made a mistake and I regretted it immediately, but it was done now and I would have to give her some explanation, and I could think of none other than the truth, at least part of it. I paid no attention the warning that told me to keep my mouth shut, but said quietly, "I know you are not playing straight with Mr. Logan, that's why."

I had never given any thought to how this girl would react to exposure; if I had, doubtless I would have imagined her taking a high hand, a very high hand, so I was amazed at the effect of my words on her. I watched the colour drain from her face, and then she clapped her hand tightly across the lower half of it. The fingers digging into her cheek distorted her face momentarily into a caricature of herself, and the eyes that looked at me over the rim of her hand held fear. It was this expression more than anything else that amazed me, puzzled and amazed me. Her hand slowly slipping down from her face, she stood staring at me, her small compact breasts rising and falling rapidly. "How did you find out?" she now asked.

"At the lake. I came into the grounds over Neete Fell. . . ."

"No!" It was her fist that was on her mouth now, as if she was blowing through it.

"When?" The question was muffled.

"Shortly after I started to work here."

"I know, I know." Again she closed her eyes. "I remember the day. I thought . . . Oh . . . my . . . God." After a moment she opened her eyes wide and said, "I must talk to you."

"I really must be getting . . ."

"Oh no, please. Give me a few minutes. Come down to the car, we can't stand here. Come down to the car. I must talk to you, please."

A few minutes ago I had actually hated this girl, but now I found myself being sorry for her. Again she had hold of my arm, but now as if she was afraid I would run away.

We didn't speak until we were seated in the front of the car, and then to my embarrassment she gripped my hand and her beautiful eyes looked appealingly into mine as she said, "I wonder if I can make you understand?"

"You can but try," I said.

"Well, you see, it all started so long ago, twelve years, or even before then. When I came home from school for the holidays, there were always the Rossiters, big Logan and handsome Maurice. Heavenly Maurice I used to call him in those days because his beauty was something not quite real. He was gay then and not a little mad, and all the girls were after him, but he always said that as soon as we both left school we would be married. He was only a year older than me. We used to play at getting married. The last time we played that game was on his eighteenth birthday. We had high jinks in the cellar. Logan was away and we all went mad, even the uncles. Logan wouldn't countenance parties, especially in the cellar, and he was right. Oh, he was right, because they always led to trouble. It was the day after this party that

Maurice took ill and there was no further talk of us getting married. I offered to marry him, I wanted to marry him, but he just laughed at me. He seemed different after his illness, queer at times. Then I went away. My mother, who was a widow, married again, a Frenchman. In a way I was glad to escape. We stayed abroad three years, but my mother's second marriage was even more disastrous than her first. We had kept on the house across the valley"—she motioned now with her head—"but that had to be sold. My mother and my stepfather separated and we came back and lived in the lodge, where we still are. And for the last four years I have been in love with two men. It is odd, but it's true."

I released my hands from her grip and, returning her stare, I said, "I think it's impossible to be in love with two men at the same time."

"It isn't, it isn't. I can't explain it. I want to marry Logan. He is good and steady and in him lies security, and oh, I do need security. But apart from that I . . . I do love him. I am greatly attracted to him, and yet Maurice has just to look at me, just to touch me and my blood turns to water. Maurice has a power that can't be explained, you can only feel it. And . . . and a year ago Maurice and I . . . well . . . we . . ."

I cut in on her here, saying sharply, "So you are quite prepared to marry Mr. Logan and keep up an affair with Mr. Maurice? I think it's . . ."

"No, no. Once I marry Logan . . ."

"Listen . . . I think you had better know that I was behind that summer-house for some time and heard quite a lot of your conversation with Mr. Maurice, and from what I remember you were marrying Mr. Logan because Mr. Maurice wanted you to."

"No! No! Oh no!" She was shaking her head vigorously. "And you can't judge me from what you heard. You don't know what it is like to come under Maurice's charm. When you're with him you never want to leave him, you'll promise him anything, and when you are away

84

from him you want to remain away but feel yourself drawn back. And another thing . . ." Her eyes opened wide now. "Whatever you do . . . listen to me carefully." She was gripping my hand hard again. "Whatever you do you must not let Maurice know that you are aware of what is between us. Even if you make up your mind to expose me to Logan, you must do it in some way other than letting it come directly from you. You don't know Maurice. You see . . ."

"Are you suggesting that he'd do me an injury? Say . . . have me pushed over the big rock like Mr. Logan was."

"No no. Maurice wouldn't do anything physical, but there are worse ways of hurting than by physical pain. And he didn't push Logan over the rock. Even if he could, he wouldn't have done that."

"No, but he knew who did it."

Her eyes narrowed at me now and she said, "You do, too?"

"Yes, I know."

"There's very little you don't know, is there? You have learned a lot in the short time you have been up at Tor-Fret."

"It wasn't my seeking; the knowledge has been thrust on me."

"All through your walking over Neete Fell and coming in the back way." She shook her head slowly. "It's funny the little things that change destiny. And you know about Weaver?"

I merely inclined my head and she turned her gaze from me, and, looking out of the car window into the slow twilight, she said, "I could pity Weaver."

"After he has tried to kill Mr. Logan three times?"

"He's as much under Maurice's spell as the rest of us."

"Is that why he tries to murder someone?"

"No, that really has nothing to do with it. It's something else that prompts him to go too far. You see, he feels that he's a Rossiter and Tor-Fret is rightly his home."

My eyes widened and my mouth opened slightly as she turned to me and said, "He was born at Tor-Fret. His mother worked in the kitchen. Weaver was born over the stables and his mother claimed no man as the father of her child, for it was an understood thing that it was 'The Rossiter', as Logan's grandfather was called. Weaver grew up here and was accepted by everyone, at least in his boyhood, as a side-shoot of the family by everyone, that is, except Logan, who could never stand him. When Logan's father died the death duties were such that it was thought they would have to sell the place. But Logan cut down and dismissed the hangers-on—there were a number of these—and one of the first to go was Weaver. But he never really went; he has haunted the place ever since and takes Mr. Maurice as his master. . . . There you have the reason for Weaver's animosity towards Logan."

I was thinking back to Logan Rossiter questioning the reason for Weaver's determination to kill him. It was understandable he would not tell me of the blood relationship. Yet why look for a stronger reason?

"But what do you intend to do about . . . about me?" The question was urgent. We were looking at each other; the girl's eyes were wide, seeming to stretch across the entire surface of her face, and I was not proof against the pleading I saw in them. If I had intended taking steps to inform Logan Rossiter of how he was being duped, I could not now have gone on with it. I said to her simply, "Nothing."

Again I watched her close her eyes, but this time in evident relief. Once more she had hold of my hand, and as I saw the glint of tears on her lashes I had the impulsive urge to put my arms about her and hold her, but I was prevented by a little voice which said, "She could be playing you up. She's just as charming a double-dealer in her way as Maurice Rossiter, and she could be laughing at you behind your back." And she forced me to bring this sore matter into the open within the next few seconds, for she said, "You are kind. Logan told me you were a kind person. He said it was in your face. I was a bit jealous of you before I saw you. He thinks you're sweet."

For no reason that was evident at this moment I found myself not only confused by her words but my heart beginning to thump, and when she added, "You know, Maurice too thinks very highly of you," I could not help but snap back, "Yes, I know. Our prim, industrious and delightfully earnest Kate. I know what Mr. Maurice thinks about me."

She had the grace to lower her head, but it came up instantly again as she said, "But he talks like that about everyone. He laughs at people, makes fun of them, but that doesn't say he doesn't like them. Take no notice of that. I'll say this in Maurice's defence—I must in fairness to him. He's suffering under a great handicap. You see, he cannot get over the unfairness of fate, he's still fighting it. I think ... I think at times that part of his mind is affected also."

She waited, and when I made no further comment she remained quiet until I said, "I must really get the next bus. I have quite a walk up from our village."

"I'll run you there."

"No, no. I'd rather you didn't."

She looked hurt and I said quickly, "You don't want Mr. Maurice to know that you took me home. Who knows but we are being watched." In trying to explain my reason for refusing her offer I saw that I had hurt her and it was my hand that went out and touched hers now as I said, "I'm sorry. I did not mean to be nasty."

She put her other hand on top of mine and through the dim light she looked at me and asked, "Are we going to be kind, Kate?"

It was such an unusual phrase for a girl of this type to be using. The term "Are we going to be kind?" was one used by children. I had used it myself for years as I had played or fought with my companions: "Aa you kind with me?" I would ask, or, "Aa'm not goin' to be kind with you." Only a short time ago, when I happened to be passing down a street in South Shields, I was interested and amused by a group of children having a squabble and one of the leaders shouting to the others, "We're not goin' to be kind with you any more, so there!" It was an idiom of the South Tyne and yet here was this educated girl asking me to be kind with her. Engendered by the distrust my employer had bred in me, my thoughts for a moment were: Is she being condescending and thinking she is coming down to my level in speaking this way? But no, there was nothing condescending about her manner; and, what was more, I no longer spoke in the idiom. At this moment the light of the oncoming bus sent a glow through the back window of the car and I made no answer to her request but said hastily, "I really must get this bus, my mother will be worrying."

"Yes, yes, I understand. And it's all right . . . Kate?"

I was half out of the car, but I turned my head and looked at her steadily. "Yes," I said, "it's all right."

I had to put the torch on going up the hill, and when I was still some way from the cottage my mother's voice came to me, saying, "That you, Kate?"

"Yes, yes, it's me."

When I reached the door she said, "What's kept you? You're late."

"I . . . I met someone," I said.

Her hand was on my shoulder helping me off with my coat. "Arthur?"

"No, not Arthur."

"I had the feeling that's what was keeping you. He was in the village just about tea-time. I was coming out of the post office and I saw him getting off the bus near *The Fox and Hounds*. He didn't notice me and I kept out of his way. . . . You haven't seen him then?"

"No. But," I added, "I think the sooner I do, the better."

"Well . . . there's something in that. By the way, I

didn't tell your father. He hasn't been too good the day."
She was whispering now.

"Is it his breathing?" I couldn't see her face because we
were standing in the passage and the room doors were
closed, but her voice told me that she was troubled. "Yes,
that, and he's off colour. In some way he's not himself.
See if you can cheer him up." She patted my shoulder
and I preceded her into the sitting-room.

"Hello . . . there." The words were spaced by a sharp
pull on his breath.

"Hello," I said, standing at his side. "Not feeling too
good?"

"Oh, I'm all right. It's your mother, she keeps fussing.
Oh, I'm all right," he repeated. "It's the weather. We're in
for a hard winter, I can always tell. Bet your life there'll
be snow afore the end of the month."

"I wouldn't be surprised," I said. "It was nippy coming
up the fell."

"Anything happened the day?"

"Yes," I said, "quite a lot. I'll tell you after tea."

And so when I had finished my meal and the table had
been cleared I told them what had transpired between
Noreen Badcliff and myself, and for once my father did
not see two sides to the situation, but said immediately,
"She's lying, I bet you a bob she's lying. No woman can
love two men at the same time . . . impossible." He
heaved a number of short breaths and was about to
speak again when my mother cut in sharply on him, "And
why not? I don't agree with you. Of course a woman can
love two men at once."

I was more than a little surprised at my mother's
championship of the girl she knew to be playing a double
game, and more surprised still when she went on and
emphatically now, "I suppose you would say it was all
right for a man to love two women at once and that he
could do it."

"Well, aye . . . yes, I would cos it's different for a man,
his temperament's different and everything. Women are

89

more single-minded, they're not capable of it; it's not in their make-up, if you know what I mean."

"One set of emotions for the man and one for the woman."

My mother, to my consternation, got up and went out into the scullery, and my father smiled towards the door and nodded to me and in a conspiratorial whisper said, "I know all her tactics. She's taken that line to get me to argue . . . thinks . . . it'll take me mind off meself." He shook his head and his smile broadened. "I'm not worrying about meself; it's her that worries; she never stops." He now held his finger up for silence, and when my mother came into the room again there was no more talk. My father and I read while she knitted. The evening was changed.

Later, when my father had gone up to bed, I said to her, "You really don't believe a woman can be in love with two men at the same time, do you, Mother?"

I put the question because I was slightly puzzled. She had been so quiet all evening, and when she was worried about my father she usually chatted and talked and went for him a bit to distract him from himself, as he had said. And now her answer to my question came, I might say, as the biggest surprise of the day. "Yes," she said, "I do believe it, for when it happens to you personally you know it must be true."

We were looking at each other, standing on the rug within the circle of light from the cream-shaded oil lamp, and I said with some wonderment, "Mother!"

"I was in love with two men for over three years. I picked your father. I didn't make a mistake, I haven't regretted it, but that doesn't stop me from even now waking up in the middle of the night and thinking of the other man . . . and knowing that some part of me, after thirty years, is still in love with him. It makes me furious when men, your father or anyone else, allows emotional licence for the male breed but not for the female. . . . All men are narrow."

I was twenty-seven and I had never been separated from my parents for more than a fortnight in a year. I would have said I knew my mother inside and out, and yet here she was appearing to me as a different woman. I could not associate what she was saying with the woman I knew to be my mother. It was like something coming out of the mouth of a fictitious character, like one of the women in Maurice Rossiter's book.

"Don't look so worried now." She touched my cheek. "I've been happier than most women, and as long as I have your father I will go on feeling like that. But life's a funny thing. Come on." She took my elbow. "Let's go up."

As I lay in bed peering through the darkness I was not thinking at this moment so much about the people at Tor-Fret, but about my mother who had loved two men. But as I went to sleep a thought wove itself along the fringe of unconsciousness and there, as if standing outside myself, I read it. It said, "I'm glad you were kind to Noreen Badcliff."

5

Things went very smoothly during the following week. Maurice Rossiter could have been the man whom I remembered during the interview, so charming and considerate was he. Even on the Tuesday, when I was an hour late, owing to my father, who was now in bed, having a rather bad turn, he did not greet me with coolness, as I expected, but was all concern and solicitude when I explained the reason for my lateness. Nor did his manner alter when twice during the week we ran into each other in the hall following my session with his brother.

Logan Rossiter was improving rapidly. His robust constitution coming to his aid, he could now hobble around. It was on the Friday of the following week that he said to me, "Dare I ask you if you can come over tomorrow morning and help me to get through this?" He pointed to a stack of work.

As I have said, because I cut my hours with Bill during the week I did Saturday morning to make up my time. I glanced up from my table towards him. He was standing with his back to the long narrow window; the pale sun was outlining him and he looked The Big Fellow again. I said, "Oh, I'm sorry; I'm due at Mr. Arnold's on Saturday morning." And then without hesitation I added, "I could come over in the afternoon, if that would do."

"Oh no, you want your Saturday afternoon . . . your weekend, to yourself."

"No, I don't; it doesn't matter, I have nothing else to do. I'll come over." I was finding now that I could talk to Logan Rossiter in a way I could never talk to Maurice, and I was surprised each time I thought about it. In fact I could almost believe that the cyncial overbearing individual did not exist, but not quite, for my common sense told me that he was still active below the surface and would break through when the occasion demanded. Because I was obliging him I was being treated to the Rossiter charm; whereas the charm was painted thick on Maurice, there was only a thin veneer on Logan; nevertheless it was definitely evident now and had successfully broken down any feeling of animosity I had towards him. . . .

So I came up to Tor-Fret on the Saturday afternoon. I came up through a gale of wind that nearly swept me off my feet. When I reached the Hall I stood inside the doorway panting to regain my breath.

Because it was my custom to do so, I went towards what I called my room to take off my outdoor clothes. There was no need for me to go near Maurice Rossiter's apartments, but I did it without thinking—force of habit you could say. It wasn't until I opened the door that I thought to myself, Oh dear, he could have been in here resting. But the room was empty, yet seemed full of noise, for the long windows in their wooden warped sashes were rattling like castanets, and from the wide chimney-piece a copper draught sheet fixed to the lower part of the chimney joined in with a running rattle of sound like a badly timed tambourine. It was likely the wind and the noise it was creating that covered the sound of my opening the door, and I was about to close it behind me, when from the next room I heard Noreen Badcliff's voice saying, "You were eager enough for me to go on with it a short while ago."

"I'm only trying to do the decent thing." This was Maurice Rossiter's voice. Yet I hardly recognized it, there was no laughter or cynical amusement in it, nor yet bitterness. If I could have associated humility with him, I would have said his tone was humble.

"And it's your idea of doing the decent thing to stop me marrying him? Had you made up your mind to blackmail me when I married him and now you've got cold feet?"

"Oh, Noreen . . . don't say that."

"Well, what am I to think? You've been breaking your neck to get money out of him, and when he doesn't respond you think it will be a good idea if I marry him and act as liaison officer between you and his pocket. Well, Maurice, it may surprise you to know that I had thought of marrying Logan long before you suggested it."

"Don't say that." The voice had changed completely. The tone was so bitter, so sharp, that the words seemed to cut through the sound of the wind, and they came to me so clearly that I started and pulled the door further open, ready to make my retreat, which I did the next moment as another burst of bitterness came from the inner room, the tone lower now, the words thick sounding. "If you married him in every church in the county, you'd still be mine. Nothing or no one can alter that now." What impression these words made on Noreen Badcliff I don't know, but they sent a chill through me.

I stood in the hall, my eyes darting about me. Where was everyone? Were they all in their different niches listening? Did they all know what was going on between those two in there? Were they all in the know except the one person who was particularly involved? As I gripped the handle and noiselessly turned it to close the door, I heard snatches of Noreen Badcliff's voice: the word "marry" and then "why?" and then on a high note two words repeated twice, "I must, I must, I must."

Still with my hat and coat on I went across the hall and mounted the stairs and tapped on the library door, the room where we now worked. There was no answer, and when I opened the door I found the room was empty and I did not enter. As I looked towards Logan Rossiter's bedroom door there came the sound of footsteps from the far passage, and Hollings appeared on the landing. As I was about to speak I heard the sound now of distant laughter, men's laughter. It was a nice sound, comforting, I thought, so different from the sound in the room downstairs.

"They're all with Mr. Stephen, madam; he was in need of company. Would you care to go along?"

"Thank you, Hollings."

Hollings preceded me along the passage, knocked on Mr. Stephen's door, and as he opened it announced, "Miss Mitchell to see you."

"Oh, come in, come in."

This welcome was not only from Mr. Stephen, but from the twins, and also Logan Rossiter, who added, "Oh, you're early. But come in and sit down."

"Come and sit near me." Mr. Stephen patted the bedspread and Mr. Bernard made way for me, while Mr. Stanley took my hand as if to assist me on to a throne. And there I sat on the foot of the bed, feeling all of a sudden very shy in the midst of these four men.

"We're just talking of weddings. Do you like weddings?" Mr. Stephen was poking his sharp nose towards me as he spoke and I made a great effort to breathe naturally and to ignore the constricted feeling in my chest as I answered briefly, "Some."

"All weddings are risks. We never had the guts to take the risk, had we?" Mr. Stephen looked towards Mr. Bernard and Mr. Stanley, and Mr. Bernard muttered, "Wise... wise."

Mr. Stephen, ignoring him, glanced at his nephew, and, as if he hadn't been interrupted, went on, "But Logan's going to brave it. Stout heart, Logan."

On this, Logan Rossiter laughed as he replied, "You may not have been married, Uncle, but it didn't stop you being a gay dog, did it? So don't talk as if you've led a lonely bachelor existence. Being saintly in your old age doesn't suit you; you're still a wicked old man."

This caused Mr. Stephen to chuckle so much that I felt his thin body shaking under the bedclothes. Then, heaving himself up, he bent towards me and, taking my hand, said, "Know what I said to those two last night?" He nodded to his two brothers. "I said if I was only twenty years younger I would've tossed me cap at you."

My face was warm and I could not but smile and reply with equal gallantry, "And if you had been twenty years younger I would have caught it."

We all laughed, and the laughter was hearty; even Mr. Bernard had joined in. But it was his laugh that ceased first and his face was straight as he mumbled, "Wouldn't mind you 'bout the house ... sensible."

I lowered my head and shook it somewhat sadly, but I was still smiling as I answered, "Some women think, Mr. Bernard, that it's the worst thing that could be said of them ... being sensible."

"Nonsense. Nonsense."

Mr. Bernard was going from the room now, and Mr. Stanley, following him, pulled faces at his brother's back. And now I rose from the bed and said my goodbyes to Mr. Stephen, promising once again to look in on him, and when I left the room Logan Rossiter came behind me. He was hobbling slowly, and I suited my steps to his as we crossed the gallery. We didn't speak until we reached the library and he was seated, and then he said, "Do you believe that?"

"What?" I did not know to what he was referring.

"About women not wanting to be thought sensible."

I looked down towards the floor. "Well, it's really hardly a compliment. When a woman is plain and has nothing else about her the best thing they can say of her is she's sensible."

"But you're not plain, Kate." His tone was emphatic. "You're . . ." I was looking at him and he at me, and we stayed like this for some moments. His mouth was partly open as if he was going to continue speaking, and then he shook his head from side to side and looked away as if he was embarrassed, yet I couldn't imagine this man ever feeling embarrassed, or at a loss for words. Nor was he, for quickly I watched him sweep away the personal platform on which he had for a brief moment stood, by saying, "Well, let us both be sensible and get down to work, eh?"

We got down to work. But as the afternoon wore on I became enveloped in a heavy feeling of sadness. It weighed on me until I had the desire to put my head down on to the table and cry, and when I asked myself what had caused this I got no reply, except that it was late autumn and the dying year had always affected me.

Nor was my sadness lessened by a visit from Noreen Badcliff herself. Logan Rossiter had left me after giving me directions with regard to the work he wanted doing. And I saw no one for the rest of the afternoon, except Hollings, who as usual brought me my tea but spoke of nothing but the weather, which was worsening considerably, until Noreen Badcliff came into the room. She tapped on the door and entered, and said, "Hello there."

"Hello."

"What is it?" she now asked. "Aren't you well?"

I could have put the same question to her, for apart from her face, which was paler than usual, there were dark rings encircling her eyes. In fact, her lovely face had a strange, drawn look; perhaps, I thought, it was the result of her doing battle with Maurice. Yet I was to remember this particular afternoon when I knew the reason for her pallor. I said now, "I might have caught a little cold; the wind was piercing coming up."

"Yes, and it's worse now. I just said to Logan I would run you back, but he's already made arrangements for Patterson to do that."

"Oh, he shouldn't. I could easily get the . . ." I checked myself.

"The bus." She was smiling, a whimsical little smile, which I couldn't resist returning, but I said, "Yes, I could just as easily get the bus."

"Well, you're not going to, not today. It was very good of you to come up, and in your leisure time too. . . . You know"—she came round and took a seat right opposite the desk—"I should hate to be tied to so many hours a day. Even if I was capable of doing anything, which I'm not." She spread her hands appealingly towards me. "I'm useless, utterly useless. Mother wanted me to go in for teaching because I was good at English. I should have loved to teach. But how can you teach when there's nothing in you? I have nothing in me. . . . Oh, I know I haven't."

How could you hate a girl who talked like this? A girl who had two men in love with her, and others perhaps, and who admitted there was nothing in her. Even with all I knew about her I could still find her endearing at this moment.

"The trouble with me," she went on, "is that I'm bone lazy. I hate getting out of bed in the mornings; the only thing that gets me up early is the thought of a horse." She smiled, and then she sighed and ended, "But I'll have to alter my ways from now on." I waited as we looked at each other. "We're going to be married on the thirtieth of November."

I knew now that she had come in precisely to tell me this piece of news. She had led up to it in a roundabout way. She had put herself over as lazy, naïve, almost unintelligent. Lazy she might be, but the latter two characteristics were a mere pretence, a mere façade to hide . . . what? I found myself once again filled with suspicion, then this in turn was swept away on my remembering what she had said to Maurice Rossiter earlier this afternoon.

Like my mother, this girl might be in love with two men. I did not know on which side the scale dipped, for dip it must one way or the other, but I was aware she was fighting in her own way as if for her very existence, and who was I to kill happiness for another. I who knew so much what the death of it meant. I looked at her and smiled as I said, "I hope you'll be very happy. . . . That you both will be very happy."

On this she stood up, came round the table and put her hand on mine for a moment, then went out without another word.

Slowly I placed my elbows on the table and pressed the cushions of my thumbs over my eyes. I was crying, but inwardly.

During the next few days the weather worsened considerably, although winter had not officially begun. The storm on Saturday had heralded winter to the fells. The morning air began to hack at your throat as if it was laden with minute icicles, and some mornings the far Cheviots were obscured by mist, and the valley where ran the Coquet was lost so completely that you doubted if it had ever existed, so levelled and impregnable was the mist that filled it. On these mornings I shrank further inside my clothes. On these mornings I longed to stay in close to the high red fire, wrapped about with the smell of my mother's cooking and the feeling of security I always experienced when with my parents.

It was such a morning as this that began the day on which I was faced with another heartbreak, a heartbreak that made my experience of two years ago seem a pale anaemic thing. And it was brought about by the very man who had caused that heartbreak.

Because of the condition of the weather I had definitely made up my mind to tell Maurice Rossiter that if he still required my services, now that the long screed was nearly finished, I would have to come up to Tor-Fret in the mornings because the nights were cutting in sharply, and even if I left the house promptly at five-thirty it still meant me walking up our fell in the near dark, which I didn't relish. When I asked Bill Arnold that morning if it would be all right my coming in the afternoons, his answer was, "You come any time you like, Kate. Make your own time, any time in the twenty-four hours. The only thing is . . . come . . . 'cos I've never had it so easy for a long time. Those books and accounts nearly drove me round the bend."

I didn't think, in fact I knew, that any similar proposal to Maurice Rossiter would get such a kind reception, and yet again I was to be mistaken as I had been so often of late.

"Yes, of course, Kate," he said. "I understand you don't want to go home in the dark, not when it's like this. It's vile. Yet you know," he added, "I would rather be here, even with the weather as it is, than anywhere else on earth. But why . . . why have we been allotted such chilling cold? It's a different kind of cold from that in any other county. Don't you think so?"

"I haven't been in many other counties, but I know I don't like it." I found I was smiling at him, as much in relief at escaping the bout of high-flown temper that I had steeled myself to receive us at the pleasant, considerate acceptance of my proposal. There was a quiteness about his manner today, and an ordinariness that was

99

disarming, but I warned myself not to be decieved by it. Yet later in the afternoon, when he called me into the other room to take some pages of the script he had been re-checking, and I saw him wince and his eyes flicker as if he had been jabbed by something sharp, I forgot for a moment his duplicity and found myself feeling compassion for him as I had done when I first met him. And he, sensing this, smiled at me and said, "You know, I don't know what I'd do without you; I don't know what I did before you came."

"You had Mr. Julian," I said.

"Yes, I had." He nodded at me. "And I thought he was good, but he didn't get through half the amount of work that you do, and took twice the time over it." He now pulled his chin into his neck and looked at me from under his lids. "I went for you like a tiger the other day, didn't I? Complaining and criticizing." He shook his head slowly. "You'll get to know me, Kate, by and by, and take those days in your stride. But remember, should I subject you to another one, don't believe a word I say. Some days I've got to let off steam or burst, and it's just unfortunate if you're the one that's in front of the steam-roller." He laughed, and I smiled as I said, "I'll remember. . . ."

The clouds were low in the sky when I left Tor-Fret. Hollings, who had been in the hall, came to the door with me and, looking out across the expanse of the terrace, said, "I'm afraid you'll get wet before you reach home, madam."

"I don't mind that very much, Hollings," I said, "as long as I get home before it's quite dark."

"Well, I should hurry," he said solicitously, "because that cloud isn't going to lift. It'll be dark soon tonight. . . . Good night, madam."

"Good night, Hollings."

I wondered about Hollings as I hurried down the fell road. He had never spoken of either his master or Maurice Rossiter since the day I had heard the voices coming up the air vent from the cellar. Yet he still appeared watchful, unobtrusively on the alert. I couldn't imagine him allowing himself to be swayed by Mr. Maurice's charm as, I told myself rather ruefully, I was. Yet in my own defence I knew that were Maurice Rossiter to talk to me seriously I would not believe a word he said. Nor would I ever be able to understand how, when loving Noreen Badcliff as he surely did, he could press her to marry his brother. I thrust aside the thought of his disability and the obstacle of money, the lack of which he gave as his reason that memorable day by the lake. No, I knew I would never be able to understand this man or his motives.

I was thinking along these lines, my body bent forward, my head down against the wind as I rounded the bend halfway down the bank, the very bend where I'd stumbled over Weaver's legs the first time I had used this road, when I only just managed to shut down on a scream as a man's figure and outstretched arm blocked my way. I actually jumped backwards to avoid contact, and then I was staring at Arthur Boyle, seeing him face to face for the first time in two years.

"I'm sorry, Kate. I'm sorry I gave you a start."

I tried to swallow and moved my chin back and forward with the effort. He was standing squarely in front of me now, his arms hanging by his side, looking like some big helpless schoolboy. He had changed in the two years since we parted, much more than I had, and some part of me even in this moment of fright was human enough to be glad about this. He said, "I had to see you; there seemed a conspiracy down there." He motioned over the fell in the direction of the village. "Nobody seemed to know where you worked in the afternoons. They all told me where you worked in the mornings, when I wasn't able to get over." He was smiling faintly now as if trying to turn it into a joke, and then his face became straight and he said quietly, "It's good to see you again, Kate. . . . My God, I've missed you. I must have been stark, staring barmy."

"What do you want?" I asked.

"Isn't that obvious? I want to see you. I must see you again, Kate."

As his hand lifted towards me I took another step back. "The person you should be seeing at this moment is your wife . . . and your child." I said the last words slowly, and with emphasis. "There is nothing more to be said between you and me, and nothing can come of you trying to see me, understand that."

As I stared at him I watched the boyish look fade from his face. His large full-lipped mouth, which at one time I had kindly termed generous, forced itself into a straight line as he pulled his lower lip inwards and bit on it before saying, "I made a mistake. I did you a wrong, there's no getting over that, but by God I've paid for it. Hell's nothing to the life I've led this past two years. If you ever wanted your revenge, then I can say you've had it. . . . Look, Kate." He took a tentative step towards me. "I'll do anything, anything if you'll put the clock back. Some men sow their wild oats early and some late. Well, you would have no reason to worry about me scattering any more wild oats. Kate . . . I'm yours for life if you'll only forgive me."

"I have forgiven you, Arthur." My voice was quiet now. "But I don't want to see you or have anything to do with you again, you must understand that."

He spread his hands out before me now, saying, "But you couldn't have changed as completely as that, not after the way you loved me. You loved me, you know you did."

"I'm afraid I have changed as completely as that, Arthur." I could say his name without any pang. "And the love that I had for you is so dead that nothing on this earth could ever resurrect it."

"Give me a chance to try again, that's all I ask. . . . I'll take it that you don't feel the same, not anything like the same, but give me . . . just give me the chance to make things up to you. Do that, Kate."

"... And your wife?"

He closed his eyes and swung his head from shoulder to shoulder. "She's never been my wife, not really. A few words yammered over you doesn't make you man and wife. . . ."

"I understood it did."

"You know what I mean, Kate; we've never been anything to each other. I just stayed with her because of the child. I married her to give the child a name. . . ."

"Well, you married her, and she's your wife. But let me tell you that if she wasn't and you were free tomorrow it would make no difference."

"It's got to, Kate, it's got to." I watched his pale complexion deepen into pink and then into red. Slowly he was being consumed by a fury of temper, the temper that I had twice before seen take control of him. And as I stared at him through the darkening light on this empty road I was quite suddenly filled with fear, and not without cause, for within the next second I was struggling within the frantic grip of his arms.

"Le . . . let me go. Let me go, Arthur. . . . Don't! Don't!" I am no weakling, but my efforts to release myself were as futile as those of a child. Arthur in this moment was mad.

His lips were trying to pin down my mouth, and as I moved and jerked my head I was vaguely conscious that somewhere on the road ahead was a moving blur, dark against the fading light. But it was only a fleeting impression, for I was swung round, my back bent over, and then my breath was almost stopped by the roughness of Arthur's mouth on mine.

For a second I thought dazedly that it was the kick I had given him on the ankle that had made him release me—that was before I took in the large lop-sided form of Logan Rossiter as he stood balancing himself on his good foot, his stick raised high over his head. To me it seemed to hover there for a long time as the two men glared at each other, but that must have been an illusion, for the yell Arthur let out came almost immediately after I was released from his grip.

"Oh no!" The cry escaped me as the stick was raised once again. Arthur was bending over gripping his shoulder. He was evidently hurt and looked dazed, and knowing him I realized that his bout of temper had subsided as quickly as it had risen. But even with the fury gone Arthur was no whelp and he advanced towards Logan Rossiter, yelling now, "You try that on again. Go on, try it on again and see what'll happen to you, as big as you are. Who the hell do you think you are, anyway? What's it got to do with you? I wasn't molesting her—she knows me."

"Do you know this man, Kate?" Logan Rossiter did not turn his head towards me as he spoke.

"Yes."

"There, you see." Arthur was now nodding vigorously. "You want to mind your own bloody business."

"Was this man being objectionable to you? Or was I imagining the whole thing, Kate?" Again he was speaking without looking at me, not taking his eyes from Arthur.

I did not know how to answer this in case that stick was wielded again, and this Arthur I knew would not stand for. There would be a fight, an unfair fight with Logan Rossiter's handicap of one damaged arm and foot. So in a garbled explanation I said, "We used to know each other but that's over. I don't want to see him again." And now I addressed Arthur, trying to keep my voice steady as I said, "As I told you, nothing can be altered. You've got to believe that. Don't go on hoping because I'll never change."

There was silence between the three of us for quite a while. My words seemed to have at last got through to Arthur, with the result that he looked utterly deflated. He was no fighter at heart, and could only whip himself to extremes when he resorted to the weapon of his temper.

"You heard what she said. Go on."

Arthur, stung once more into some retaliation, barked, "I'm going, but not on account of you. Get that clear. Likely you and I'll meet up again . . . when you haven't got your stick with you."

"If I had the use of my arm I would have no need for a stick . . . Now, go on!"

Arthur turned towards me, but I could not look at him. My head was hanging now because I felt sick, and I had the dread on me that I was about to vomit. But I saw his feet turn away, and then he was lost in the thickening dark.

I stood with my hand tightly pressed across my mouth. Nothing seemed to matter now except that I shouldn't be sick. Then Logan Rossiter was standing in front of me, his voice low and questioning, "Are you all right, Kate?"

I didn't answer, for besides the feeling of sickness I was shivering all over, and there was a weakness in my legs such as one experiences following shock. Then to my own surprise I found that I was crying, and not just crying with the tears dropping down my face, but with them gushing from my eyes, blocking my nose and choking me. It was then, in this moment when I couldn't fully appreciate it, that I felt the strength and tenderness of Logan Rossiter's hold, for his arm was about me. At first I experienced no amazement that my head was lying on the broad expanse of his chest, and my wet mouth was pressed on to his shirt in the vee above his waistcoat, for, like a distraught child, I was spilling words out, telling him who Arthur was, or had been. In broken, choking snatches I even told him about the girl. When the break-up between Arthur and myself had come two years ago I couldn't remember crying like this, nor talking like this. It was as if it had all been bottled up inside me and now the stopper had been cork-screwed out and I was experiencing a sense of relief that I hadn't known before. I had no encouragement from his voice, for he had not spoken, only from the pressure of his arm, the pressure that seemed to be changing my life, for I was now aware that standing within this circle I was a different being.

At last I stopped talking, and sniffing and gasping, I raised my face from his chest and looked up at him. I looked into eyes that seemed to be waiting for mine. I stared into their depths until I became lost and could see nothing but them. They covered the face of the fells, they covered the dominion of my entire world. I was aware of my heart racing, racing towards something terrifying, something beautifully terrifying. But I was not racing towards this thing alone, I was aware that what was happening to me was also happening to him. We had both left our surroundings, our responsibilities, our world, and were in some dimension where emotion alone mattered. Although I was still standing within the circle of his arm, we weren't close. Then, like two people coming together following long and lonely separation, we were joined. His grip had tightened about me and was forcing me into him. My arms were about his neck, our mouths met, and we were lost.

How long the kiss lasted I have no recollection; I only know that I was brought back to this planet with a bang, for I felt myself actually being thrown off him. It was as if an electric shock had wrenched us apart. I stood for a moment at arm's length from him, swaying and dazed. He was glaring at me as if he hated me, and I became overwhelmed with a feeling of utter, utter dejection. I knew what it was to be rejected, but this feeling was comparable with nothing I had experienced before. I had been rejected by Arthur Boyle and that had hurt, but in comparison this was like having the skin ripped off your flesh while remaining conscious of it.

Logan Rossiter was now no longer looking at me, for his big body was turned from me as if in shame. Once again I knew I was going to cry, cry tears that would wrench my being in two, but I could let no one witness this crying, least of all this man. I swung blindly away, and my feet were lifting to run, when his hand caught me, and so swift had been his effort to reach me that he almost overbalanced, and me with him. And again we were clinging to each other, and now he spoke my name in a way that no man had used it before. It was like a loving caress, but it was also, I knew, a farewell. His voice was thick and almost lost in his throat as he muttered, "Kate. My God, Kate." Then, "Forget this. You must. . . . Oh, Kate."

I could not look at him, and I made no answer. He put a little distance between us and his hand was only lightly on my arm when he spoke now. "Come on up to the house; I'll get Patterson to take you home. Come, Kate."

I shook my head. "No. I'm . . . I'm all right. . . ." I nearly added, "I'll miss the bus." If I had, I am sure I would have subsided in a bout of hysterical laughter.

"He'll be waiting at the bottom of the hill. You don't want that, do you?" His voice was soft.

No, I didn't want that. I didn't want any more conflicts tonight; all I wanted was to get home and think, and sort this out. But did it need sorting out? There was nothing to sort out. Just a plain statement of fact. I was in love, in love I think for the first time in my life, because this was a different feeling from anything I'd had for Arthur. This lacerating, choking, even shameful feeling was quite different. Why it should be I was at this moment incapable of explaining to myself.

His hand now came to move me forward, but I remained stubbornly still. Like some young bewildered girl I tossed my head, muttering, "I can't go back; they'll want to know why. . . . Asking questions . . . I can't."

"No one will ask you any questions, Kate. There'll be no one about at this time. The uncles will be in the cellar and Maurice resting. You can stay quietly in the breakfast room until I get Patterson . . . come on. I can't let you go down there alone. Come, Kate . . . come."

Like a child who didn't know what she wanted to do I allowed him to lead me back up the hill. It was dark now, but we needed no light, nor did we walk together. I said he led me back, but there was no contact between us.

Far from the uncles being busy in the cellar they were walking across the hall when Logan opened the front door, and they turned their surprised glances on me, and in a moment they were at my side exclaiming, and asking questions. Above their heads Logan Rossiter's eyes were saying to me, "I'm sorry." Then quite abruptly he thrust them aside. "Come into the drawing-room and sit down, Kate," he said.

"Did you fall?" exclaimed Mr. Stanley at my back.

"Fright . . . had a fright?" put in Mr. Bernard. "Get you a drink? Settle you."

They were in the drawing-room now, and it was Mr. Stanley who pressed me into the deep low comfort of the settee in front of the fire, saying, "There you are now, settle yourself." Then, looking up at his nephew, he asked, "Well, what happened?"

I could not see Logan Rossiter, for he was behind me, but his voice sounded tired when it came to me, saying, "She was attacked."

I wanted to turn and protest. I hadn't been attacked, not in the way he implied, but I remained staring towards the fire while the old men exclaimed, their voices high with indignation, "Attacked! Did you see him?"

"Yes, yes, I saw him."

"What you do?" It was Mr. Bernard asking the question.

"I couldn't do much, I was rather handicapped. What I did was with my stick."

"Did you know the fellow?" asked Mr. Stanley. There followed a small silence, a waiting silence, then Logan Rossiter spoke again, saying, "No, I didn't know him, but Kate did. And if you don't mind, don't bother her any more tonight with your questions. I'm going to see Patterson. What about that drink you were going to get, Uncle?"

108

"Yes, yes." Mr. Bernard bustled away behind the couch and Mr. Stanley with him. And I laid my head back, drew in a deep breath and made an effort to relax my tensed nerves and to quieten my racing mind.

I had not been in this room before. What I could see of it showed a surprising amount of comfort. Deep armchairs, faded chintz, old furniture. Looking at it from my mother's standpoint the whole place was in need of a good clean, but this didn't detract from the character of the room and I realized that at one time this had been an elegant place. My gaze was fixed on the portrait of a horse and rider that dominated the whole length of the broad mantelpiece. A part of my mind was wondering vaguely which Rossiter this was when I was startled by the voices of the present-day Rossiters coming from the hall, both Logan's and Maurice's together, and it was not difficult to gauge that they were once again having a battle of words. And I was brought upright in my seat as Logan Rossiter's voice came to me, muted, yet clear, crying, "There's no need to have her here at all, she could take the work home."

And now Maurice's voice high and excited, shouting, "Where I have my work done is my business. You were quite willing that she should do yours here, weren't you? Why didn't you send it down to the office?"

"The circumstances were quite different. . . ."

"Oh yes, of course, my dear brother, I forgot. When you want things your own way the circumstances are always different."

I swivelled round on the couch and looked towards the old men. They had been gazing towards the closed door and now they turned as one to me and shook their heads, and it was Mr. Bernard who muttered jerkily, "Like tigers those two, not brothers. Hopeless . . . hopeless. Always the same. Never change."

The voices from the hall were now becoming indistinct as if they were moving away, but Maurice's voice, even higher now, came to us crying in answer to something

Logan had said, "Or else? . . . I do what you order or else? What does that imply? That if Mr. God Almighty isn't obeyed he'll cut off my allowance?"

It was as if Logan Rossiter had suddenly sprung out of a room and into the hall again, because his voice was clearer than ever now as he cried, "Don't be such a blasted fool. All I'm asking . . ."

"You're not asking, you're telling me. As usual you're telling me."

It looked as if the battle was going to rage afresh, when Mr. Stanley, squaring his bent shoulders, marched to the door and into the hall and joined his voice to that of his nephew, and nothing was distinct any more.

By the time Mr. Bernard came round to the front of the couch and handed me a glass of wine the house was quiet. Abruptly he said, "Drink it up", and, literally obeying him, I drank it up. In two gulps the wine was gone. At another time it would have appeared as a sacrilege to the old man, but not tonight. He took the glass from my hand and nodded his white head and then disappeared behind the couch again.

I sat wondering now why Maurice Rossiter had not told Logan that we had already discussed altering my time, and that he was agreeable to it. Very naturally he had been nettled by his brother's approach. He was not to know that Logan was disturbed, not so much because I had been attacked, as he put it, but because for the few brief seconds—or, like me, had he felt it an eternity?—he had been wafted out of his ordered world. He had allowed something to happen that he would have definitely condemned in others. There was a tinge of bitterness in my thoughts now and I encouraged it, for as long as I could feel bitter I would not cry.

There came a knock on the door and there stood Patterson. He looked across at me and said, "When you're ready, Miss."

I was ready now. I rose from the couch, said goodbye

110

to Mr. Bernard, who patted my hand in a fatherly fashion, and then went into the hall.

Did I expect to see Logan Rossiter waiting at the door to say goodbye? I don't know. But I do know that when I found the hall empty I was overcome by a strange feeling, and as I stepped on to the terrace my mind presented me with a still stranger thought, for of all people it was of Weaver's mother, the woman who had given birth to Weaver in the room above the stables, that I was thinking. She had been used by "a Rossiter". What her life had been I don't know, but I had a good idea that happiness hadn't played much part in it. I hadn't been used by "a Rossiter", but I had been as it were thrown off by one. I could still feel the impact of that electric current that sprang between Logan Rossiter and me a short while ago, and he had undoubtedly created the current. Weaver's mother had remained here all her life. Perhaps once touched by "a Rossiter" she was unable to get away. The bitterness coming to my aid again, I said to myself, "It won't happen to me. I'll get away from the Rossiters, all of them, and Tor-Fret and all it stands for." For what did it stand for? Unhappiness. For who was happy in this house?

My mind was lifted from myself for a moment by the voice of Patterson, saying, "Careful how you go, miss."

Patterson was a quiet man, much younger than Hollings or Bennett, and I couldn't remember having spoken to him until this night, and then it was only to thank him for his escort. He went before me down the road swinging a lantern, letting the light shine at my feet. When we reached the main road he looked about him sending the rays of light here and there. He was, as he had doubtlessly been ordered, looking for the man. Then we walked along the road to where stood three workmen's cottages clustered together in a little dip. At the side of these was a barn-like structure which Logan Rossiter used as a garage. Within a matter of minutes I was in the car and on my way home.

When we reached the point in the road where the lane led off up the fell towards the cottage, I thanked him and said, "I'll be all right now." And to this he answered, "I'm to see you to the door, miss. Mr. Logan's orders."

I did not argue, and now it was I took the lead up the steep fell path. As we neared the house my mother's voice hailed me, and when she came within the rays of the lantern I saw the quick widening of her eyes as she peered at my companion. "This is Mr. Patterson, Mother. He . . . he has seen me home from the house."

"Good evening." My mother inclined her head towards the dark figure.

"Good evening, ma'am." Now Patterson turned to me and said, "Goodnight, miss."

"Goodnight and . . . and thank you, Patterson, it was very kind of you."

"Not at all, miss. Goodnight."

"Goodnight, Patterson."

I went past my mother and into the house, but she did not follow me for some seconds, and when she came into the light of the sitting-room there was a half-smile on her face as she began, "That was short and sweet." Then looking at me fully she exclaimed, "What is it? You've been crying. What is it, lass?" I sat down in the armchair near the fire and dropped my head wearily back into its worn comfort as I said, "Arthur met me as I was coming down the road from the house. It was getting dark and I think he went mad for a time." Then I lowered my eyes. "Mr. Logan came on the scene and . . . and there was a fight of sorts."

"Oh, my God, lass. Did he do anything to him, I mean Arthur?"

"No. Mr. Logan hit him with a stick. His arm was still in a sling, but Arthur was in a rage and . . ." I shook my head quickly and finished, "It's over, it's over."

"You're upset, lass. I knew you would be when you came across him." She came over to me and, putting her hand on my head, stroked the hair back from my brow, and the gentleness was too much for me, and once again I was crying, helplessly now, and she was kneeling by me talking softly, "There, there, now. Cry it out and let it finish. As you say, it's over. There, there. But, it has upset you. Don't let your father see you like this. I've got a nice tea for you. Come along, wash your face and have something to eat. Oh, lass, don't cry like that. . . . I've never seen you so upset, not even when it happened."

I couldn't tell her that I wasn't crying over the loss of Arthur Boyle, but over the irrevocable loss of something not fully realized, something just glimpsed, some world where reigned love. Not just an everyday love that helped you to suffer your existence, but a love that coloured life with almost unbearable intensity, a love that was part-wonder, part-pain not unmixed with fear, fear of the wonder fading, fear of the day when the pain would no longer hurt. It was a love like that, and all I had seen of it was a glimpse, and now it was gone, gone for ever.

6

The Kate that presented herself at Tor-Fret the following afternoon was not the earnest, prim, industrious Kate; it was a washed-out Kate, yet a new Kate, in which bitterness at the moment was uppermost. Why should this have hit me? I didn't want any more emotional tangles, I had had enough. I had been quite content to go on living outside of love, except the love of my parents. This was to have been enough for me, yet here I was in an emotional state I'd never dreamed possible. In the dark hours of the night I had asked myself angrily how, when I had heartily disliked the man, when his presence had filled me with unease and trepidation, when he very sight of him made me steel myself against his sharp sarcastic utterances, how, knowing all this, I could have fallen in love with him. Because it was as simple as that—I was in love with Logan Rossiter. And yet I could not apply the word simple to this feeling. It was anything but simple; it was something larger than myself, something that I was being caught up in. . . . And what of him? Did he feel the same? When I asked myself this question I had been standing at the window looking into the black night that coated the fells and the valley and the river that separated Tor-Fret from this house and me. Is he awake? I had asked myself. And the answer came bluntly, No.

My father had said men felt differently. Their emotions were keyed to a different pitch. Yet in that moment on the hillside Logan Rossiter had, like me, been lifted on to another planet. Yet, when he realized the significance of what was happening, he had thrust me off. Make no mistake about that, I had told myself. He had been shocked at what had hit him and would have none of it. There would be no intrigue between this Rossiter and myself. He was no Maurice. . . . But a man can love two women at the same time my father had said, and my mother had said the same thing about a woman. I doubted, even allowing for the wildest conjecture, whether Logan Rossiter would love two women at once; and if he should, strangely I knew that I would not want to be one of them. This feeling that had broken loose in me would, if given licence, demand something equal, or even greater than itself, in return. Either that or it would remain alone. I had nodded out into the lonely night and had whispered aloud, "It will remain alone all right, there is no doubt about that." I had sense enough to know what I, with my homely attractions, could in no way supplant a girl like Noreen Badcliff. I was also straight enough with myself to realize that if I left Tor-Fret it wouldn't be because I had given in my notice. I knew I couldn't do this, it was as if I were tied to the place by unseen shackles.

This morning my mother had tried to dissuade me from

going to work, but I assured her and my father that I was perfectly all right. I also assured them that I had seen the last of Arthur; yet I doubted this.

Bill Arnold had said, "You look under the weather. You'd think you'd been up all the night." To this I replied that I had. I'd had a nagging toothache. It was the first excuse that came to my mind, and I was in a bit of a dilemma when he suggested that he'd run me into Alnwick and the dentist, for he said, "There's nothing that will wear you down more than toothache."

I lied further by telling him that it was a tooth I'd just had stopped, a matter of an exposed nerve; nothing could be done about it. It came and went. How glibly one could go on when the necessity arose. . . .

As I went up the hill towards Tor-Fret the sun was shining. It was a brittle shine, yet the light was soft on the heather and turned the dying patches into cloaks of velvet. Yesterday I would have stopped and drunk in the changing scene, and would undoubtedly have thought that there was no place in the world to compare with this, this particular corner of Northumberland. But today as I looked over the hills I wished myself miles away. Any place in the world but here.

Remembering the exchange in the hall between the brothers last night, I steeled myself for what Maurice Rossiter would say on the matter. And as so often had been the case with me I received the reverse from what I expected.

As I crossed the terrace I saw the contorted figure of my employer standing with his back to the long window, and when I opened the door from the hall into the room I braced myself against the onslaught.

Evidently Maurice Rossiter was waiting for me, and his approach took the wind completely out of my sails. To say the least, it was kind. "How are you feeling, Kate?" he began as he hobbled towards me, even before I had taken off my hat and coat.

"Oh, I'm all right, thank you."

"Well, you don't look all right. You still look shaken up. I'm very, very sorry you were upset in that way."

I went towards my desk and he followed me, saying, "Tell me how it came about?"

I looked up at him. I did not know how much Logan Rossiter had told him of what I had spilled out in my distress. And then again I could not imagine Logan telling him anything after their clash in the hall. But he might have told the uncles and the uncles could have passed it on to Maurice, I didn't know. So the best thing to do, I saw, was simply to tell the truth. And this I did.

"It was a man I was engaged to two years ago," I said. "We disagreed and he married someone else, and now he finds it was a mistake. He was trying to convince me that I could rectify it. I couldn't see eye to eye with him."

I had related this coolly, dispassionately, like someone else, not like myself at all, and this was proved in the next moment when Maurice Rossiter, after looking at me with a critical expression for some moments, threw his head back and laughed. And he was still laughing as he said, "You know . . . you know who you sounded like? You sounded just like Logan. You could in fact have been the solicitor himself making a statement to the Bench. Oh, Kate, you're delicious . . . Oh, now, don't look like that. I don't mean anything derogatory. Please get it out of your head that I hold you in anything but the highest esteem. You know what I think?" He leant on the desk now towards me, his manner one of high good humour. "I think if I had the proper use of my limbs you'd consider me a real bad lot, capable of any kind of roguery. I have seen this in your eyes, Kate. You have very telling eyes, you know."

I had expected my employer to be on his high horse, and here he was laughing and joking with me, talking as if we were life-long friends. Talking as if every word he had shouted in the hall last night hadn't been a blow hitting out at Logan. Perhaps he had some cause to hit out . . . I wouldn't know. Yet this constant change of manner made him suspect to me. Ignoring what he had said, I came back with, "Referring to what you said yesterday, Mr. Maurice, it will be all right if I came in the mornings?"

"Certainly, certainly. I said make your own time." His words were clipped now.

I was looking up into his face. "I could be here by nine and leave at twelve. Would that suit you?" I said.

"Yes, yes, definitely. Of course, of course. That's settled, then."

On this he turned abruptly away from the desk and hobbled into the bedroom, and I was left with a stronger feeling still that what had transpired in the last few minutes had come from the façade of the man, and that underneath he resented the fact that I, and not he, had suggested the alteration in my time. And in this moment I glimpsed a truth about him that was later to be proved: Maurice Rossiter resented any change being brought about in his daily life that hadn't been suggested by himself.

Later the uncles came in and enquired how I was, and I could smile at them and say I was quite all right now. One patted my shoulder and the other my head, and then they changed positions and one patted my arm and the other my hand. At another time I would have laughed and thought, They're treating me like a Great Dane. But I was soothed inside by their presence and their thoughtfulness. . . . I liked the uncles.

At three o'clock as usual Hollings came in with the tray. And after unnecessarily rearranging the tea-things he spoke to me, but with his attention still centred on the tray. "I'm sorry to hear about the incident last night, madam," he said.

"It's over, Hollings, and I'm all right."

"It wasn't Weaver, by any chance?"

"No, no, it wasn't Weaver. I happened to know the man."

"Oh. Oh, I'm sorry, madam."

"It's all right, Hollings."

When he had left the room I thought, at least his master doesn't tell him everything, for then he'd have known it wasn't Weaver I had been struggling with on the road. . . .

Five minutes before I was due to finish my work Patterson, after knocking on the door, entered the room. He did not say anything but looked towards me.

Maurice Rossiter had been on the point of going into his room, taking with him part of a new story I had started on some days earlier, and he turned about and looked towards Patterson but did not speak. Then he went into his room and the door banged behind him.

The noise had made me start, and when I looked back at Patterson his eyes were directed towards the floor. I wanted to say to him, "There's no need for you to come, thank you," but I felt the uselessness of argument. He was carrying out Logan Rossiter's orders and, like Hollings, I gauged that Patterson was Mr. Logan's man. The banging of the door had somehow confirmed this.

On our journey down the hill Patterson was more talkative than he had been last night. He spoke first of all about the weather, and then about fishing. He was a fisherman and I gathered before he had said very much that salmon fishing was the one joy of his life. He was still talking of fishing when we got into the car, and by the time I got out at the bottom of the fell road I knew also that his master was a fisherman, and that they fished together.

It was still daylight when we neared the cottage and because of this he did not come to the door, but, raising his hat, said, "Good evening, miss," and then added, "It isn't many people who like to talk about fishing—I mean ladies." And when he had gone I smiled rather whimsically to myself. There had only been one person talking about fishing that I knew of and it hadn't been me. Another man was deluding himself. But in Patterson's case it was a harmless delusion.

My father was downstairs when I arrived home and his smile was warm on me as he said, "Hello, there, lass."

"Hello, dear, how are you feeling?"

"Oh, grand, me own self again. I've told the winter where to go because I'm having no truck with it."

I smiled at him and he pulled some papers from the head of the couch, saying, "I've got somethin' to show you."

"Now let her get her tea, Tom," chided my mother. "You can go into that after. Come on, lass, sit down. I've been baking all afternoon and I don't want to see it go stale."

I looked towards the laden table, but it didn't whet my appetite. Yet I knew I would have to eat to stop them both from worrying over me.

After the meal my mother exclaimed, "Well, you won't get fat on that." And then she added, "I'll make a pan-hackelty for the supper."

Panhackelty, a mixture of potatoes, onions and meat or left-overs done slowly over the fire, was a winter evening favourite of mine. My grandmother had first introduced it to me when I used to visit her on the Tyne. But the thought of it on this particular night only made me think, Oh dear, oh dear. And then my father, catching hold of my hand, drew me to him and, pulling me down into a chair near his, he said, "Have a look at these." And he thrust on to my knee a number of catalogues showing on their covers types of shining machines—motor-cycles. I gazed at him in amazement until, selecting one quickly, he said, "Oh, them others are what they sent along, this is what I want you to look at." And, opening the folder, he pointed to the picture of a scooter, saying, "Now wouldn't you like one like that?"

"What!" I looked from him to my mother, who was standing at the kitchen door, a tea-towel in her hand, smiling. "What," I asked them, "do I want with a scooter on these hills?"

"You won't be riding it on the hills, daftie." My father

pushed me. Then, becoming serious, he added, "It's like this. We thought that if you had a mind to get a job in Alnwick, or even Morpeth, and you were independent of the buses, you could do the journey in no time. And it would be a sort of pleasure to have a thing like that." He dug his finger at the catalogue while still looking into my face.

"What about the winter?" I said.

"Oh, they soon clear the roads if there's a heavy fall in the winter. You won't be out in it half so much as you will be if you stick at that job on the fell top. Look, lass. We've been worrying for some time about you having to go up there. And now that that fellow's having to bring you home ..."

"He's a nice man."

"We've nothing against him, it isn't him; but somehow we're not happy about you being there at all, are we, Kate?" He looked towards my mother, and she, coming across the room, stood before me and said quietly, "I would leave that place if I were you, lass. I've got a feeling about it, I'm uneasy. Have been for a long time. This was my idea." She pointed towards the catalogue. "And I thought it would give you a bit of an interest and take you out a bit. It isn't always winter and you know you're too cooped up with us. We're not young any more."

"You speak for yourself." My father nodded at her, then, turning to ne quickly, he said, "But your mother's right. We appreciate all you do for us, don't think otherwise, lass, and God knows it'll be a sorry day if you were to leave us, but you want younger company. You haven't been across the doors but to go to work for over two years now, it isn't right. You're young and"—his hand came out and stroked my cheek—"and you're bonny. You're me own, and I suppose I shouldn't say it, but you're bonny. You're far bonnier than your mother was at your age and she had looks. Isn't that a fact, Kate?" He looked up at my mother, but she did not answer him, she was looking down at me and I could not meet the tenderness in her eyes. I dropped my head and tried to get rid of the lump that was rising in my throat, and before it reduced me once more to tears, as I knew it would, I muttered, "I can't leave there, not yet."

"But why, lass?"

"He . . . he depends on me."

"The crippled one?" This was my father.

I nodded. Here was another lie, but how could I speak of the thing that tied me there, this new-born emotion. Even its effect of humiliation had not the power to arouse my pride and make me leave Tor-Fret. Not yet at any rate, I now told myself. I would wait until the thirtieth of November. Something might happen before then, something that would come between Noreen Badcliff and him. . . . Not through me. No, not for a moment did the thought enter my mind of giving this girl away, for, oddly enough, I liked her. I liked her for herself, yet at the same time I hated the very thought of her need of Logan Rossiter. For it was this need—and from whatever source it sprang I did not know—that would make her marry him.

My father's voice came to me as if out of a thick mist, saying, "You're not for it, lass?"

I shook my head slowly, and my mother's hand came on to my shoulder, gripping it firmly now, and her voice was bracing as she said, "Well, don't worry, it was only an idea. Now, come on, no more crying. There's nothing gets you down so much as crying. A little is all right, it's a relief, but enough is as good as a feast."

The lump in my throat was forced to subside. My father gathered the catalogues from my lap now and my mother, thrusting the tea-towel at me, said, "Come on, give me a hand, I've got a stack out here."

As I went towards the kitchen my father said quietly, "I think I'll play a bit." And a few minutes later as I stood silently drying the dishes the little house was filled with strains of Beethoven's *Für Elise*. As I listened I was soothed and once again thought, This is all I want. This peace. This close unity. Yet my parents were aiming to thrust me out like a chick from the nest. Their very love for me told them I must fly and so they had thought up a scooter. Some part of me smiled at this. Me on a scooter. I had never had the nerve even to ride a bicycle.

So from the following morning I began my new time at Tor-Fret. It was different coming up the steep road at this time of day. Some mornings everything within a few yards of my feet would be obliterated by patches of mist. Then I would step out of it and into a wonderland of pearl sunshine. Other mornings, through the clear white light the contours of the fells and the distant mountains would take on different shapes. This was caused by laggard patches of mist and isolated tufts of low cloud which from the distance had the appearance of being caught for the moment in clefts on the peaks.

And the house, too, seemed altered. I would encounter Patterson in the hall, mopping and dusting in his own fashion. I had not known previously that he worked inside. He always gave me a pleasant greeting. Apparently, too, he cleaned Mr. Maurice's apartments, for on the first morning I was there he came into the room and said, "I'll see to this later."

There was much more bustle about the house in the mornings. I could hear Hollings talking from some distant place. Perhaps the butler's pantry, a small room between the kitchen and the dining-room. I judged he was chatting to Patterson. Then, too, the uncles showed me another side of themselves and their activities. I had imagined they spent the best part of their lives down in the cellar seeing to the wine. But no; apparently they, too, fished, for I saw them going across the terrace the first morning laden with paraphernalia as if they were off on a long, long trek.

In changing my time I had not expected to encounter Logan Rossiter, and during the first week we did not come face to face, yet on the third morning when I came up the hill, a morning when the sun was shining brightly, I saw in the distance a man on horseback. The animal was picking its way among some heavy scree on the hillside, then was brought to a halt near a high boulder, and I was reminded of the picture that hung above the mantelpiece in the drawing-room.

October was drawing to its close and November would soon be upon me. I thought of it in this way: it was like a month of doom. And yet the sensible streak in me told me that if anything should put off the marriage between Noreen Badcliff and Logan Rossiter it would make no difference to me, except that I might be deluded into hoping. And when I got this far my thoughts invariably turned towards Weaver's mother. What had she hoped for? I had seen nothing more of the man Weaver, and this feeling of sympathy towards his mother didn't alter my feelings towards him.

It was at the beginning of the second week of my changed time that I heard Logan Rossiter talking, but again we didn't meet.

Maurice Rossiter did not get up—at least he did not make his appearance in my room—until about half-past ten or eleven in the morning, but this particular morning I heard the brothers talking as soon as I entered. The voices were indistinct across the long length of the room, but when I was seated at my typewriter I could hear snatches of the conversation which I admit I did not close my ears to. For once, the voices were not angry. Logan Rossiter's in particular had a reasonable sound, although his voice became much louder as he said, "Nothing on God's earth will make me sell any more land, Maurice. Now don't let us fight over this, and I want to remind you that I won't be persuaded to do so by Noreen. . . . Now, now. Don't get het up. Let's talk quietly for once and put our cards on the table. You don't want to see the house sitting like a giant in a backyard, do you? And that's what she'll look like if any more land goes. And there's not enough to run sheep on as you

123

suggest. It's out of the question, for it would mean engaging a man and providing him with a house. It can't be done. Anyway, we gave up all ideas along those lines when we sold the farms, you know we did."

And now Maurice's voice; it, too, quiet, reasonable. "That would be quite a narrow strip to let go. Quite unnoticed at the bottom of the hill. Nobody wants to buy land on the heights."

"I've told you, Maurice. I couldn't bear to go down to that road each day and see bulldozers hacking the land to shreds, and then rows and rows of little houses springing up like a fresh batch of mushrooms every morning. If they would erect one or two decent ones, then I might have consent; but no, when these fellows buy land these days they've got to pay for it, and they get their money back by crowding as many houses on it as possible."

"You were quite willing to let it go for the hospital site."

"That was different. I didn't like the idea, not really. There would still be bulldozers, yet the end was more in keeping with the surroundings."

"You know, Logan, you amuse me at times. Your logic is very odd. You won't have a few rows of houses holding three or four people in each because you imagine there'll be too much coming and going. Yet you will suffer a hospital, or, as it would be, a sanatorium, and cars lining the roads on visiting days, and people walking up to this our very door out of curiosity, visitors and patients alike. Had you thought about that?"

"Yes." There came a sigh. "Yes, I'd thought about it all, and I still feel that the end justified my views. But, anyway, don't let's talk about this again, Maurice. It only creates bitterness. Both the houses and the hospital are out of the question. As I tell you, I'd rather sell the lot than have any more bits chopped off."

"And you'd never do that?" This was a question.

"There's no saying what I might do." There was a different note in Logan Rossiter's voice now. "I could do just that, why not? The whole place is like a millstone round my neck; in fact, my neck is breaking with it. . . . Believe me, I could do just that."

"You don't mean it." Maurice's voice had changed, too. "You can't even think about it. What would happen to the uncles? Don't forget you have your responsibilities."

"You, Maurice, reminding me of my responsibilities! That is really amusing. The uncles could be taken care of. They are getting old, and things don't matter so much to them. There are very nice guest-houses along the river where they would survive . . . fishing all day; they would survive, oh yes."

"You must be mad." Now Maurice's tone was full of anger. "They were bred here, they can't stay away from the place for a week. And what about the others? Hollings, Bennett and Patterson? Especially Hollings and Bennett, they would never survive anywhere else."

"They could be taken care of." Logan's tone was more moderate than ever. "They could all be taken care of for less than half that it costs to keep them here. But there, don't upset yourself, it won't happen. I'll do nothing of the sort as long as I'm not driven too far. I'm just keeping my head above water now; I shouldn't even dream of having the top floor redecorated, but it will have to be done. One last word, Maurice; when you're feeling unduly bitter about my meanness remember this place was never meant to be run on a solicitor's practice."

There was silence now and I heard the click of a door, and then another sound, one that I hadn't heard before, a dull thump, thump, thump, thump. It was some minutes before I realized that Maurice Rossiter was banging his fist, either into his pillow or the bed itself.

The conversation I had overheard had repercussions. Although later that morning, when we met, Maurice Rossiter was civil to me, I could see it was with an effort. He made no such effort, I noticed, when speaking to the uncles, or Hollings, or Patterson.

From time to time during that week when I looked at

125

Maurice I knew that he was thinking, thinking deeply, pondering on something, and I got an inkling into what this was some time later. It happened on a Wednesday and the first of November. The month I dreaded had come upon me.

The house was a bustle now because the decorators were up on the first floor. The whole atmosphere of the place had changed. Everything seemed to be hurrying towards an end and I too began to imbibe this feeling of hurry. I realized now that the sooner it was over and done with the sooner I would pull myself together.

I found on my desk this particular morning a small pile of quarto sheets. These were two articles that Maurice Rossiter had discussed with me the day before. He seemed to be working at a feverish pace now. He had stopped me going on with his second book—which, by the way, in my opinion, was much better than the first— and had taken to writing articles, and these I found were far superior in writing and interest to either of the novels. One was dealing with the nature of the fells from Durham to the Cheviots, the other was on wine-making. The pages were higgledy-piggledy and I blocked them together to get them straight. But one piece wouldn't go into place, it insisted on sticking out from the side. Its texture and colour, too, was different from the quarto paper, and when I pulled it from among the sheets I saw it was only half the length of the quarto, also that it was a letter. It was open and my eyes took in the heading straight away . . . Darling Maurice. Perhaps I shouldn't have read it. Perhaps I would have blamed anyone else in my place for reading it. But the fact is that I did read it, and if I had been harbouring any hope of something preventing Noreen Badcliff's coming marriage, the words I read quickly dispersed it.

"Darling Maurice"—my eyes flew across the lines of writing—"What you suggest is impossible. Why, at this late hour, have you changed your mind so completely? I have been begging you to marry me for months and

126

always you have been adamant in your refusal. Even up to a few weeks ago. I have given my word to Logan now and I must keep it. You say you want to do the decent thing . . . well, I'm trying to do it, too. Although God knows it would be better for him if I were to break it off. But I must go through with it, Maurice, and you must believe that nothing you can say now can alter my decision, because, Maurice—I don't say this with the intent of hurting or in any form of retaliation—I want to go through with it. Not that any one on this earth can take your place, but, darling, I am tired and not a little frightened. And I have reason to be.

"If you were to examine your motives, darling, you would recognize, I am sure, that your frantic offer of marriage at this stage is made, not to placate me as much as to hurt him. Although you have gone so far as to deny this emphatically in your letter, knowing you, I can see no other reason for it. Darling, you will always be dear to me and not for a moment do I regret the wonderful times we've spent together. One last thing I would beg of you, Maurice: don't draw me into argument when we meet. Don't try to press me, or change my mind; it won't be any use and it will only upset me. Please . . . please be kind to me because you have a part of me that can belong to no other. Noreen."

Please, please be kind to me. . . . Are you kind with me? . . . Please, please be kind to me. That phrase alone stood out from all the letter. This girl begging Maurice Rossiter to be kind to her, as she had begged me. There was a need in her for love and comfort as great as the one that filled the huge void within me. I was sorry for myself and my own plight, but I was equally sorry for her. And oddly, in this moment, for Maurice Rossiter. Yet how hopeless was the suggestion he had made to her, for if she had consented they could never have stayed in this house. As I remembered him saying, he needed this house, he needed its space, its kind of comfort. He needed the kind of attention commanded here as his due.

Yet he was willing to throw it up if she would marry him. But how and where had he imagined they would live? For he depended on his brother for everything he had. I couldn't puzzle it out and I didn't try. What I was concerned with at the moment was putting the letter back between the sheets of paper, and when I had done this I asked myself: What now? If I went on typing the articles I would eventually come to the letter again. The sheet was about half-way down, there was about an hour's work before I would have come to it in the ordinary way. What if he didn't discover its loss before then? I moved it rapidly nearer to the end. But I need not have worried. Before ten minutes had passed the door burst open and he came into the room in his pyjamas and dressing-gown, his dancing step so pronounced as to be almost pitiful. He did not give me any greeting but started to speak right away as he moved towards my desk, saying, "Those articles, have you started on them? I have mislaid some papers. Have you come across . . . ?"

I looked towards him and, making my voice ordinary, even a little apologetic, said, "I haven't got very far yet, I've just done the first page."

Even before I had finished speaking he had whipped the script from the table, and, supporting it against his withered arm, he flicked through the pages. Then stopping, he placed his hand flat on the top page and pressed the papers around his arm until they formed a cuff, and, smiling at me in a sickly fashion, he said, "I've just thought of something I want to alter, it won't take me long. In the meantime, I wonder if I could trouble you, Kate, to go and tell Hollings that I need him for a minute. . . . Would you mind?"

"No, not at all." I got up immediately and went out of the room in search of Hollings. I knew that if I had only crossed the hall and then gone back into the room he would have had time to remove the letter and the articles would have been on my desk again. But I didn't hurry. I found Hollings in the pantry and I gave him the message.

He was cleaning a lot of very dirty-looking silver which I guessed hadn't seen the light of day for many years. This was in preparation for the thirtieth of November, no doubt. He put down the ornate sugar bowl and said hastily, "Has he had a turn, madam?"

I shook my head. "No, he didn't seem ill. He just asked me to fetch you." As he loosened the apron round his waist he said, "It wouldn't surprise me if he did have a turn; he's been walking the floor every night this week." On this he hurried towards the bedroom door and I went more slowly towards my own room.

Evidently Maurice Rossiter was deeply troubled. Because of his infliction he liked rest, yet he had been walking the floor. My pity for him mounted, yet at the same time I was still suspicious of his motives. Why at this late stage did he want to break up the marriage between his brother and Noreen Badcliff, when only a few weeks ago he had been all for it, even commanding her to marry Logan? Was it because he realized now that he would be no better off financially with Noreen as Logan's wife? That in some way, once she became his sister-in-law, he would lose his power over her? As she had once accused him of doing, had he hoped in a subtle way to blackmail her and now could see the futility of it? I didn't know.

It was just on twelve o'clock when I finished the two articles and I took them to his room. I knocked and opened the door, expecting to find him, as I usually did at this time, propped up on the couch writing, but today he was sitting near the window, his elbow on a small table, his hand covering his face. He did not seem aware of my presence until I spoke, and then, turning his head towards me, he said, as if coming out of sleep, "Oh, it's you, Kate."

"I have finished them, Mr. Maurice," I said.

"Oh, all right. Thanks, Kate . . . thanks." He still continued to stare at me, then he said something that surprised me more than anything that happened at Tor-

Fret. Even the discovery that I was in love with Logan Rossiter had not the element of surprise that Maurice Rossiter's words had as he said, with a kind of unbearable sadness in his tone, "Kate, I wish I was dead."

My mouth dropped slightly open, my eyes widened, and with my head leaning sideways I walked towards him, and, standing at the opposite side of the little table, I exclaimed, "Oh, don't say that, Mr. Maurice."

Looking back at me, the sadness hanging like a cloak from him, he said, "I'm ten different kinds of a devil, Kate. I'm not a nice person. I demand a great deal of sympathy because of my affliction, but I don't deserve it. I really don't need it. I'm sufficient unto myself, but I must demand, I must have . . ." He broke off and I moved my head slowly. In this moment I was being overwhelmed with pity, genuine pity, for I felt that this was not an occasion when the man before me was playing on my sympathy, striving to arouse it. He was in some kind of mental anguish. I said softly, making excuses now for him to himself, "Of course you're not bad, Mr. Maurice, you're no worse than the next. We are all weak in one way or another." And now I smiled, trying to lift him out of this depth, adding, "And you know what they say of the devil? He isn't half bad when you get to know him."

He answered my smile now by a stretching of his lips, and he nodded, then sighed, and, lying back in the chair, asked me, "Why do people tell you things, Kate? Do you find that everyone you come in contact with talks to you?"

"No, not particularly," I said.

"The twins talk to you. Uncle Stephen talks, to you. Even dour Hollings talks to you, and that's something from Hollings, I can tell you. . . . And my brother, the astute lawyer, he's talked to you, hasn't he?"

We were moving away now from the plane of pity on to dangerous ground, and I said, still looking him straight in the face, "I took Mr. Logan's letters down, that's all, so of course he had to talk."

He smiled now more widely. "One of my devils is at work . . . I'm probing, Kate, and not without reason, but you're very diplomatic. But as I said, everybody talks to you, even Noreen." Our eyes were holding now and I was on my guard. Definitely one of his devils was at work and it surprised me when, speaking through him, it said, "You had a long talk in the car the other night. What did you talk about?"

I stepped back from the table. I felt my face closing as I answered, 'We hadn't a long talk, Mr. Maurice. I sat in the car for a time with Miss Badcliff and we talked about . . . Well, we talked about the things that women do talk about."

"Kate . . ." His voice was low and urgent, and he stretched his hand across the table towards me. "Believe me when I say to you that it's important for me to know what she said. There's a reason why I want to know, it concerns us all . . . Logan, too. Him most of all. I feel you know much more than you say, Kate. I see it in your eyes. Tell me . . . tell me what she said, what she thinks. I used to know, but now . . ."

At this point his eyes suddenly lifted from me and looked upwards. There was nothing to attract them but the sound of a wood-pigeon cooing. When he lowered his eyes again to mine he seemed, for the moment, to have forgotten the gist of what he had been saying, and then, recalling it, he exclaimed, as he pulled himself to his feet, "It was unfair of me to ask. Anyway, I might have known you'd keep mum. You'd make a very good friend, Kate."

Those were the very words that Logan Rossiter had said to me some time ago. But I couldn't see any woman being friends with this man. His mistress, yes, but not a friend. He was a man who couldn't have a woman friend. She would either love him or hate him. Perhaps both, but she could never be friends with him. I said, "Goodbye, Mr. Maurice."

"Goodbye, Kate," he answered. "And forget about the last few minutes. I'm a neurotic individual . . . let's face it."

"Goodbye," I said again. And again he answered, "Goodbye, Kate."

Thoughtfully I put on my hat and coat, and thoughtfully I went down the hill. There had been a heavy shower of rain, but now the sun was shining, and hollows here and there were glistening like patches of silver, and my eyes were taken into the distance by the gleam of these patches. I was looking towards my left to where the land flattened out into a wide stretch before dropping steeply downwards again. And then I saw an odd thing happen, an amazing thing—a thing that made me imagine I was suffering from an hallucination. I saw the figure of a man standing at a point on the flat piece of land. One minute I saw him standing in the sunlight and the next minute he had disappeared. It was as if he had fallen down a crevasse. It wasn't an impossibility for anyone to fall between a cleft in the rocks on these fells, but that particular stretch of land appeared like pasture-land, and yet I told myself there could be a crevasse there which I couldn't see from this distance. Lower down, where the hill flattened out into the valley, I could see sheep grazing. Was the man a shepherd and had he fallen? No, no. I rejected the idea. It was as if he had dissolved into the air. I hurried farther down the road now to get a different view of the field, but this view only confirmed what I had already imagined. The field was pasture-land, giving way to bracken as it rose to the next fell. I looked back towards Tor-Fret, I looked around me. Behind any of the mounds dotting the hillside a man could be lying watching me, and my movements would be reported to Mr. Maurice. This knowledge prevented me from cutting across the fells to the field to investigate, but as I reached the road I determined that tomorrow morning I would get off the bus a stop earlier and make my way towards Tor-Fret from the direction of that field.

The incident struck me as odd. It had not left me with the impression that the man could be lying hurt. . . .

That evening, while sitting round the fire, my father said to me, "Would you like to go and stay with your Aunt Peggy in Durham for Christmas?"

I turned on him wide-eyed. "And leave you two here?" I said, bringing my mother into my glance. "Don't be silly."

"You like your Aunt Peggy, and there'll be a houseful and it'll be jolly."

I drew in a breath and then said, "I couldn't imagine anything more tedious or more wearing than being jolly with Aunt Peggy and the rest at Christmas. No," I nodded my head at them. "As dull as you two are I'll stay here and put up with you."

My father, laughing now, gave me a playful dig, and as I resumed my reading I thought here was another effort to throw me out of the nest.

Since the night I had returned home so distraught my father hadn't asked me for an episode on Tor-Fret. And I seemed to surprise even myself when quite suddenly I lifted my head from the book and said, "A funny thing happened on my way home today."

On this my father let out a bellow, saying, "You sounded just like a comic on the wireless, lass."

"Well, it wasn't anything comic." And then I told them of the man I had seen disappearing into the ground. And when I had finished, my father said, "That seems funny. I'd take a dander across there tomorrow morning on your way up. Perhaps you'll find out where he went. You didn't think he was hurt?"

"No."

"I would do nothing of the sort." My mother had risen from her chair, her face full of concern. "I don't like the things that go on up there, and I'm telling you straight, lass, I won't be happy until you leave there."

As I looked back at her trying to frame an answer I knew that in spite of the secret burden of misery I was carrying I would not want to be deprived of one minute of my time at Tor-Fret. I knew that the lost feeling I was experiencing now would be nothing compared to the overall misery were I to cut myself off from that house. Apart from the feeling I had for its master, the house itself had claimed me also. So I could give my mother no answer. I merely shook my head and returned to my book.

The following morning I got off the bus at the stop before Peter's Well and I walked straight from the road up the steep heather bank. There was no path at this point. The morning was dry and cold, with no sun. It was the kind of morning when one would take a sharp walk, so if I was spied approaching the path directly across the fells I had the excuse that I needed to stretch my legs.

Distances are deceptive. I had to do quite a hand-over-hand scramble to reach the actual field where the strange occurrence had happened yesterday. And when I stood on its edge looking downwards I saw, tracing itself in a zigzag way to the road below, a path which started from a point of the field further along from where I was standing.

Yesterday, from where I viewed it, this stretch of land had looked level, but now I saw that it was uneven in patches, and I felt a little silly when I realized that the man could have dropped flat and been hidden by one of the heather-covered mounds, for the fields were not all grass. Yet, nevertheless, I walked in the direction of what I imagined was the spot where I had seen him disappear, but when I reached it the ground showed no crevasse, only small mounds and clumps of dying bracken. And it was as I looked towards the bracken that a slight sound came to me, a gentle pleasant sound, which I recognized as a trickle of water over stones. I walked towards the sound and, bending over the bracken, I saw a ditch with a rivulet of water running away towards my right. This was nothing strange, for the fells were streaked with rivulets running to the rivers. But what was strange was where the water came from. I had moved slightly upwards towards my left now and there I discovered how the earth had swallowed up the man. Sticking out from the bracken and the slope of the ground was a drainpipe, a large culvert; it must have been four feet deep, large enough for anyone to walk into if they bent down. This then was the explanation of the man vanishing. But why should he go into the culvert? I stood still and lifted my head and looked upwards in the direction of Tor-Fret. I couldn't see the house, not any part of it, but I knew instinctively that this drain led to it, and there came back to my mind the voices in the cellar, and Mr. Stanley talking of the drain door.

As if I'd been discovered looking at something very private, I swung round and hurried away. And before I reached the path that led to the house I knew for a certainty that the man I had seen dropping into the earth yesterday was Weaver, and that he had been on his way to Maurcie Rossiter. Going back to the time when I was standing opposite to my employer, and going over what happened during that time, I could again see the point where his manner changed, where he put an end to the conversation. It was when he had raised his eyes to the ceiling at the sound of the wood-pigeon, and it came to me that I had heard that wood-pigeon on different occasions.

By the time I reached the house I was shivering with apprehension and I expected someone to say to me immediately, "Poor Mr. Logan!" But my imagination had run away with me. I was greeted almost cheerily by Hollings. There was the clatter of ladders being moved and the jangling of pails from the upper floors. And on my desk I found a note from Maurice Rossiter which read, "Take half an hour off and go and have a word with Uncle Stephen, he's been asking for you."

With my new time-table it had been almost impossible for me to visit the old man. So, shortly after ten o'clock, I went up to Mr. Stephen's room and I found him very depressed and very grumpy.

At first he did not show any pleasure at my arrival, and not until after I had made the usual enquiries about his health and showed signs of cutting my visit short did he seem to come alive. And almost at once he gave me the reason for his grumpiness. "Have you heard the latest?" he said.

"The latest?" I repeated. "What about?"

"The wedding."

I remained silent, and he, hitching himself up on to his pillows, leant towards me and went on, "Hole in the corner, that's what it's going to be. Marrying early morning, ten o'clock, then going straight off, and not coming back here for a drink or anything. Can you imagine it? And they call that a wedding."

Still I said nothing, and he continued, "It isn't him, it's her. He was quite prepared to make a bit of a splash, even talked about it a week or so ago, but now first thing in the morning, and straight off. Huh! I did think I was going to see a little jollification in this house before my time was up. But jollification, they don't know the meaning of it these days; not the young ones. . . . Why does she want everything quiet like that, eh? They could have come back here and had a drink and then have gone off, couldn't they? But no, straight from Alnwick they go. . . . Now what do you think of it, eh? I know what his friends'll think. Mean, they'll say, mean."

It was impossible to tell the old man what I thought of it, truthfully thought of it, so I said, "She doesn't like fuss."

"Noreen not like fuss? funny, Huh! Wildest piece for miles she used to be, skittish as a mountain goat, and now no fuss. . . . Huh!"

He was slumping down on his pillows now, and his old wrinkled face losing the temporary firmness his temper had given to it, he smiled at me, and, reaching out for my hand, held on to it like a child clutching at an elder, and his voice matched his age and pathetic appearance as he said, 'Funny thing about weddings. Do you know, there's never been a wedding from this house. Funny thing, but I've always wanted to see a wedding from this house. Right back in the family men have married women away from the house. My great-grandfather met a woman in Spain and married her; my grandmother was a woman from the wilds of Cornwall; fey she was, I remember her well. She was married down there, it was all done before she had seen this house. My own mother was French and it was in France that my father married her; she was another fey one. They are all a bit fey in this family, have you noticed that, Kate?" He was grinning widely now, and I shook my head at him as he went on, "And Logan's mother. Ah, she was a bonny woman, was Logan's mother. My brother came across her in Dublin. I can see her now the first time she came in through the hall door. She was big and stately. Bigger by inches than her man. Logan is the spit of her. She didn't like it here. Her nature was happy and gay and she longed for the life of Dublin. . . . But she didn't stay long, anyway. She died she did." He laughed gently here. "She talked like that. That's what she would have said. . . . She died she did. Oh, I can remember her well, and at the last it seemed as if she was glad to go. . . . You know something?" He was gripping my hand with a renewed strength now and he craned his skinny neck forward as he whispered, "This house doesn't take to women—not foreign women, anyway. You know what I mean? I've a funny idea it wants someone belonging to the soil on which it stands, to the rocks and the crags and the screes, to the high fells. . . ."

Now he thrust himself back on the pillow and raised his hand at me as he said, "And that is why I had such hopes of Noreen. She was born in the county, she belongs. And yet"—his voice sank—"she won't be married from the house."

Aiming to soften his disappointment, I said, "But it's

usual, you know, for the bride to go from her own home to the church."

"Fiddlesticks. Nonsense. They should do as they do in America: be married in the house, that's the place for marriages. Have your priests, and your parsons, but let 'em do it in the house. They've got to live in the house. They've both got to carry out the 'I will' in the house, so why don't they start where they mean to carry on—in the house? But, anyway, they could have come back, couldn't they? After they had done it they could have come back." His voice was pathetic now.

Yes, I thought, they could have come back. If there hadn't been Maurice Rossiter to look at the bride with eyes that made her remember what she was desirous of forgetting, then she would have come back. But as it was, I thought, she was doing the wise thing not to face Maurice until she was settled in her new life. With such thinking I turned a knife between my ribs, but there it was, it was something I had no power to alter. I could only hope that they would both find a certain amount of happiness. Yes, I could hope that, especially for him. This love that had been sprung on me was already great enough to desire this.

The old man now brought the conversation on to a personal level by exclaiming, "I want my coffee. Hollings never brings it before eleven. An' I want it black. I'm as dry as a stick."

This gave me an excuse to rise to my feet. "I'll go and tell him," I said. "Goodbye now, Mr. Stephen."

He blinked at me and smiled his toothless smile, saying, "I like seeing you. Will you come up every morning?"

"I can't promise every morning, but I'll try to slip up as often as I can."

"Yes, yes, do . . . I like seeing you. . . ."

In the kitchen I found Hollings and delivered Mr. Stephen's message, to which he replied, "He's not getting it black, madam. 'Tisn't good for him." He gave me, what was for him, a smile. And I returned it, then went to my room.

I did not see Maurice Rossiter until about fifteen minutes before I was ready to leave. His manner was cheerful, too cheerful to be natural. There was no reference to our conversation of yesterday. He talked only of his work. He expressed great satisfaction with the articles, and told me he had done another.

More for something to say than anything else, I remarked, "You must work all night." And to this he answered. "I do very often." And I was left with a picture of him sitting propped up in bed during the small hours of the night writing, writing one of his devils out of his system.

7

When I look back I can remember very little of what transpired from the beginning of November until the day of the wedding. Only one thing stands out, the rest were mundane happenings, such as my mother insisting I have a fry before I went to work. This was because she said I was getting scraggy. It was true I had lost weight, but I could never see myself as thin, let alone scraggy. And then there was the Sunday that Rodney brought his girl from Amble up to see us, and my mother asked them to stay to tea. And when they had gone my father had looked at me with his head on one side and said, "You're not regretting anything in that quarter, are you?" To this I replied, "Oh, Father, don't be silly." And he answered, "Well, you didn't sound very bright at tea and I thought you might be regretting something." Again I had said, "Don't be silly."

And then there was the morning of the first really hard frost, a black frost. There was a patch of ice outside the door some yards long and impulsively I slid along it, much to my parents' amusement. As usual they had come to the door to see me off, and my father had cried laughingly after me, "Enough of that now. You wore enough shoes out when you were a bairn; don't start that all over again." I waved to them from the bend on the hill. Braced by the steely air, I became almost joyful, intoxicated you could almost say. But it did not last for long. Before I reached Tor-Fret I was sober once more.

But the one thing that remains clear in my mind took place one morning as I was once again going to visit Mr. Stephen. It was about a week before the actual wedding day. The decorators had finished their work in the rooms on the left side of the landing, and the door of one room was ajar, and in spite of myself I had to stop and look in. It was furnished as a sitting-room, and from where I stood I could see a moss-green-coloured couch set at right angles to the fireplace. It was standing on a red Turkish carpet, not the ordinary hard red that inclines to purple, but a scarlet red with a yellow and green pattern, and the walls appeared a creamy grey. The glimpse afforded me drew me to the threshold of the doorway and then into the room, I had just noticed that the curtains were the same soft green as the couch, when a voice from somewhere behind me, said, "Do you like it, Kate?" As I started round I put my fingers to my lips and muttered apologetically, "Oh, I'm sorry."

"Why be sorry? What is there to be sorry for?" Logan Rossiter stepped from where he had been standing at a bookcase in the corner of the room and came towards me, but not too close. When he stopped and looked at my flushed face he said quietly, "Don't be disturbed like that, please. I'm so glad it was attractive enough to draw you in. . . . Do you like it?" he asked again.

"Yes, yes I do, very much." I took my eyes from his face and looked around the room now, taking it in as a whole, and as I did so I knew a feeling of deep envy. "I think it's very beautiful."

"I hope . . . I hope Noreen thinks so too. She hasn't seen it yet."

My eyes were on him again, and his were tight on my face as I replied, "No?"

Now with a quick movement he stepped behind me and closed the door, then, coming and facing me again, nearer this time, he said quietly, "I wanted to see you, Kate, to have a word with you. To tell you how sor——"

"Please. Please don't. Don't talk about it." My hand was out as if warding him off. I couldn't bear to hear him apologise for what had taken place.

"But it was my fault——"

"It was nobody's fault. It's over and forgotten, please. . . ." I looked at him appealingly.

"All right, Kate, as you wish. But there's still something I'd like to tell you. I feel I must tell you, if only I can find the right words."

Now I experienced a terrifying feeling, a racing through my system that made me want to cry out. I didn't want to be confronted by another Arthur Boyle. The thought was unbearable. Arthur had met a girl in a train and because of her I was thrown aside, rejected. Although I would not forgo one minute of the time Logan Rossiter and I had clung together on the hillside, I did not want to be another "girl in the train" and that "The Big Fellow" should lose my respect by becoming a mere Arthur. Although if he walked out on Noreen Badcliff an hour before the wedding it would be nothing less than she deserved, yet he was not to know this. If he retracted now he would, in his own mind, be letting down a lovely girl, a girl he had known all his life, and admired all his life . . . had loved all his life.

He now put up his hand and patted the air, and so meaningful was the gesture that I almost felt it on my flesh. Then, as if he had been travelling alongside my whirling thoughts, he now said, "I understand you, Kate. All that you'd like to say, all that you want left unsaid . . .

141

I understand. The only thing, the final thing I will say to you is, if I caused you any distress, please forgive me."

My throat was tightening but before it gave me away and choked my voice I managed to say, "There's nothing to forgive, nothing. Goodbye." And I paused before adding, "I hope you'll both be very happy."

He made no answer whatever to this, and after a second, during which we again looked at each other, I turned and opened the door and went out. I remember that I did not go on my way to visit Mr. Stephen but returned to my room.

That's all I can recall of that month, until the wedding day.

Have you noticed that the weather seems to match itself to certain happenings? This is not always so, but I think the weather was in keeping with the events that followed Logan Rossiter's marriage to Noreen Badcliff.

For days now my father, looking across the vast expanse of land that formed the fells, had watched the weather signs. The startling squalls. The clouds dropping on distant peaks as if bent on sweeping them away. Then intervals when everything stood out against the stark white light peculiar to this part of the country. And he would say to me when I returned home at night, "We're in for it; it's going to be a winter and a half, you mark my words."

Then on the eve of the wedding the world became still. The cold was intense; and when I returned home that night with my heart as chilled as my face, my father said, "This'll break in a storm, you'll see. There's hardly a blade of grass moved all the day; there'll be snow 'afore the morning." And my mother said, "I saw a grey wagtail the day; it's a long time since I've seen a grey wagtail. It was lovely and yellow underneath; oh, it was bonny. I put out some bread, but it didn't come near, but a missel thrush did. By, he golloped it up. Oh, I'm sorry for the birds days like this." And my father put in now, "I'm

142

sorry for anybody outside days like this." Then turning to me, he added, "You won't be going in the morrow, anyway, I suppose?"

I turned from his keen glance, and, settling myself in a chair before the roaring fire, I replied evenly, "Yes, I'm going in."

"But he won't be working surely . . . not on his brother's wedding-day?" This was from my mother, and I cast a glance at her, saying, "Well, he's told me to come in and that things are to go on as usual."

I turned from their probing stares and looked into the heart of the fire, and there I could see Maurice Rossiter when he told me that things would go on as usual. It had never dawned on me that he would want to work on this particular day, and certainly I had not thought that he would expect me to come up to the house, even if there was to be no reception. It was as I was leaving the room that I turned to him and said, "You won't want me tomorrow then?" I took it as an accepted fact that he wouldn't require my services on this day, but he had turned a completely blank countenance towards me as if I had said something utterly idiotic, and then he had asked in a voice that was too calm, "Why not?"

"Well, the . . . the . . ." I found I was stammering in confusion. "Well . . . the wedding."

"I'm not getting married.'

I was completely nonplussed and showed it.

"It is my brother who is getting married and there is to be no reception, so why shouldn't we go on as usual, Kate?"

I had looked at him blankly for some moments before I was able to say, "Very well, I'll come in."

I thought now that cruelty was such an integral part of Maurice Rossiter's nature that he couldn't help but inflict it on himself. I could not blame him for inflicting it on me, not on this occasion, for he was ignorant, at least I prayed he was ignorant, of my feeling towards his brother. I told myself I would die of shame if what had transpired between Logan and me was ever made known to him.

My father now put his book down and took off his reading glasses as he said, "Listen to that. There it comes, the wind." And my mother, seating herself on the other side of the hearth, a stocking in her hand, clicked her needles together and smiled at me, but, speaking to father as if he were a frightened child, said, "There's no need to worry. The house has stood many a gale and not a stone moved. I think it will ride out another." She pulled a face at me, then concentrated on her knitting, and I lay back in my chair and opened a book and looked at its pages without seeing the print. . . . This time tomorrow it would be all over.

My father, as if he had discovered himself to be a prophet, shouted from the landing the next morning, "What did I tell you, Kate? Snow, heavy. Have you seen it?"

Yes, I had seen it, and I called back to him, "You were right."

Later, down in the kitchen, my mother said, "You're not going out in this, lass, surely? You'll get down this hill but what about getting up to the house?"

"It isn't thick," I said, "and it won't lie. It's much too early for it to lie. It's just a shower.

"Oh. Don't you bluff yourself. The sky's laden with it. Your mother's right. You stay put."

"I must go," I said. And I knew I must go. I was glad now that Maurice Rossiter had insisted that I go. I could not have borne to stay penned up in the house all day thinking. I had to do something, and struggling against the elements was as good a way to forget myself as any other.

As yet the snow was nowhere thick enough to stop traffic on the road, but the people in the bus, like my father, prophesied more to come. But my father had been right. It was one thing getting down the hill into village but quite another getting up to Tor-Fret. And when I arrived, chilled to the bone and quite out of breath, I was greeted in the hall by the twins, who quite openly were amazed to see me. "Why, Kate!" said Mr. Stanley. "What brought you up here in this? We're in for a good thick blanket, didn't you know?"

Mr. Bernard, now peering into my frozen face, said, "Maurice? Maurice tell you to come today?"

"It's all right," I said. "I . . . I wanted to come. I'm not in the way, I hope."

"In the way?" Mr. Stanley replied while Mr. Bernard shook his head. "No, of course not, Kate." And then he patted my arm and said, "It's nice to have you here at any time, but I think we're more glad of you today. It's a funny day today."

The two old men now looked at each other and nodded in agreement; then, turning to me, they waited for me to say something. They looked very old at this moment, and pathetic, sort of lost. What was it about the men in this house that brought to me a sense of not only loneliness, but aloneness, as if each in his own way was encased in a private world from which he was groping, groping in vain for a hand to anchor to?

I made myself smile and say, "I'm glad I've come then."

And now Mr. Stanley, brightening, said, "We'll have a glass of wine, eh, instead of coffee. You'll join us in a glass of wine, Kate, won't you?"

"Yes, I'll be glad to, thank you. Tell me when you're ready." I turned from them and went into my room. It struck cold; the fire had just been lit and was still sullen, so I sat with my coat on for some time—in fact, until the big old wall-clock in the hall boomed ten. Then I stopped my typing and let out a long breath. . . . It was done. It was over. Now it was up to me to pull myself together. It was no use repining or thinking any more about it. I wasn't the first woman in the world, I told myself, that this had happened to, and I could do one of two things. I could become maudlin under it, full of self-pity, asking why? why? why? Or I could use it as an incentive to drive me to do something with my life. As my parents were aiming to throw me out of the nest, then I must also tear myself from the magnetism of this house and one of its occupants. I was a good secretary, I knew my own worth, I could go away and get a decent post, say, in Edinburgh, or London even. And who knew what might happen to me there? Yes who knew?

It was as I was injecting myself with this brave philosophy that I heard the thumping, the same kind of thumping I had heard before, the thump of a fist being beaten into the bed or pillow. And, turning my eyes towards my employer's door, my resolutions fled and for a moment I cried inwardly for us both. And then the uncles came in.

"How 'bout this glass of wine?" Mr. Bernard cried. Then added, "Where's Maurice? Not up yet? Dear, dear." As he made his way towards the intersecting door it opened and there stood Maurice Rossiter fully dressed.

I had known this man for a number of weeks now. I had seen him in varying moods, which altered his face accordingly. But never had I seen him as he looked at this moment. His skin was so white as to appear powdered. His eyes seemed to have fallen back into their large sockets and were merely dark pools, yet bright with a strange light. I had once, many years ago, shone a torch down a deep well and I was reminded of this incident now. Candidly I was appalled at the change in this man, and pity for him once more flooded over me. The old men, too, were vitally aware of their nephew's mood, and their manner was tender. Mr. Stanley spoke first to him, saying, "Ah, there you are, Maurice. Come on, come on, we'll have a quiet glass together. What do you say?"

And now Mr. Bernard, going forward, began in his staccato manner, "No restrictions, no rationing, not today. Sample some of the bottles, eh? Eh, Maurice? Sample some old bottles, that's the stuff."

Maurice Rossiter now shambled forward and passed the old men, making for the chair before the fire without speaking. I felt that he could not speak. If his face was anything to go by his feelings were so ravished at this moment that he was incapable of any utterance. And now Mr. Bernard, hoving over him, pointed towards the fire and spluttered, "Look at that, dead as a door-nail. Morning like this. Where's Patterson?" He turned from his nephew and was making his bustling way towards the door when he was stopped by Mr. Stanley saying quietly. "Leave Patterson alone, Bernard, he's got his hands full. There's a grand fire in the drawing-room, come on. Let's all go there. And you, Bernard, go and bring the bottles up. . . . Go on."

"Yes, yes, that's it, that's it." Mr. Bernard scurried out, and Mr. Stanley, looking at me, said, "Come along, my dear. We'll go to the drawing-room. Maurice will follow; won't you, Maurice?"

Not for the life of me, even knowing all I did about Maurice Rossiter, could I have left him sitting there in his lonely pain, and so I bent towards him and said, "Won't you come? Come now."

He brought his eyes from the struggling embers of the fire and looked at me and blinked once. I was sure he had not been aware of my presence until this actual second, and now he inclined his head forward and, pulling himself up on to his feet, went out of the room. Mr. Stanley and I, keeping well behind him to give him, as he always needed, room to swing his body.

As Mr. Stanley had said, there was a grand fire in the drawing-room, and the room itself looked inviting, for it was filled with snow-light from outside and fire-light from within, and their mingling lent to it a charm, a comfort and a charm.

We had hardly seated ourselves round the fire when Mr. Bernard bustled in with three bottles in his arms. "Brought a bottle nineteen-fifty-two up. . . . Remember? Christened it Tor-Freto."

"Good. Good." Mr. Stanley was now acting like an excited boy, an act no doubt put on to bring Maurice out of his depression. He clapped his hands together and shook them as he exclaimed, "Wait till you sample this. It's as good as your Austrian Petite Tokay. Two years in the barrel it was, smooth as a liqueur. And what else, Bernard?"

Before Mr. Bernard had time to reply Maurice Rossiter said flatly and quietly, "I'd like a drop of hard stuff."

Following this request there settled a silence on us. It only lasted for a matter of seconds, but during it the two old men exchanged quick glances, and then Mr. Stanley said soothingly, "Now you know there's none left, Maurice."

"I'll have a drop of the fresh."

"You won't! You won't! Deadly." Mr. Bernard was now spluttering in agitation. "Another year at least. Two better. Remember last time. Don't want ..."

"All right, all right." Mr. Stanley now silenced his brother, but not before he had cast in my direction a very uneasy glance. I knew that "hard stuff" referred to whisky. . . . Did the uncles make whisky? But it was illegal. I recalled the workmanlike corner of the cellar. Was that where they made it? I wouldn't know.

"This one is very good, Maurice, warming." Mr. Stanley picked up the bottle his brother had referred to as "Tor-Freto" and proceeded to pour out the wine. He did it with a slow dignity as if he was performing a ceremony —I think he always looked on the serving of wine in a ceremonious light—and then we all had a glass in our hands, and for a moment there was another awkward silence. I say for a moment, but this one seemed to me to go on for an unbearable length of time, and then thankfully it was broken by Mr. Stanley raising his glass to eye-level and saying, "Well, let us drink to them."

It is usual to repeat a toast but no one replied, "To them." Mr. Bernard inclined his head, that was all, then raised the glass to his lips, as did Mr. Stanley, and the wine was on my tongue when it almost spluttered from my mouth as the stem of Maurice Rossiter's glass snapped in two. As the wine soaked into the carpet we all looked down, and the strangest part of it was there was no exclamation of any kind either from the old men, myself, or Maurice Rossiter. No "Oh dear!" or "How did you manage that?" or "It's all right, I'll get you another." There was not a single word spoken. The atmosphere had an eerie feeling. If I can explain it, it seemed pregnant with a force that pressed against all of us, even its creator. And there he sat, staring before him, not into the fire, not at the picture of the rider above the mantelpiece, just before him, looking, I thought, into his own mind and watching the torture manufacturing itself. What would have happened next I don't know, but the old men and myself were diverted by the sound of the front-door bell ringing. We all looked towards the drawing-room door as if it was a means of escape, and then Mr. Stanley exclaimed in a high tone, "Who can it be on a morning like this? Hollings wouldn't ring. Anyway, it's too soon for him to be back."

I hadn't up to now known that Hollings was out, but I knew that there would be only one place he would go this morning. I knew that for this occasion Logan Rossiter would have preferred Hollings to do him this service rather than anyone else.

Now there was a tap on the drawing-room door and Patterson opened it, and in came the minister. The man was blowing on his hands, his face a ruddy beam. He seemed in high fettle, which is more than I could say for anyone else in the room. For the twins' greeting had, I thought, a coolness about it. As for myself, I felt that odd tremor of fear as when I had first come face to face with this man. Evil in any shape is a force to be reckoned with, but when it is hiding under an authorized cloak of goodness its power becomes terrifying. Yet the presence of this man—I couldn't think of him as a minister—

seemed to lift the dark depression that was weighing Maurice Rossiter down. For although he didn't smile at the visitor, he greeted Fallenbor in a tone that was almost normal. "You're just in time," he said; "you must have smelled it." He looked towards his uncle, and Mr. Stanley went to the side table and poured out two more glasses of wine. In the meantime the minister had taken his stand with his back to the fire, and he rubbed his buttocks vigorously as he beamed around him, saying, "What a day! Do you know, I had almost to claw my way up the hill. It's early this year. . . . Well, well." He extended his hand towards Mr. Stanley and, taking the glass, went on, "Isn't this nice! Thank you, Stanley, thank you." Then, raising his glass and bowing slightly to one after the other, he sipped at the wine and his round eyes widened, and, looking towards Mr. Stanley again, he exclaimed in a loud voice, "Ah! Ah! This is special, isn't it? Of course, of course, what am I thinking about? It's for a special occasion. Well, I will drink to it, but not alone—come along." He chuckled now as he held up his glass.

I did not sip the wine again but watched Maurice Rossiter closely, and couldn't but be surprised when I saw him put the glass to his lips and drink in quite an ordinary fashion. It was evident that the minister was having a soothing effect upon my employer, and this became more evident still when in the next moment, placing the glass on a low stool at the side, he looked towards the man and said, "I'm glad to see you, Fallenbor. I was in the doldrums; I want cheering up. Tell me something to make me laugh."

I couldn't bear to hear this man playing the raconteur. Doubtless he could tell an excellent tale, but I didn't want to hear it, or listen to him. So, rising to my feet, I said, "If you'll excuse me, I'll get back to my work."

"There's no need, Kate, there's no need." It was the first time that Maurice Rossiter had addressed me since I came in, and, looking at him, I said quietly, "I would rather if you wouldn't mind, Mr. Maurice."

He was looking straight up into my face now as he said, "As you will."

I handed my glass to Mr. Bernard and smiled at the old men, then, inclining my head towards the minister, I went out of the room.

When I opened the door of my room it was to find Patterson peering out through the snow-smeared window. He turned quickly on my entry and, looking towards the fire, said, "It's going all right now, miss. Couldn't get it to brighten at all today." And then he added, "I was on the look-out for Hollings. If he doesn't come in a little while I'll go down the hill. He'll have a job to make his way, it's getting worse."

I looked past him towards the window. I could see nothing now but the snow-flakes falling gently on to the drift on the low sill. "I'm going to find it a job to get home, too," I said.

"Well, if I go down I'll see if the road is clear enough and I'll take you in the car."

"Mr. Logan didn't take the car then?"

"No, no. They were going south by train. And Mr. Rankin, his partner, picked them up at the bottom of the hill."

So he had had someone with him besides Hollings. As I turned to my desk, Patterson, looking towards the window again, said, "Awful day for them really," and then he added with a little smile, "Well, I don't suppose they'll mind, do you?"

I turned my head towards him. As I said, I liked Patterson. He was a kindly man, uncomplicated. "No, Patterson," I said, "I don't suppose they'll mind."

"I wouldn't in his place, at any rate." His smile was broader now and I dared to say, "Nor I in hers." We both laughed now as if it were a joke, a private joke, and then he went out, leaving me alone.

Nor I in hers. As I repeated the phrase the common-sense Kate asserted herself, saying, "Stop it. Get some work done. Get down to it." And my weaker self obeying her, I got down to it.

It was just on twelve when Mr. Stanley entered the room, saying anxiously, "I'm afraid, Kate, you'll have to wait awhile before venturing out. Patterson isn't back yet. He went down to see if Hollings had arrived on the eleven-thirty bus, for he would have come straight back. Hollings isn't the one to stay out. Never moves really. So he must have got held up somewhere."

"Oh," I said, "I'll be able to manage. I've had two winters on the fells, I'm quite used to snow."

"Have you been to the front door?"

"No."

"Well, go and have a look out; it's no use looking out of the window."

I went past him through the hall and opened the front door on to a massed white world. I knew it had been snowing steadily, but I hadn't realized how heavily and how thick it was lying. Under the portico lay about three feet of drift, and I gauged that it must be anything up to a foot in depth beyond. That wouldn't be too difficult for walking on the level, but on the steep fell road it was another matter. I turned to where Mr. Stanley stood behind me and said, "I see what you mean. I'll wait until Patterson comes back. Yet it's hard lines on him having to go down again."

"Oh, Patterson's tough, he's fell-bred. Come in, dear, and shut the door; the blood in my veins is very, very thin." He smiled at me, then added, "Leave what you are doing; come along, come and join us. There's only Bernard and I. We're upstairs with Stephen; the minister is entertaining Maurice."

And so, not a little worried, I went upstairs to find Mr. Stephen in a very querulous mood. Unlike his brothers, he was not hiding his disappointment over the wedding. And he greeted me immediately with, "Serves them right; serves them right, doesn't it? Don't deserve any better weather."

"Now, now . . ." Mr. Stanley began, only to be shut up abruptly with, "Never mind 'now, now'. You won't stop me saying what I think . . . not until I'm dead."

"Not then." This staccato quip came from Mr. Bernard, and the twins laughed together. Then Mr. Stephen, turning to his one remaining pleasure, asked, "What's for lunch? Not the usual, I hope, today."

"Grouse, man, grouse." Mr. Stanley was leaning towards the bed.

"Grouse. Ah, who brought them in? Logan?"

"No, Patterson. He was out with Burrows on the lower farm."

"Well, that's something . . . grouse." The old man smacked his lips, then added, "Pie or roast?"

The twins now looked at each other in enquiry, then Mr. Stanley said, "Roast. Roast, I suppose, if nobody's told Bennett otherwise. Bennett can't stand pie himself." Again the twins laughed.

It was half an hour later that I went downstairs with Mr. Stanley to ascertain whether Patterson had returned with Hollings, and before we reached the kitchen we knew that they were back, for we heard Patterson's voice saying, "There now, there now, take it easy, let me get them off you," and when we entered the kitchen it was to see Patterson kneeling on the floor pulling off Hollings's snow-encrusted boots. The old man was leaning back in a deep cane chair. His face was rimed with snow, and there was a ridge of hair on his neck sticking out like miniature icicles, where the snow had caught him between the collar of his coat and the bottom of his cap. He turned his weary eyes towards me, and I gave an exclamation of concern as Mr. Stanley, hurrying to his side, exclaimed, "My God! Hollings, you look all in. As bad as that, is it?"

It was Patterson who answered, "It's as bad as anything I've seen for many a long day, sir. Bus got stuck a mile away, he had to walk. No traffic moving at all. I don't know how we got up the hill . . . I really don't."

"I'll get you something . . . warm you inside." Mr. Stanley scurried from the room, and Patterson, getting to his feet, inclined his head to me and said, "You're not going to get down there yet a while, miss."

"But I'll have to, Patterson; my people will be worried."

"They'll be more worried if you get stuck out in that. It was as much as I could do to get up the hill. I'm telling you, I wouldn't risk it, miss. In fact it would be madness; it's blowing a blizzard. If it stops, well, that's another thing, I'll get you down. But it's not only getting you down, it's getting you there."

Yes, it was getting me there . . . home. I said now, "I'll have to get word to my people somehow. The wires aren't down, are they?"

"No, not that I know of, not yet. But they won't last long in this, the wind is enough to crack a steel plate in two."

I was about to turn away when Hollings's hand came wavering towards me, and his voice was weak in his throat as he said, "Don't risk it, madam. Don't risk it."

I nodded at him and turned towards the kitchen door, but before I could reach it it was pushed open and there entered Maurice Rossiter. He rolled a few steps, then supported himself against the long white scrubbed kitchen table, and, looking first at Patterson and then at Hollings, he said, "Pretty bad out then?"

"Yes, sir." It was Patterson who answered for Hollings. But now Maurice Rossiter, his eyes still on Hollings, asked the old man pointedly, "And how did it go?"

Hollings, easing himself straighter in the chair, and turning his head fully towards Maurice, replied, his voice seeming to gain strength, "Very well, sir; it went very well."

The old man and the young man surveyed each other for a full minute, and then Maurice Rossiter made a deep obeisance with his head before turning away. I was holding the door open and he passed me without a word, and I followed him. And when we were opposite my door I said, "Would it be all right for me to use the phone, Mr. Maurice? I'll have to tell my people I won't be home for a while."

"Yes, Kate; yes, certainly." He spoke over his shoulder and added, "You must stay for lunch." I looked at him and saw that he was smiling, and I realized that already he was carrying quite an amount of wine.

I crossed the hall and went into the room that I had entered on the first morning on coming into this house, the room where Logan Rossiter had scathingly repeated my name.

It was with a feeling of thankfulness that I contacted the exchange, and in a few minutes Rodney's voice came to me muffled and unfamiliar, but when he knew who it was speaking he exclaimed, "Oh, it's you, Kate. Where are you stuck?"

"Up at the house," I said.

"Well then, you stay there. Don't attempt to come down here for a while. The roads are blocked and it's blowing a blizzard."

"But my mother and father, Rodney, They'll be worrying themselves sick."

"They'll guess that you'll stay put. Anyway, look, don't you worry. I'll have a shot at getting up to them."

"Oh, will you, Rodney? That's good of you."

"Don't you worry, Kate. And if I manage it, I'll give you a ring back. That all right?"

"That's fine, Rodney. I'm sorry to trouble you."

"No trouble at all, you know that, Kate. By the way, I hear the big one, the eldest's getting married the day?"

"Yes, yes. It was this morning."

"How did they get down?"

"Oh, they went early. They didn't intend to come back, anyway."

"Lucky for them. But what a day for it. Ah, well. Are they having any jollification?"

"No, Rodney, no jollification."

"Well, that's a pity; it would have passed the time away. You'll get something to eat though, surely?"

"Yes, I'm staying to lunch."

"Good. Now don't worry, I'll have a shot at getting up to the house . . . take some bread with me and things and then if I can I'll ring you back. How's that?"

"Thanks, Rodney. You are so kind. Goodbye."

"Goodbye, Kate."

I put down the phone and my mind was easier. . . . That was until I sat down to lunch.

Maurice Rossiter sat at the head of the long dining-table, which was only half covered by a cloth. The table would, I am sure, have seated two dozen people comfortably, and doubtless in the not so distant past it had served that number often. But now we sat at one corner of it, I on Maurice Rossiter's right and the minister opposite me on his left, the twins one on each side of us. My employer's manner had undergone a complete change. I myself could hardly believe that this was the same morose creature of a few hours ago, and of the two facets I knew which I would have preferred, for his wine-inspired gaiety was getting on my nerves. But apparently it did not upset the uncles in this way. I think they preferred to have him cheerful and had slackened their restrictions on the wine to keep him so. The minister too, I noticed, had also drunk deeply, if his flushed face was anything to go by. He refused nothing, either of wine or food. And it was hard to see how he could talk so much while eating, and drinking so rapidly, but talk he did, and in a very amusing fashion, even I had to admit this.

Maurice Rossiter was for pressing me to empty my glass, saying, "Come on, Kate; come on, stop dithering. You've been playing with that for the last half-hour."

I'd had two glasses of wine with the meal and with the one I'd had earlier this was more than enough for me. Its effect I termed as feeling nice. And I did feel nice. The past was pushed just a little way behind me now; I could look at it without straining. I was enjoying sitting in this dining-room that smelt of leather and smoke, and whose walls had once been red but were now a delicate pink where the paper showed between the huge pictures of men and women . . . all Rossiters. I liked the look of the old-fashioned silver and the way the meal was served. Patterson was serving today; poor Hollings wasn't yet up to it, I supposed. Yes, I was feeling nice . . . mellow, and all due to the uncles' home-made wine. I knew lots of people who made homemade wine, but I knew that they didn't make wine like this. I can remember my father saying of my grandmother's efforts: "She calls it parsnip and says it tastes like whisky. . . . Whisky, huh! Boiled turnip water would be a better name for it." Yet as much as I had enjoyed the wine, I knew that I mustn't have any more. And I was placing my hand over the top of my glass to prevent Maurice Rossiter refilling it when I and the rest at the table were distracted by the sound of Patterson's raised voice coming from just beyond the door. He was saying, "How did you get in here?"

I recognized the voice that answered him and was quick to pick up the glance that passed between my employer and the minister. The voice was that of Weaver, and it was not low or even of ordinary tone as befits a servant in his master's house, but came loud and defiant as he cried, "The way Aa've come in many another time. An' let me tell you Aa've more right than you in here. . . . Go on, house-boy, tell Mr. Maurice."

"By God! If Mr. Logan was here he'd kick your backside over the topmost fell and I'd help him."

"Aye, ya would, Aa know. An' . . . well, he isn't here, is he? An' not likely to be, so go on."

"Go on yourself, don't give me orders."

I was amazed at the change in Patterson's voice. Then the next moment the door was thrust open and there stood Weaver. He was wearing a ragged snow-covered top coat, the collar turned up, and he still had a cap on his head.

Mr. Bernard had risen, his face red with anger as he

cried, "Get out, away, do you hear? This minute. Away you go."

"Not so fast, Uncle, not so fast." It was Maurice Rossiter speaking, and he put his arm across in front of me and pulled at Mr. Bernard's sleeve, adding, "Sit down, sit down." Then, because Mr. Bernard showed no sign of obeying him, his voice changed to a deep growl as he said, "Logan is no longer here remember. I'm head of the house at present, Uncle, the next in line. Maurice Alastair Rossiter, the next in line . . . sit down. . . . And you, Weaver." He now waved his hand, beckoning Weaver further into the room, and his tone became lighter, even jocular. "Come in, come in. Is it a drink you're after? Well you've come on the right day."

Mr. Stanley had now risen from the other side of the table, and, looking towards his nephew and ignoring the fact that his brother had been told to reseat himself, he said with quiet dignity, "We'll leave you then, Maurice. Come, Kate." He motioned me to my feet, but as I made to rise Maurice Rossiter's hand became a grip on my arm as he said, "Stay where you are, Kate. We're all friends together, for this day at least."

"I . . . I would rather, if you don't mind, Mr. Maurice. I . . . I'd rather get on with some work."

"Let the young lady go." It was the minister speaking. It was the first time he had looked at me directly, or addressed any remark to me during the meal, and again he repeated, his voice soft but insistent, "Let the young lady go, Maurice. It's better so."

Maurice Rossiter's hand came from my arm and I rose to my feet and went down the long table, past Weaver without looking at him but knowing all the time that his eyes were hard on me. Mr. Bernard had walked by my side, and at the bottom of the table we met up with Mr. Stanley, and together we went out of the room, across the hall and into the drawing-room without exchanging a word.

I could see that the old men were deeply troubled,

and, thinking that they might want to talk, I made an excuse to leave them to themselves and returned to my room. Not, I'm afraid, to work—I wasn't feeling like work. Nor was I feeling nice any longer. I was feeling frightened. . . .

By three o'clock in the afternoon the storm had increased if anything, and the sky was so low and dark that it was like late evening. Intermittently there came to me sounds of rumbling laughter. Maurice Rossiter and his two companions were still in the dining-room and the sound made me ask myself, What if I have to stay the night? This thought drove me in search of Patterson, and I found him in the kitchen talking with Hollings and the old cook.

"Is there any chance of me getting down to the road, Patterson?" I said. "I feel I must get home."

It was not Patterson who answered me now but Hollings, saying, "We've just been talking about it, madam. It would be asking for serious trouble to let you go in this; even if you got down to the road there would be nothing running. There's nothing for it, I'm afraid, but that you must stay the night. It's almost dark now . . . look." He pointed to the window.

Now Patterson turned to me. "We were thinking, miss, that the best place would be Mr. Logan's office. It's a small room and I'll put a fire on. The couch is comfortable. You'd do fine in there, I'm sure, miss."

I looked from one to the other rather helplessly, and said, "Thank you. . . . Very well." Then, turning from their concerned gaze, I went back to my room, the feeling of fear more pronounced now.

At four o'clock the phone rang and I went to answer it. It was Rodney. He had managed to get to the cottage and my mother's message to me was definitely to stay put, not to risk coming down while it was like this, and not to worry. I thanked him warmly and was reluctant to ring off.

Although I told myself that there was Patterson and

159

Hollings and the uncles in the house, the feeling of fear grew. The only one that could make any impression on Maurice Rossiter, or rather on his two companions, would be Patterson. There were two camps under this roof—one, with the exception of Patterson, being made up of old men. This I knew was the main cause of my fear, and was not unreasonable, knowing Weaver and judging the minister. . . .

Looking back, I don't know exactly at what time I left my room and went into the study. I think it was some time after eight o'clock. I'd had tea with the twins in Mr. Stephen's room. It had been a quiet affair, devoid of laughter. I had come downstairs about five o'clock. When I refused an evening meal Patterson had brought me some hot milk and biscuits . . . that was about half-past seven as far as I can remember.

It was about this time, too, that I first heard the sound of distant laughter coming as if through the floor, as indeed it was. Maurice Rossiter, the minister and Weaver were now in the cellar. There had been heated words between the uncles and Maurice in the hall about this move, which had ended with Mr. Stanley saying in a voice pathetic with pleading, "Have what you like, but don't touch the brew, Maurice . . . please."

What was the brew? Was it the hard stuff that Maurice had wanted this morning, the raw whisky? If so, the effect this would have on top of all the wine he had drunk was something I didn't want to think about.

As Patterson was about to leave the room he had said, "I'd stick a chair under the knob, miss. It mightn't be necessary, but you never know—men in drink are queer creatures. There's no key. Never been any need for keys in locks in this house, not having any—" he paused, "well, ladies about—not for years, anyway."

My foreboding fear drove me to ask him, "Will you be in the house all evening, Patterson?"

"Yes, I'll be about. I sleep over the stables, as you

know, but I'll see things are all quiet before I go over the night. Don't worry."

And so assured, up to a point anyway, I had gone into the study. It was a cluttered room, but comfortable, and it was warm. And about it hung the presence of its owner. I sat down on the couch that was to be my bed, but did not even take my shoes off. Looking back, I realize I had been ready to run from the minute I had seen Weaver enter the dining-room. Even with the wind howling like a battalion of demons round the house, I think I would have risked throwing myself on its mercy rather than have been confronted by either Weaver or the minister in drink. Strangely, I did not include my employer in my fear.

At times the house, but for the noise of the wind, would become free of all sound, and I thought . . . I hoped, that sleep had overtaken the three men in the cellar. Then hope would be whipped away by the smothered echo of their laughter breaking through once more.

I put my feet up on the couch but made no attempt to read. I could only sit taut, thinking. I thought quite a bit of the sitting-room at home, and of my mother and father, and I hoped they weren't worrying. I thought of many things, but I tried not to let my mind touch on Logan Rossiter . . . or his wife. This title, when I'd thought of it earlier, had pricked me like a sting.

At what point I dozed I don't know, but it was the sound of a door opening that brought me stiffly awake. This door had a particular sound of its own, being the front door. It was built of massive oak and had a chain on the back which jangled when the door was moved either one way or the other. I turned my head in the direction of the hall. Had Patterson come in by the front door? No, I rejected this idea; the stables were across the courtyard right opposite the back door. . . . I hadn't stuck a chair under the door handle. . . . I was swinging my legs from the couch when the study door burst open and I actually screamed at the sight of the figure standing there. . . . The Big Fellow himself. Rimed with snow from head to foot, he looked like something inhuman. In fact, had I not associated the opening of the front door with his appearance I must have thought he was some fearsome apparition. He showed no surprise whatever at seeing me, but with slow lifting feet, as if he were still treading the snow, he moved towards the couch. Putting out his arms and groping like a half-blind man at its back, he stepped round it, then, flopping down, he dropped his body sidewards and lay there panting for some minutes. With one great intake of breath he turned his frozen face towards me and with a weary lift of his hand indicated that I close the door. Up to now I had been too stupefied to move; I had just stood, my hand to my throat, gaping at him, but at his signal I sprang forward, and when I had shut the door I was back like a flash to his side. And now words poured out of me. Words of compassion, of enquiry, of amazement. "Oh, Mr. Logan! Oh, Mr. Logan! What's happened? How did you get back? Where is . . .? Let me take your coat off." My hands were fumbling at the button of his great-coat when wearily he thrust me off, which simple action, I knew later, went towards saving his life. And now pointing to a cupboard that stood next to the window, he spoke for the first time. "Get me a drink."

Again I was flying to his bidding. There was half a bottle of whisky, a syphon of soda, and a glass in the cupboard. Within a minute I had filled the glass to the rim and was holding it to his lips. He swallowed it in one draught, then closed his snow-laden lids for a fraction before handing me the glass and saying, "Another."

When he had finished the second glass he lay back against the couch again, and his breathing gradually became steadier. All the while I stood in front of him, until at last, realizing the condition of his clothes, I said, "Let me take your shoes off, you must get changed." Then I added, "Where is Mrs. Rossiter? Has anything happened?"

162

For the first time he brought his gaze to bear fully upon me, then, drawing his hands down over his now running wet face, he shut me out for a moment, before saying, "Where are they?"

"Who?" I asked as if I didn't know what he meant.

"There's no lights in the front. Is he in the dining-room?"

"You mean Mr. Maurice?"

He nodded his head slowly at me, and as he did so there seeped into the room again the echo of laughter.

Definitely it wasn't the first time that he had heard that echo, for immediately his eyes were drawn towards the floor. And as he stared at it I felt my throat tighten and constrict my breathing, and then the fear was flooding over me, so much so that for a moment I seemed to lose my head. I was kneeling on the floor ripping his hands as I beseeched him, "Please . . . please wait till tomorrow. Whatever it is it can wait till tomorrow. There'll only be trouble. Please, Logan." The name came naturally.

His eyes were on mine again and his hand came out towards me and pushed me gently aside, but even so I over-balanced and fell on to my hips. And from there I watched him, still with slow snow-weighed step, move towards the door. He had opened it and was in the hall before I had pulled myself to my feet. And he was half-way down the passage towards the cellar door when I came up with him. And I clutched at his arm with both hands, which did not hinder his walking at all, but now he spoke quiet quietly and evenly, saying, "Go away, Kate."

The laughter came louder here but still distant, and then it lashed harshly at my ears like a lusty wave, for Logan Rossiter had pulled open the cellar door.

As I watched him descend the first few steps the laughter was still high, which indicated that as yet they were not aware of him. I was at the top of the stairs now and could see over the rack dividing compartments of the cellar. In the little room where the uncles had wined me were a number of men. I could just see their heads and there were more than three. And then one of them happened to look up, and it was me he saw, not Logan, for he gave a yell of drunken glee. Following on this there seemed to me to be a crowd of men spilling themselves through the partitions into the main space that fronted the stairs. But when they had once gathered there, their faces all turned upwards, the cellar became quiet as if it were night and the whole place was about its own business, the business of fomenting the wine that gave the uncles so much pleasure, in making and sampling. And the quiet was not broken by any of the gaping men below but by a whisper coming from behind me, saying in awe-stricken tones, "Oh, my God, what is this?" I had no need to turn, I knew it was Hollings, and now his hand was gripping my shoulder and his mouth near my ear was hissing, "Go to the stables; quick, get Patterson."

If Logan Rossiter's life had depended on my obeying this order he would have lost it, for I found it impossible to move, to tear myself away from this scene. There on the bottom step stood the master of the house, and about ten feet away was his brother supporting himself with the aid of his stick and a stout rack against which he leaned his back. I could see that although Maurice Rossiter was mad drunk he was still capable of feeling amazement, for his eyes held a glazed sort of wonder as he gazed towards Logan. Just to the side of Maurice stood the minister, again I should say leaned, for he and another man, whom I had never seen before, were supporting each other, swaying gently together as they, too, gaped. Standing to their side was yet another strange man, a small man, the build of a pit man, short and wiry. But away from them all, standing alone, was Weaver. If anything he was more drunk than any one of the other four, yet more steady on his feet. He seemed to be braced by the sight of the man who had thrashed him more than once.

And it was to Weaver that Logan Rossiter spoke first, yet he embraced the rest of the company with a sweep of his great arm as he thundered, "Get out! Get out, you scum!"

"Put us oot?" It was Weaver who had spoken. No whine in his tone now; he was fearless with drink.

It was at the instant when Logan was on the very point of springing on this man that Maurice interrupted with a high cry of, "Ho . . . hold your ha . . . hand, my de. . . . dear brother. These are my friends, all my fri . . . ends. . . Always have been. Don't you recognise them?"

Logan, taking one step nearer to Maurice, brought to me the awful conviction that he was going to pounce, not on Weaver now, but on his brother. And I almost cried out in protest. Logan Rossiter wasn't drunk, but at this moment he was in a worse state. He was mad. But Maurice seemed undaunted by this; perhaps he was too drunk to recognize the danger. Still bracing himself against the support of the partition, he stuttered, "C . . . come on, t . . . tell us, what's brought you home so early? the s . . . snow blocked the line? . . . Where's y . . . your dear wife?"

On this there came a loud hiccoughing laugh from the minister, to which Weaver added a thin whining sound like the neighing of a horse.

Logan Rossiter was standing stock still now staring at Maurice. The laughter frittered itself out and there was silence again, and they waited for him to answer the question. Which he did, slowly bringing each word up from the agonized depth of him. "It's all been one great howling laugh, hasn't it? And your friends undoubtedly enjoy your confidence. . . . Well, let them laugh, let them laugh as much as they like, it's going to be their last laugh. . . . You ask where my wife is, Maurice?"

Now his voice became level, even calm, and he finished with a staggering statement. . . . "She's in Newcastle, in the hospital having a miscarriage." The voice changing now came like the crack of a steel whip. "As if you didn't

know, you . . . you devilish swine!" He was standing over
Maurice, towering over his crouching figure, his two fists
quivering above his head. But he did not bring them
down. It was doubtful whether he would have had time
to strike Maurice before the others were upon him, for
they were all waiting at the ready. And now motionless, I
watched Logan's arms drop to his side as he moved
swiftly back, putting a safe distance between them. My
eyes were drawn to Maurice again, for I sensed that
Logan's news had come to him, as to me, with a breath-
checking shock of surprise. Then a strange thing happened. Maurice, pulling himself from the partition and
with the aid of his stick only, stood erect. He seemed to
grow straight before my eyes, as he said, almost as if he
were sober, "Really!"

"Y'uve got one ower on him this time, be God I'll say
ye hev, Mr. Maurice." Weaver's head was lolling on his
shoulders with his laughter.

"Be quiet, Weaver." Maurice lifted his stick and waved
it towards the man; and now, addressing himself to
Logan with a hint of the old sarcasm in his voice, he said,
"So Noreen is having a miscarriage. You couldn't, of
course, stay with her. Oh no, because you had to tear
back here to wreak vengeance on her se . . . seducer. Is
that it? Well, now I've news for you, my de . . . ar
brother, for you mean business, don't you? So we'll all
put our c . . . cards on the table. This is the end, so why
not? Why not indeed? . . . Well." He paused here and
with a swift stroke of his hand wiped the sweat from his
face. "Well, I have great pleasure in informing you, The
Rossiter . . . The Big Fellow, that Noreen is not your wife
and never could be, for she happens to be mine and has
been for years. . . . There now . . . how do you like
that?"

I had moved slowly down the stairs, Hollings behind
me. And I knew that the uncles were behind him. I saw
Logan Rossiter move his head and look round the cellar,
taking us all in, even those on the stairs. His glance, for a

166

moment, was like that of someone whose senses had been knocked out of his body by a terrific blow. And now looking at Maurice again, he said in a voice that did not carry any conviction to me, "You're mad, stark staring mad."

"Oh no I'm not. Ask our dear friend, the Reverend. He married us; didn't you, Fallenbor? It was the night before this happened to me." Maurice patted his side. And you, my sanctimonious spoil-sport, were away from home, so we decided to have a party and we called in all our friends. And after the party Noreen and I thought it would be a good idea if we were to get married. And Weaver here and the Reverend accompanied us, dancing across the fells. Isn't that so?" As the confirmation to this came, he went on, "There was one other. You remember Lawson? My dear friend of college days, Lawson. He acted as best man, and about a week later the devil took him in a road accident, you remember? But that's how it happened. Noreen and I were married. She, I must admit, thought it was a game. I have never disillusioned her. But she's my wife, Logan . . . my wife. But I was quite willing to loan her to you, for it was all to my benefit to do so. Yet my conscience tried to force itself through at one point and I did my best to persuade her not to have you, but to marry me, yet once again. But she would have none of it, and now I can see why. Yes, I see why. She didn't want to make me a father, for I'd be rather a handicap as a father. Dear, dear, considerate Noreen."

Logan Rossiter was still standing before his brother, but his body looked no longer taut—it looked limp. I was crying for him; with every pore in my body I was crying for him. It was as I made a step towards him that Mr. Bernard's voice came yelling from the stairs, spluttering it its anger. "Don't believe him, Logan; don't believe him. That old reprobate Fallenbor, he couldn't marry them. Illegal. Illegal. Only be married in church. He had no church, not at that time. And what about banns? You know the law."

"He's right, Logan. He's right." This was Mr. Stanley shouting now. "I'm ashamed of you, Maurice, ashamed to own you. Get the scum out of this cellar, and this minute. Get you out, Fallenbor . . . And you, Weaver. . . . Out!"

On this Weaver stepped forward, shouting, "Neebody's goin' a order me oot; Aa'm a Rossiter, same's you. Weaver ain't me name, Aa'm a Rossiter, an' don't forget it." He was now flaying his fist up towards the staircase and the old men. Perhaps it was this that broke the spell that was on Logan Rossiter, this claiming of kinship with his house and forebears, for, like a panther springing from a tree, his body hurled itself on to the man, and as their locked bodies struck the floor the sound made me retch.

I was in the cellar proper now, my back against the rough white-washed rock, my hands gripped in front of my breast. The other men had moved away from the contorted struggling bodies on the floor. I saw Logan Rossiter's fist pounding Weaver's face, and Weaver using both feet and fists in retaliation. I had no doubt in my mind that Logan would overpower this man. But I also had no doubt that when he had finished with him the other two crouching men would then set about him. This thought made me turn and yell up the staircase: "Get Patterson! Get Patterson!" I don't know if anyone even heard me. I only know that in the next moment my hands were clasped tightly across my mouth as I saw what was about to happen. Logan and Weaver had rolled near a rack of bottles and Weaver, freeing one hand, was groping blindly and madly at the rack. I saw him grip one of the bottles by the neck. I saw his knee wedge itself in Logan's stomach and his teeth clamp on Logan's ear like a ferret on a rabbit. This was enough to give him leeway. Logan released his grip for a second and that was all this crafty vermin wanted. His arm swung sideways and the bottle crashed down on the side of Logan's skull. But it did not break, nor did Weaver let it escape from his hold. As Logan fell back and my scream rent the cellar I closed my eyes tightly, but I could not close my ears to the sound of the sickening crunch as the bottle descended once again on Logan's head.

A great moan filled the cellar. It seemed to rise above the cries and yells from the staircase. When I opened my eyes again it was to see a bloody crumpled mass that had once been "The Big Fellow". I could hear myself screaming as I ran towards him, and when I knelt by his side I moaned between crying, "Oh, my God. Oh, my God." I could see no feature of his face for blood, and I had nothing to staunch it with except a woollen coat I was wearing, and I tore this off and tried to wipe his face clear. I ascertained enough with my frantic efforts to know that the blood was coming from a slit which started above his left eye and went up into his hair. As I worked I cried and talked and moaned, and was only dimly aware of the bustle around me. I didn't realize for some time that the staircase was clear and the cellar door closed, but when I did I also took in the fact that Mr. Maurice was going for Weaver and that the minister was trying to calm him down. I was holding my blood-soaked coat tightly against Logan's head and was about to appeal to them, any one of them, for help, when Mr. Maurice, shaking his stick at Weaver, yelled, "You bloody fool! You won't get away with this so easily. Haven't I enough to contend with? He'll put you along the line. I've told you." And now I found myself straining up from the inert body at my side and yelling, "And I'll see he goes there. If it's the last thing I do I'll see he gets his desserts for this," I think I must have been quite frantic myself. My hands were covered with blood, my clothes too. My eyes were blinded with tears. I was bawling and jabbering like someone demented. You hear of women being cool and calm in an emergency . . . I'm not one of them. It was in this state that I was pulled to my feet by the taller of the two strange men. I struggled to free myself

169

from his grasp, but he held me firm and pushed me towards a bench, and, forcing me to sit down, he stood over me, with his hands pressed tight on my shoulders. Weaver was just a few yards away and he was yelling at Mr. Maurice. "An' Aa've told ya, him nor neebody else'll put me along the line. Aa'm goin' to see this through finally, once an' for all. Anyway, ye hate his guts as much as me, but if ye've got cauld feet get up above and leave it to me."

"Get out! Go on, get out." Maurice was swaying towards Weaver now, his step wildly erratic, but Weaver did not move. And when they came abreast Weaver's hand shot out and, gripping Maurice by the front of his coat, he said, "Ye can't frighten me, Mr. Maurice, ye never have been able to. Aa've let ye play ya game of master, it's suited us both, but now it's ended. There'll be no more high jinks in this cellar, for ye or neebody else. So . . . are ye in with me or oot?"

"You're not going to touch him any more." Maurice looked at the bruised and swelling face of this man in whose veins ran the Rossiter blood, who, as he was forever claiming, was a Rossiter, and his tone now had a despairing note when he went on, "He's had enough. It could be serious as it is." I saw him glance towards the prostrate figure of his brother. And then he ended, his voice dropping, "He'll need a doctor in any case, and how are we going to get one up here?" It appeared to me that Maurice Rossiter was now stark sober.

"Good enough," Weaver cut in quickly. "We know where we stand. Smithy?" He now jerked his head to the smaller of the two men. "Bottle them both up."

"Mr. Maurice an' aall?" There was amazement in the man's voice.

"Aye. . . . Mr. Maurice, an' aall."

The minister had been standing aside during this, casting his furtive eye every now and again to where Logan Rossiter lay. He was now evidently nervous and apprehensive, and Weaver's question startled him when it came at him, "An' what about you, parson, eh?"

"Well"—there was even a little laugh from this obnoxious individual—"you know me, Weaver, I'm just passing through. Still, I advise you to go carefully. This could be a very nasty business for . . . for us all."

"Aa understand, parson, divn't worry. Yer hands won't get mucky. Leave that to Weaver as ye've aalwiz done, ye and Mr. Maurice here." And now Weaver actually pushed Maurice backwards on to the bench on which I was sitting. The backwards jolt must have been painful, for I heard Maurice stifle a groan.

But I wasn't worried about him, only about Logan, and, pointing to the spreading pool of blood, I cried, "You've got to do something. Let me go and get some bandages. He could die. Do you hear? He could die!"

Now followed something that I want to try to forget, yet even in my dreams it keeps recurring and I wake up choking, and spluttering and spitting out wine. . . . No, not wine . . . whisky.

"Ye'd better drink it," said the short man, handing me a glass. "It'll be easier that way for us aall." As the man forced the glass into my hand Maurice Rossiter cried, "Look, leave her out of it. She has nothing to do with this."

"No?" said Weaver. "Only help to push us along the line."

"There are others besides her who could be used as witnesses, don't you realize that? Don't be such a damn fool, let her go."

"The old boys think too much of this here cellar an' their whisky-still to split. Anyway, they'd nivver hev the guts."

"But what's the object in bottling her?" Mr. Maurice now demanded.

"Ye leave that ta me. Aa was aalwiz full of good plots. Remember, Mr. Maurice? Aa could give ye yarns for yer writin'." Weaver was laughing.

171

I looked up into the repulsive and battered face of Weaver now and said in a quiet voice, trying to appeal to the better part of him, "I don't care what you do to me, only do something to stop the bleeding. Mr. Logan could bleed to death."

"Worried, are ye? Aa thought ye might be. Aa knew ye're all in up to ya neck the first time. Aa clapped eyes on you. But ye leave The Big Fellow to us. Whichever way he'll peg oot he won't bleed ta death, that ain't my idea. There's plaster in me sack. Smithy . . . stick some on."

"You're forgetting Hollings and Patterson in your calculations." Maurice's voice sounded tired now.

"Hollings won't squeak. He's got a couple of nieces this side of Amble. He likes them. He won't squeak. As for Patterson, there's a woman livin' in Gateshead who'd very much like to know where he is. She's been lookin' for him noo for a long while. Aye . . . there's reasons why they'll aall keep their mooths shut. . . . But this one's different."

He was pointing his thumb towards me, and Mr. Maurice put in harshly, "Don't be such a damn fool, man, you're mad. You think trifling things like that will stop Patterson or Hollings getting you what you're asking for? And you, Smithy, and you, Connor, use your heads. If anything happens to my brother you'd be as guilty as he is."

"An' what about yersel, Mr. Maurice?" Weaver's voice was quiet.

"I know all that's going to happen to me, Weaver. My number's up as well as yours. I know quite well what's coming to me, so look . . . let's call it a day. You go on out your usual way and take these two with you and leave him to me." He nodded towards Logan."

"Oh no. No no." Weaver shook his head slowly. "Either way Aa know what Aa'm in for. Aa've got nowt to lose, Mr. Maurice. In for a penny, in for a pound, that's me. When he comes round he'll hev me hounded like a fox.

After the night there'll be nee chance for me around here. This is the finish. So Aa'm goin' to de things me own way as Aa aalwiz intended te. . . . Keep goin' with the stuff, Smithy, and you an' all, Connor." He pointed towards a barrel over in the corner. And Smithy and Connor kept going.

The stuff was raw whisky, the hard stuff that Mr. Stanley had warned Maurice about touching. At first it merely burned and ripped at my throat while I spluttered and coughed. But by the time they had forced the third glass between my lips my whole body seemed on fire, and my resistance was noticeably less. So expert were they in making me drink that I knew that this was not the first time by many a count that this trick, if you could call it such a thing, had been worked. The voices were now becoming very indistinct. I could not take in what was happening around me. There was bustle of a sort, and once, when I raised my head from the table, I imagined I saw Logan Rossiter standing on his feet. I did hear Maurice's thick trailing tone saying now, "Don't force me, I can take it." My whole body was now like a flaming furnace and I was drunk. This, I thought, is what it feels like to be drunk. It wasn't a bad feeling except for the burning. I didn't care what happened any more. At one period I imagined that someone was kissing me; who it was I didn't know. But I knew when they were pulled away from me. Nothing mattered now. Nothing, nothing.

I was sitting upright again, and then I was on my feet, and a voice from somewhere far off said, "They were on the spree together, it's a clever idea." And another voice said, "She'd hev to hev a coat, aye, she'd hev to hev a coat on. What about this?"

I felt like a baby being dressed. Then with my feet dragging I was walked through a door and along a passage, and now I was pushed on to my knees, and I was crawling. I seemed to be moving towards a swaying lantern, but I never reached it, it was always just that much ahead. Then a hand gripped my shoulder and pulled me on to my feet again. It was all very confusing. At one period I had a great desire to rock with laughter. It was then I walked on ice and slipped and fell on my back. When I was dragged to my feet my head struck the roof and I had to walk bent forward. I remember thinking I was like Alice in Wonderland and wanted to laugh again. Then I was on my knees once more and the lantern, swinging in front of me, showed a round hole and, beyond, an expanse of whiteness. Now I was pulled to a halt and there was a confused mingling of bodies about me, and curses and directions. But nothing mattered, nothing mattered any more. I was quite happy inside and quite warm. I was lying against someone, close, pressed tight to a body. It felt nice. The voices faded away from around me. A great silence settled on me, and I slept, deeply, deeply. . . .

"Wake up! Wake up!" The hissing sound had been probing my befuddled mind for a long time. It was like a faint echo from across the fells. "Wake up! Wake up, will you? Sh! . . . sh! . . . don't make a noise. Come on, wake up . . . wake up, miss." My head began to wag violently as if it was being rocked off my shoulders, and I gasped and spluttered, "Wh . . . what is it? Leave over . . . leave over."

"Listen, miss, it's Patterson. Listen, wake up."

I didn't care who it was, I was too far douched in sleep. And then I almost yelled out, and would have done if a hand hadn't been clapped across my mouth. The snow that had hit my warm flesh running down between my breasts had the effect that Patterson intended it should. My eyes sprang open and I sat gasping as I pulled my clothes away from my body.

"Are you awake?"

"Ye . . . yes." I was awake and that was all. My head was not on my shoulders but dizzying in a space some distance from my body.

"Listen. Sit up . . . careful or you'll bump your head against the pipe."

174

I pulled myself on to my knees, groping at Patterson in the dark. I had not the vaguest idea where I was until Patterson said, "Don't move now or you'll tumble into the snow, you're on the end of the drainpipe."

On the end of the drainpipe! If I had been told I was sitting on the edge of a volcano I couldn't have felt more surprised. I tried to make my befuddled brain grasp at the significance of this, but I couldn't get anything clear. And then my head was brought down from its height and somewhat nearer to my shoulders, when I heard Patterson saying. "Sir. Can you hear me, sir? Look, wake up, sir ... come on, drink this."

With a flop that actually shook my body my head fell into place, and now I remembered but still dazedly, but nevertheless I remembered the sight of Logan Rossiter lying on the cellar floor in a pool of blood. I put out my hands and wildly groped about me until Patterson caught hold of my arm and his calming voice said, "Steady, steady. And quiet, miss. Make no noise."

"Is he . . .? Is he . . .?"

"He's coming round. . . . Come on, sir, finish this up. Try now." There was a long groan, and then I heard Logan's voice muttering thickly, "Oh, my God. Oh, my God."

"It's all right, sir. Look, I've tied up your head. Do you think you could get on to your knees?"

"No. No, leave me." His voice was very tired. "Leave me alone."

"No, sir. Come along. Get on to your knees."

"I can't, Patterson, I can't."

"M . . . make an effort, p . . . please. Please try." It was my own voice that was imploring him now and it was stuttering, not only with the effects of the drink still very much upon me but with my shivering, for now my whole body was shaking as if with ague.

"Come on, sir, give it a try. If you can once get up out of the drain you'll be all right. I've brought the sled. You remember the old sled?" His voice was now as soft as a

175

woman's, and as persuasive, as if he were humouring a child.

"Leave me be. Leave me be." The voice faded away.

I felt Patterson's breath on my face now as he said, "Lower your feet into the snow and see if you can stand up. Here, sit on the edge of the pipe."

With Patterson directing me, I sat on the edge of the drain and lowered my feet down into the snow, and when I stood up the bottom of the pipe came to my waist.

"Now," said Patterson, "if I get him out do you think you can hold his weight against the edge of the pipe until I pull him up out of the ditch?"

"Yes, yes," I said, not knowing whether I could or not.

I couldn't see anything that Patterson was doing, and my mind didn't imagine anything, for I, in this moment, became wholly concerned with myself. I was shivering from head to foot, and in my fuddled, bemused, unnatural state I was only barely aware that my feet were in running water, that the storm was over and the thaw had set in. All I wanted was to drop my head forward on to the icy rim of the drain and sleep. I was not concerned with self-preservation, yet it was the preservation of the man lying in the thawing ice that got through to me and warned me that if Logan Rossiter sank into the snow, Patterson would never get him out until it was too late. When I felt the bulk of him against me I pressed my body to his and, putting my hands under his armpits, I gripped as far up the icy circle of the drain as it was possible for me to reach. In this way I kept him upright until Patterson's hands were groping over us both. I felt the clothes on Logan's body lift upwards, and automatically I heaved too. As he was dragged up over the edge of the ditch his body made a tunnel in the soft snow, and a few seconds later it was through this that Patterson dragged me also.

I can't remember if I helped to get Logan on to the sledge. I can only remember wondering why there was no light, no torch being used. I faintly recollect Patterson's voice hissing, almost angrily at me, "You'll have to pull back harder than that or I won't be able to hold it." How he ever did hold that laden sledge from running amock in that white sloping wilderness is still a mystery to me. My job, I understand now, was to pull on the back of the sledge and so act as a brake. I can remember twice lying quite flat in the snow and Patterson pulling me to my feet. He's told me since he did this five times. I do remember, and with a sense of shame, that when we finally reached the road I was bubbling out loud, crying unrestrainedly like any child. I remember also saying to Patterson, "Are we going to the cottages?" and I can still feel my sense of amazement when he said abruptly, "No." And I can hear him adding fervently, "Thank God the plough has been along." I now started to jabber, crying, "I can't go on, I can't go on, I feel sick. I want to be sick. want to sit down."

"Well, sit down." His voice was hissing at me, really angry now. "Sit by him until I get back, and don't make a sound, I'm telling you, don't make a sound."

I was only too thankful to sit down. I could just make out the huddled form of Logan as he lay with his knees up on the short sledge. And I remember I sat close to him and took hold of his hand. Then I must have lain my head on his body and slept again, for I actually yelled out when Patterson dragged me to my feet. And there, as if it had been conjured out of the air, was the dark bulk of the car. I did say to him, but not as plainly as I'm stating it now, "But you'll never get the car along the road—it's madness trying." Yet I longed to get inside the car, into its warm shelter. But again he had to force me to get up and to help him get Logan on to the back seat, for I was reluctant to do anything but follow my own need, which was to drop where I stood and sleep, just sleep.

"Keep him upright against the back; don't let him fall over." It was just as I was admonished harshly to do this that Logan stirred and spoke.

"Patterson," he said.

"Yes, sir."

"Where . . . where am I?"

"You're in the car, sir. Don't worry."

"What time is it?"

"Oh, I should imagine . . . somewhere around one, sir. Now don't worry, we'll get you to a doctor."

A light suddenly sweeping over the car from somewhere along the road made Patterson bang the door and get into the driving seat, and after two quick attempts on the starter the car moved forward. I was still supporting Logan, but now I felt his body move of its own accord into a more comfortable position. As he did so I mumbled a question to Patterson that was going round in my mind. "Why didn't we wait?" I said. "There was someone coming with a light."

He did not answer for what seemed a long time, and then he said, "Someone was coming all right. Connor lives in one of those cottages."

I became quiet. I was shivering less. The slight rocking of the car lulled me. And then I was woken yet once again from sleep by Patterson saying, "This is as far as we can go."

I shook my head and drew in a deep breath, making an effort to regain my senses. "Where are we?" I asked.

"As far as I can make out quite a step from the village. The snow plough is just ahead, this is as far as it's got. Now look, I'll have to get to the village somehow and get help and phone a doctor. You lock yourself in and don't open up for anyone but me. You understand?"

"Patterson." The voice was just a whisper.

"Yes, sir."

"I'm . . . all . . . right now . . . I . . . I can walk it."

"No, sir, out of the question. Just you rest. Stay with miss here, I'll be back."

He pushed up the handle which locked the door, then banged it, and I settled back into the deep comfort of the

178

car. My shivering had almost stopped, but I had a weird feeling, a sick weird feeling, and the desire for sleep was heavier on me than ever, so without effort I allowed myself to sink into it. . . .

I don't know how long it was after this that I heard Patterson's voice again, and not only his but a number of other voices, two of them so familiar that I imagined that the car had been got through somehow into the village. The voices I recognized were those of Bill Arnold and Rodney. It was Bill's voice that came to me as if from the end of a tunnel, saying, "Well, as we've got to go back to the village, anyway, I'm for taking him there." Then Rodney's. "It's him we've got to think of; the quicker he's between sheets, I should imagine, the better. We can, with a big push and two of you going ahead, get him up to Kate's place in under half an hour. But it'll take every bit of a couple of hours to get through these road drifts back to the village. And I bet you what you like, a lot of this fell will be clear of snow. The wind'll have whipped it off the slopes and down into the valley. You know how it does."

"But will the doctor get up to him?" said a voice.

And another answered, "But aye, there's the track leading up from yon side of the village, almost straight as a die. Rodney said he went up there yesterday to tell Kate's folk. Didn't you?"

It was many hours later when I thought of the man's description of our road being as straight as a die, and wondered what kind of a road would qualify in his mind for a winding one. But now there were hands on me easing me out from the car, and Rodney's arms were about me, his voice tender and soothing as he said, "Aw, Kate. Aw, Kate. Now don't worry, you're going to be all right."

I opened my eyes with an effort, and just glimpsed the swinging lanterns and the bustle of men before I was overcome with the dreadful feeling of nausea again. It was a frightful feeling like nothing I had experienced

179

before, and to my own disgust I was crying again, and whimpering now, "I want to go home. I want to go home."

"You're going home, Kate. You're going home."

It seems dreadful to think now, but I had forgotten completely about Logan, for my whole body and mind was consumed with sickness. I felt myself being half carried through the snow. Then this gave way quite abruptly to the feel of hard rock under my feet. Whoever was on my other side now turned and shouted, "It's as he said, it's clear." A voice ahead was calling, "This way. This way, to your right there. That's it."

I lifted my weary lids and glimpsed the fairy-like scene created by the swinging lanterns. Then, with a suddenness that was startling, my whole stomach turned a somersault and I was sick. And Rodney and the other man held me up, and Rodney soothed me as my mother would have done, saying, "That's it, get it up. The more you get up the better. There you are, there you are." And the other man said, "Phuh! Whisky!" And somehow this filled me with deep shame.

I began to shiver again and I can't remember anything more of the journey except that I looked upwards and saw a blaze of lights, and deep within me my soul cried out: You're home, you're home. And then my mother's voice swept over me, repeating two words, just two words, "My God! My God!" And this went on for a long time.

There followed confusion and bustle and voices, then quiet, quiet that I likened to the peace of Heaven. I was in my own room and my mother was undressing me, still at intervals repeating the two words, "My God! My God!" She said other words, but these were the only two that seemed to get through my bemused, whisky-fogged brain. And then I was in bed and nothing mattered—nothing, nothing at all.

8

"I'm sick. Oh, Mother, I'm sick."

"You'll be all right, lass. Lie still."

"I want to be sick."

"No, you don't. No, you don't. There's nothing more to come up, you just feel like that. The doctor has given you something. You'll be all right in a little while, just sleep."

"Oh, I am sick. And my eyes are funny, Mother. I can hardly see."

"That'll pass, my dear. Just you go back to sleep."

I realized nothing, only that my body and mind were consumed by this dreadful sickness, and I wanted to die. I remember waking up and it was dark again, except for a night light that seemed to bob up and down like a cork on a wave, and through it I saw a shape sitting by my bed and I thrust my hand out to it and fell asleep yet once again in the firm grip of my father's hands. . . .

It was forty-eight hours later when I drank my first cup of tea, and, looking at my mother, asked wearily, "How is he?"

"Holding his own."

The reply brought me from the pillows and I whispered, "He's that ill?"

"Well . . . well, the head'll mend as quick as those things are able to, but"—she turned her eyes from mine —"he's got a bit of a chill, and no wonder. You were lucky, my girl, to get off so lightly, but with him, with the loss of blood and all that—well, he's got pneumonia."

As I pushed the bedclothes back my mothers hands stayed me quickly. "Where do you think you're going?"

"I'm getting up."

"That you're not. Not today, or tomorrow either if I know it. . . . And the doctor. You've been poisoned, lass, with that stuff."

"But I'm all right now."

"You will be until you stand on your legs. Doctor's orders, you stay put there the next couple of days at least."

"Can I just look in and see him?"

"No, you can't. He doesn't want to see you or anybody else—not at present, anyway."

"Who's looking after him?"

My mother was busily tucking the clothes round me, and her hands stopped and her face lengthened as she said primly, "Who do you think? I may not have got any certificates, but don't forget I did five years in the hospital. There now, and nurse's orders." She patted my cheek gently. "You stay put. . . ."

For the next two days I stayed put. The sickness had left me, but I had to admit to myself that I still felt ill. It was on the afternoon of the fourth day that my mother showed Patterson into my room, and awkwardly he took a seat by the bedside and smiled at me.

"How you feeling now, miss?"

"Oh, I'm all right, Patterson."

He nodded his head at me. "You're lucky, you know. You could have been much worse with one thing and another. By"—now his head moved from side to side slowly—"I've never seen a woman as drunk as you were." Patterson meant this in a jocular way, he was making light of the matter for my sake, but I couldn't take it in a light way. It seemed to me, at this moment, shocking that I had been paralytic drunk and that the dreadful feeling of illness was nothing more than a hangover, a giant hangover.

"But you know," he went on now, "it's just as well you were bottled. It would have been a good thing if Mr. Logan had taken on a similar load, for he wouldn't have got pneumonia then. But if he hadn't kept that coat on things would've been worse. He wouldn't have lasted this long, I'm sure. Pity they didn't bottle him, too." Then seemingly noticing my expression, his own became grave and he said, "I'm not trying to make light of things, miss, not really. The stuff could have killed you, raw spirit like that, and then the exposure."

As I looked at this man I thought to myself: I owe him my life, as does Logan Rossiter, and I put out my hand impulsively and touched his, saying, "If it hadn't been for you . . ." I shuddered, then went on, "How did you know?"

"Well, miss." He cast his eyes downwards. "It was like this. I came to the top of the cellar stairs and saw how things were going. Mr. Logan had then been knocked out. You see, I had been over in me room for not more than ten minutes; it seemed impossible for all that to happen in so short a time, but it had. So . . . well, I made myself scarce. I knew Weaver, I knew that he wouldn't finish there. I also knew that it's only on the films that one fellow can beat four, especially if they're hurling bottles. So I used a bit of brain against their brawn, so to speak. I went back to my room and lit the lamp as if I was settled in there for the night. I knew one of them would come looking for me. So my idea was to tackle them just like that, one at a time, or even two, but not four." He smiled shyly. "But they got one over on me. It was simple They just barricaded the door and I couldn't get out. Well, not for a long time, because you see they also locked up Hollings and the old gentlemen. But they didn't bother with Bennett; they reckoned he was too old to do anything, and he'd never taken sides, had Bennett. He wasn't too old to come and get me out, but that was some time later, because he had to bide his time until the coast was clear, or doubtless they would have brained him. And he's too old to stand knocking about, is Bennett."

"Where are they all now?" I found I couldn't name the minister, or even Weaver, without feeling sick again, and I'd had enough of feeling sick

"Well, miss, you know the saying: As ye sow so shall ye reap. Well, Weaver's idea was to finish Mr. Logan off by simply leaving him in the drain and letting the cold do its work. His mad idea was that when he was found with you, miss, stinking of spirits as you were, the reason for yours deaths wouldn't be far to seek. You'd been having a party, you were all drunk, there'd been a fight, and that was that. You see, it wasn't an unknown thing to happen at Tor-Fret, at least in the old days when Weaver was a boy at the turn of the century. And Weaver, miss, never grew up, not really. Weaver wasn't bad, he was just a bit mental. The one that was bad and still is, is Fallenbor."

"Where is he now?" I asked.

"Weaver, miss? Well, at this minute he's in the mortuary in Alnwick. They must have all parted company, taking a number of bottles with them, and Weaver was so dead drunk that he fell asleep in the snow, just like he left you. They found him stiff in a thicket at yon side of the lake. He was making for a cave—there's lots of caves round there, you know, miss—in the outcrop of rocks hidden by the bracken, and he spent most of his days there, and nights too. But he never reached there that morning. As for Connor and Smithy, well, they are comfortably settled in jail at the moment."

"In jail?" I was sitting up in bed bending towards him. "And Mr. Maurice?"

His eyes moved downwards. "Mr. Maurice has been in a bad way the last few days, miss. Something like yourself, very sick. Also with him is his conscience."

"What will they do to him?"

"Nothing. Oh, nothing, miss. It said in the papers he was the victim of that little band of thugs, too."

I screwed up my eyes as I repeated, "In the papers? Is it in the papers?"

"Oh yes, miss, it's been big headlines. It was big headlines the first day; but big headlines, like everything else, are soon forgotten. Other headlines take their place. You see, miss, Mr. Logan isn't unknown in this part of the world, and he was married that day. Although he did it quickly, everybody knew he was getting married. It all seemed a funny business, and there's been talk."

184

I nodded slowly. "Miss Noreen . . . I mean Mrs. . . ."
"As far as I can gather she's still in the hospital in
Newcastle. It's all caused quite a bit of a scandal."

My mind was working now, pushing me back. I was in
the cellar once again hearing Logan Rossiter's words.
"My wife is in Newcastle having a miscarriage." Then
Maurice's voice, crying, "Your wife? She's never been
your wife." I said now very quietly, "About Mr. Maurice
and Miss Noreen being married . . . was there any truth
in it?"

"Well, they're trying to find the minister, miss. There's
bets on all sides. You see, there's certain laws about marriage. It's got to be in a registered place and if there are
no banns there's got to be a special licence. I think there
can be two kinds of special licence, but I'm not up on
that subject." He smiled wryly. "I was married once. It
was in church and that was binding enough—God
knows," he added, the smile twisting his mouth now.
"But if you want my opinion, that was all a bit of a game.
Mr. Maurice liked to think it was legal to have one over
on Mr. Logan. They've never hit it off, miss, never. You
couldn't imagine them being born of the same mother,
they're so different. Yep mind, Mr. Maurice has his
points. I don't dislike him, but he's not Mr. Logan. Never
could be, not for me."

I felt sick again but with a different kind of sickness
now. This sickness was not created by raw spirit but
oozed from the depths of my heart. I hadn't been in any
condition to think what it would mean if Maurice's decla-
ration proved to be true, yet when Patterson disproved it
in such a way I could not but believe him. It was as if I
had been living in hope for days that something would
happen to annual the marriage. Perhaps my subconscious
had been at work, for now my disappointment rose to the
surface of my mind like a tidal wave and swept away any
secret hopes I had been harbouring. But Patterson was
speaking again and I brought my wandering attention to
him. "But you know, miss," he said, "It's my private opin-

ion that Mr. Logan should never have married Miss Noreen. Mr. Maurice was really the one for her. I could never understand it really. They were both after her years ago, but it seemed as if she preferred Mr. Maurice. So Mr. Logan gave her up without much of a battle, as if he wasn't greatly concerned like. And then recently she swings from Mr. Maurice back to him . . . and there it was, what could a man do? For she's an attractive girl, is Miss Noreen . . . Mrs. Rossiter I should say."

"Yes, she's very attractive, Patterson, very attractive."

Perhaps it was the tone of my voice that brought him to his feet, for he said now, "Look, I'm tiring you, I must go. But I'm glad to see you as fit as you are." Then in an effort to cheer me up he bent towards me and, smiling, finished, "By, you did give me a time that night. I had more trouble with you than with Mr. Logan. The times you fell in the snow flat on your face. I can laugh at it now, but it wasn't funny then."

"No," I said, managing to smile at him, "it wasn't funny then. Goodbye, Patterson, and thank you very much . . . very much."

"That's all right, miss. I hope that tomorrow you'll be up."

"Yes. Yes, I'll be up tomorrow. Goodbye, Patterson."

"Goodbye, miss."

I got up the next day, and with legs that wobbled and with a head still a bit swimmy I went across the landing towards my parents' room, and, knocking gently, I opened the door.

The man in the bed was not The Big Fellow, he was no one that I knew. His head was swathed in bandages, his cheeks were hollow like those of an aged man, and his face was very red. His eyes were open and held me from the minute I entered until I stood by this side, and then he spoke to me. "Kate," he said, "how are you?"

I could only swallow and stare at him and prevent myself from dropping on my knees and laying my head on the bed and giving vent in a spate of tears to the emotions that were choking me.

His breathing was coming in short laboured gasps, and he said now, "Lot of trouble . . . to your people . . . lot of trouble."

I shook my head and forced the words steadily through my lips. "It's no trouble. No trouble whatever. . . . Only get . . . well." My voice cracked on the last word, and he nodded and reached for my hand.

At this point the door opened and my mother entered. She was evidently surprised to find me there, but she said quietly, "Well now, who told you to get up? Away to your bed."

I drew my fingers from Logan's clinging grasp and, turning, went silently out of the room. I waited on the little landing for her, and when she came out I said to her, "I'm not going back to bed, I'm going to nurse him."

She stood looking at me hard for a long moment, perhaps it was a matter of minutes, and whatever she saw in my face she did not comment on, she simply said, "All right, have it your own way. Only remember this. He's very ill; the doctor says it'll be touch and go. We've got to be prepared for that. There's one thing in his favour: constitutionally he's strong. So we can only do our best and pray to God he pulls through. The crisis is some way off, but it will come."

On this she turned and went down the stairs, and I went into my room and got dressed. My body was cold again, but with fear. A person in his low state could easily release his hold on life if that life appeared too complicated to take up again. And God knew, his must appear to him more than complicated at this stage.

We were into December and Christmas near, but this fact did not matter to me. Our house during the next few weeks became more like a hospital ward, with Patterson as the running orderly, running between it and Tor-Fret. Every day he helped to lift and wash and change his master; sometimes it was me on the other side of the bed, sometimes my mother. Sometimes he kept a night watch with my father, sometimes with me. We all insisted that my mother must have her rest at night, for the strain was now telling on her, and although she would not admit it she was very tired.

The crisis came and it passed and it left just a shadow of The Big Fellow. But the shadow required more careful nursing than the man had done. As I had foreseen, Logan lost all desire for life. Sometimes in the middle of the night he would wake and, groping for my hand, would hold it and repeat my name, saying, "Kate . . . Kate," in a weary kind of way. I had been embarrassed by this the first time it happened because Patterson was sitting in the shadows, but no longer did it embarrass me. I didn't mind now who knew what I felt for this man, and I would grasp his hand and try to infuse my natural robust strength into him, willing him to get better, willing him to have the desire to live.

Then one day—it was the second of January—he sat up and smiled. I had been sitting by his bedside all night and had gone to my own bed about eight o'clock in the morning. In the afternoon, before going downstairs, I had quietly opened the bedroom door and there he was lying back on his pillows, more raised up now, and on the sight of me he pulled himself up a little further and he smiled. And his voice was different when he said, "Hello, Kate."

I was crying now and I did not try to hide my tears, but I stood near him and answered, "Hello, Mr. Logan."

He took in a long thin breath before saying, "No mister, Kate, no mister."

"As you wish."

"It's snowing again," he said, looking up into my face.

"Yes, it's snowing again." I nodded at him, then looked towards the window, and when I looked back at him we both smiled, we even laughed together—a weak laugh on his part but nevertheless a laugh. Snow would always be significant to us.

He said now, "Sit by me, Kate."

"I've been doing that for weeks," I said.

"I know. I know. I'll never be able to repay you, or your people . . . your mother is a marvellous woman. They're both very fine people."

"I think so." In an endeavour now to make him smile again I said significantly, "And my mother's name is Kate."

The effect was what I had played for, and he smiled enough to bring a fullness to his hollow cheeks. And then he said, "Oh, be kind to me, Kate, although I don't deserve it."

There was that phrase again, "Be kind to me." How meaningful it was and how strange the people who used it. People who you would never dream needed kindness. I was reminded in this moment of Noreen Badcliff, and inevitably then came the thought that, to all intents and purposes, this man was still married to her. But I sat on near him, talking to him, but not now touching his hand. Nor did he make any attempt to touch mine. He was on the road to recovery, he did not need my strength now. . . .

From this day the pattern of the house changed further. There were visitors. Logan's partner came twice within the next fortnight. On his second visit he brought another distinguished-looking man with him and they were a long time upstairs talking. But some time before this Patterson brought the uncles over. It was as if during the time since I had last seen them they had put on a great number of years. Perhaps it was only within the walls of Tor-Fret and their own environment they appeared younger, for when they came into the sitting-room of our small house they looked two old, two very old shrunken men. Their delight at seeing me was almost pathetic, and I was both moved and pleased by it.

It was my mother who took them upstairs, and when

they came down again, Mr. Bernard, the grumpy, stiff, taciturn Mr. Bernard, was crying. My mother gave them tea, and my father, being a really tactful man at heart, talked fishing, and by the time Patterson came in to take them home before the light failed, they looked a little like the Mr. Bernard and the Mr. Stanley that I remembered, yet not quite.

And Hollings came; he came a number of times. It was nice to see Hollings again. And on one of his visits he took me aside and handed me a letter, and to my surprise he said, "It's from Mr. Maurice. He would like an answer, madam."

The letter was brief and to the point. "Dear Kate," it said. "Can I ask you to come up and see me. You will be doing me one last favour if you will comply. Yours sincerely, Maurice Rossiter."

I lifted my eyes from the letter and said to Hollings below my breath, "He wants me to go up."

"I know, madam. Will you come?"

I hesitated before saying, "Yes. Yes, I suppose I had better. Tell him, I'll come. . . . Tomorrow afternoon."

"Very well, madam, thank you." He said nothing more concerning this during his visit, nor did I.

Naturally I did not mention this request to Logan, but that night, when I took his drink up to him, he said to me, "Sit down, Kate, just for a minute. You've been flitting about like a migrating bird these last few days. What is it? Are you troubled about something?"

I sat down, and then looking at him straight in the face I shook my head, and said, "No. No, I'm not troubled. Why should I be?"

"Yes, why should you be? Your life is uncomplicated. How could it be otherwise living in this house?" His voice was slow and weary-sounding again. And then quite suddenly, reaching for my hand, he bent towards me and asked, "Can we talk, Kate? Not just pleasantries. And forget that I was ever ill. I'm ill no longer; I'll soon be up and about. . . . Not that I want to get away, believe me.

190

In spite of everything it's been like . . . well, like going into retreat. But now I want to talk to you. . . . You understand?"

I shivered and looked away for a second before bringing my eyes back to him and saying, "Yes. If you want to talk, talk."

"Tell me"—he lay back on the pillows again but still kept hold of my hand—"what did you feel like when that . . . that fellow let you down?" It was a surprising question. I thought he had wanted to talk about himself and Noreen Badcliff—I couldn't think of her as Noreen Rossiter—and of course he did, only he came to it in a round-about way.

I closed my eyes for a moment and thought back, and then answered him truthfully. "Like death," I said.

"So humiliated that you felt that you wanted to crawl into a hole and die?"

"Yes, something like that."

"Did you hate him?"

"Yes, I loathed him for a time, and myself for being such a gullible fool."

"It's good to know that one isn't alone with such feelings." He thrust his body forward now and, releasing my hand, placed his palms flat on the counterpane, and with his head on his chest and his words rumbling and indistinct he said, "I hate her so much that even now I feel I could kill her." His body was shaking with the intensity of his emotion.

I shook my head. "Don't feel like that, not so bitterly . . . at least not against her. She wasn't all to blame; Mr. Maurice was to blame and . . . and you yourself."

He did not lift his head but raised his eyes and looked at me from under his brows in a questioning way, and I answered the question with, "You shouldn't have left her dangling between you for years. When Mr. Maurice wouldn't marry her . . . you should have done something if . . . if you cared for her enough."

He straightened up and lay back against the head of

191

the bed and, looking towards the ceiling, said, "Yes, you have something there, I know you have. In a reasonable frame of mind I can see it myself, but"—he brought his eyes down to me—"apparently he thought he had married her. Yet he couldn't have been sure as to the legality of it, or I'm positive he would never have let me go through with it."

"I think he would." My voice was quiet as I thought of the devils that were at work within Maurice, and I repeated, "I think he would, and you've got to face up to that, too." Then I asked a question that had been niggling at my mind for days, weeks in fact. "Have they proved that the service was legal?"

He was looking down at his hands now, examining his nails, and his tone was one I couldn't translate as he said, "No, Kate, they found it was illegal. My marriage to her stands until . . . until it is annulled and . . . and I can do nothing, legally speaking. There is no question of adultery. The act . . . er . . . only becomes such when either of the parties is married." He closed his eyes now. "Our marriage can only be annulled if she refuses to consummate it." Now his eyes came up slowly to meet mine, and I blinked once or twice but continued to look at him. At last I had to rise to my feet in case my hands went out to him for he had made no gesture towards me. Not outwardly anyway; I had only the look in his eyes to go by. I stood a little away from the bed now and said, "Good night."

"Good night, Kate," he answered, but as I turned from him he stopped me and in a flat tone added, "Just a minute. I think I'd better tell you. Tomorrow I'm getting up and as soon as I am able I'm going away. Although, mind"—he moved his head slowly—"I'll hate to leave this house and your people, but I've stayed long enough. I'm going abroad for a time, Kate."

"Abroad?" I had turned squarely to him now. "You'll be away . . . long?"

"I'm not quite sure, Kate." He screwed his eyes up

192

tightly for a moment. "I can't go back up there, not yet a while. Nor can I face my friends and acquaintances in the county. I suppose I'm not big enough—inwardly, at any rate. These things die, I'm told, a natural death. Well, as soon as I feel this one is quite dead"—he pointed now to his chest—"inside here, too, I'll come back. You understand, Kate?"

I tried to keep all feeling from my voice as I said, "Yes, yes, I understand."

I turned quickly about and went out of the room and across the landing, and as I sat on the side of my bed, my head in my hands resting against the rail, I told myself it was best he should get right away. But, being a woman, I also told myself there was a danger in it for me. Men did strange things, even strong ones, big fellows, they did strange things after going through an experience such as Logan had. They jumped off on the rebound, and in a foreign land there would be many ready to catch them.

I went to bed, and there returned to me the feeling of emptiness that I had lived with before the night on the fell road when Logan Rossiter and I had kissed.

9

The following afternoon I sat facing Maurice Rossiter in the very position I had taken up when I had first come for interview, but this was not the same Maurice Rossiter. The man opposite to me had changed in his way as much as his brother had. All the devils seemed to have died in him, or fled. There was no bite of sarcasm in his voice. There was no pain-inflicting glint in his eye. He went on speaking to me as he had been doing for the last quarter of an hour. He was saying now, "You came in, Kate, at the beginning of the end. In fact I think you heralded it.

Noreen told me of the day you took the top road and came down by the lake."

I could still blush at the memory and I lowered my eyes from his. He went on, "You became entangled with us, but, believe me, I never wished you any harm."

"I can believe you, Mr. Maurice."

"I am leaving here tomorrow, Kate."

"What!"

"You seem surprised. But what else is there for me to do? It would be quite impossible for Logan and me to live together in the future. Quite out of the question, you can see that."

Yes, I could see that, but I hadn't been able to see a solution, for I couldn't imagine Maurice leaving this house. He went on, "I'm going across the valley to Noreen's. Strange as you may think it, I consider her my wife, although officialdom says differently. If I hadn't been eaten up inside against fate and the blows it had dealt me, I would have done as she wished years ago and there would have been none of this. But there, life is very strange. The pattern is set at the beginning, and, do what you may, you are kept in the tracing lines. If it wasn't so, you wouldn't have come into our lives, Kate, and there wouldn't have been Logan for you."

"Mr. Maurice!" My tone was one of high indignation, mixed with amazement.

"Don't get on your dignity, Kate." He smiled quietly at me. "And this isn't one of my old devils speaking. I'm just stating what you know to be a fact."

"But how ... how did ... ?"

"Don't worry, don't worry, Kate. No one would have guessed. No one had the least suspicion. None but my henchman who was lying in the bracken the night the man molested you. He was still lying there when Logan intervened and he saw what followed. Oh, please. Oh, please, Kate, don't hang your head like that. There's nothing to be ashamed of."

"I'm not ashamed of it, Mr. Maurice."

"Then don't act as if you were, Kate. Remember, Weaver, bad as he was—kept a still tongue about it. And you must give me my due, I didn't taunt you with it, did I? Nor him, not even on the night of the show-down."

No, that was true enough. He had not mentioned it and he could have done. As Patterson said, Mr. Maurice had his points.

"You know"—he was smiling kindly at me—"if I had been in his place I would have gone ahead. For the fact that he had let himself go with you proved that it wasn't a surface feeling. Oh, I know my brother, Kate. He would rather crucify you than allow his feelings to divert him from the straight road. There couldn't be two people more opposite than Logan and I, that is why we could never pull together. But in my own defence I would say that people of my timbre are easier to live with. You will find his high principles trying at times, but you won't mind. . . ."

"Please, Mr. Maurice, please. There's no talk of anything like that."

"All right, Kate, all right. But there will be. When everything is cleared up there will be, you mark my words. . . . It's funny." He smiled wryly. "It only takes a matter of minutes to tie two people together, yet even in the most straightforward cases it takes weeks, even months, to untie them. You see, Noreen is answering the law by living openly with me. What more could they want? Apparently a signing of papers and an appearance at court. When? In their own good time. But eventually we'll be . . . as we were."

I hoped so from the bottom of my heart; but to change the conversation I said, "How is Miss Noreen?"

"She is very well, Kate. Oddly enough, she's better than I've seen her for years. In fact, I can say that she has grown up—if you know what I mean. I must tell you something." He leant towards me. And now I glimpsed a little of the playful side of the old Mr. Maurice as he said, "She's learning to type."

This brought a smile to my face, but I said, "Why not? Anyone can type."

"I hope so, Kate."

"Is it the lodge you're going to?"

"Yes, it's the lodge. I'll find it different." He glanced round about him, then looked towards the window. "There's no long view. But still, I've had a long view all my life. I, too, must grow up and look at the world that's close about me, I'm a very selfish individual, Kate."

I did not contradict him but said, "I feel that you'll be happier there somehow, and you'll work better."

"You mean that my work will improve?"

"I didn't say that."

"All right, we'll let it pass. But now Kate . . . I want to tell you why I asked you up here. It's simply this. I want you, in your own way, to pass on to Logan what I could never say in a letter. I want you to pass on to him what I've told you: that I'm going and he can come back whenever he likes. I know he will never come back as long as I am under this roof. And, you see, the old uns depend on him. I depended on him, but now I must learn to stand on my one good leg. But the old uns are different—the uncles, and Hollins, and Bennett. They can't be thrust aside, they can't be left to rot, and only he can see to them."

I did not speak. I realized that Maurice Rossiter was making sacrifices which would probably be the making of him. I said, "I will tell him, Mr. Maurice."

"There's something else, and this is very difficult to talk about. I have always accused him of being tight-fisted. All my life since my father died I have fought with him over money, and now I hear through his partner that he has made me an allowance and almost trebled what he allows me now. That won't have been easy for him. I can't write to him. I can't do anything about it. Will you, Kate . . . will you tell him . . . ?" His voice was thick now and trailed off

"I'll tell him," I said softly.

As I rose to leave he held out his hand and asked, "Would you come and see us sometime, or is it too much to ask?"

"I would only be too pleased, Mr. Maurice."

"I'll leave it to you then, Kate. Goodbye."

"Goodbye. Don't worry, everything will be all right."

"I hope so, Kate, I hope so. Thank you. Thank you for coming. You'll see the uncles before you leave?"

"Yes, of course."

"Goodbye, Kate."

"Goodbye, Mr. Maurice."

When I reached home my mother was in the sitting-room. She turned her face to me and smiled, saying, "Well, how did it go?"

"Very well," I said. "Very well."

I looked towards my father, who was sitting, his head on one side, waiting for me to relate my visit, and I said, "It's nearly the last episode, I'll give it to you later on."

He nodded and said, "Good enough, lass, good enough."

My mother, motioning her head towards the ceiling, now remarked, "He's up and in his clothes. By, it's taken it out of him, he's nothing but an outsize skeleton."

When I went into the bedroom and saw Logan sitting at the window I had to endorse my mother's description. He was nothing but an outsize skeleton.

"How do you feel?" I asked.

"Wobbly, very wobbly. It's surprising. You think you can walk a mile when you're in bed. Dear, dear, I've never felt so weak in my life."

I looked at his face, at the second scar, the one that reached now from the corner of his eye socket and went up over his brow and well towards the top of his scalp. The jagged line would pale a little more, I knew, but it would always be in evidence. The line running up from his lip to the corner of his nose, the result of Weaver's first attack on him, and then the line from his eye disap-

197

pearing into his hair, gave the impression that someone had tried to slice off that side of his face. I wanted to touch his cheek and say, "Oh, my dear." But instead I sat down at the side of the small hearth and, bending forward, I picked up a piece of wood and put it on the fire. And as I straightened up I said, "I've been up to the house."

"Oh?" I knew his face was turned towards me.

"Mr. Maurice sent for me."

He asked no question but sat in silence, stiff silence, and so I went on talking. And in my own words I gave him Mr. Maurice's message. I did not look at him during all the telling, but when I finished I turned towards him and found he was looking out of the window. He did not speak, and when I rose to my feet he made no effort to keep me in the room and I went out and down the stairs.

My parents were both in the kitchen, and I did not refer to anything that had transpired upstairs, nor yet could I begin the episode for my father, but I said, apropos of a question that had not risen in the house for the last few weeks, "If Bill hasn't got anybody yet I'll start again on Monday. I'll manage on half-time during the winter. I don't want to go into the town again—not yet, anyway."

"No, lass, of course not." My mother glanced at my father, and he, coming to my side, said, "Look, there's no need for you to take up at Bill's again if you don't feel like it; we can manage fine, there's nothing to stop us. We've done it afore."

"Thanks, Father," I said. "But if Bill's post is still open I'll continue there."

The post was still open and so I continued to work for Bill. And for quite a while I was a source of interest in the village. Bill said I was good for business, for people were always dropping in, having discovered they wanted paint or brushes or some such. When I was confronted with old newspapers and asked if this or that was true, what could I say? Was I looking forward to being called as a witness against Smithy and Connor? they asked. No, no, I wasn't. It was difficult to be evasive, in fact it was quite impossible. But I was most thankful for one thing. No one was shy in using Logan Rossiter's name, which meant that they hadn't an inkling of my true feelings.

10

"By, I do miss him," said my father. "The house isn't the same. Can't get used to the quietness. He had some good crack. What he didn't know about fishing wasn't worth learnin'. Aye, he was a nice bloke." He laid aside his book and looked towards my mother. She had a stocking in her hand again and for the first time for many weeks she was knitting, but she made no attempt to endorse his words, so he said to me, "Do you suppose he's there now?"

"Yes," I said, "he'd get there about tea-time."

"By, here one minute, Switzerland the next." My father shook his head. "It's unbelievable when you think about it, isn't it?"

"It would be," said my mother caustically, "if he had done it in a minute."

"You're so sharp, lass, you'll be cutting yourself . . . you know what I mean, don't you? I wonder if he'll write?" finished my father now.

"He'll write," said my mother. "He said he would and he will."

They talked like this for quite some time. It was a two-sided conversation and I wasn't drawn into it. They were my parents and they weren't blind. They knew how it was with me, but they pretended that they didn't, on the

199

principle that if you don't acknowledge a thing exists it can't hurt you. They were terrified of me being hurt again; in fact they felt I was in the process of being hurt. Mr. Logan Rossiter from Tor-Fret . . . and me? Well, things happened like that in books but not to their daughter. Not that she didn't deserve the best. Oh, yes, she was their daughter and the highest in the land wasn't good enough for her . . . in theory. But when it came down to actual practice, then their workaday souls were troubled. And mine was troubled, too.

Yesterday afternoon Logan had said goodbye. We were standing in this room alone and he had taken my hands in his and looking steadily at me he had said simply, "I'll be back, Kate, I'll be back." That was all.

What did it mean: "I'll be back." Of course he'd be back, but did it hold any special significance for me? Couldn't he have promised something, given me hope?

Last night, as I had lain thinking, my eyes dry and burning, I had clung to Maurice's explanation of his brother's character. He was so high principled he would crucify you, Maurice had said. Yet he could have said some word to me, some telling word, couldn't he? I asked myself. Just one word. Yet was he not, in his own eyes, still a married man? And in mine was he not still on a par with Arthur Boyle? No. Not any more. Not any more. . .

Then there was the business of the rebound. He might look live a living skeleton, his face might be scarred, but nevertheless this in no way detracted from his innate attractiveness. I spent the early hours of the night torturing myself with pictures of all the women he would meet. Slim girls dressed for winter sports. They appeared alluring creatures. Everybody appeared alluring except myself, for my body with its ample curves was not built for slacks, or tight jumpers.

My mother's voice broke in on my thoughts now, saying, "I shouldn't be surprised at seeing him back in a week or so."

This was meant to soothe me, and I thought to myself:

I should. He wouldn't be back in a week or so. Nor was he.

The first letter I received from him began, "My dear Kate." It told me of the journey, of the comfortable château high up on the mountainside. And in the line before the end, he said, "I miss you, Kate." But this was qualified, as he went on, "and your mother and father. I'll never be able to repay you all."

"What does he say?" asked my father. The letter was such that I could hand it to him and say, "Read for yourself." He read it, then read it out aloud to my mother, who was working at the sink. The only comment she made was with her eyebrows—she raised them high.

It was shortly after this that Patterson came to the house again with a request that I should go up and see the old gentlemen. They were rather lonely. So once again I started going up the hill to Tor-Fret. My first visit was deeply moving, for Mr. Stanley and Mr. Bernard held my hands and hovered over me as if I were someone who had been lost to them, someone whom they feared they would never see again. Hollings and Bennett too, their greetings were such they warmed me and made me feel wanted, especially that of Hollings, for he treated me with deference that endeared him to me. One thing I noticed immediately: they seemed all so much older. The twins seemed to have aged even more since the visit to our house. The only one who appeared the same as when I had last seen him was Mr. Stephen. This was probably due to the fact that he had not been present on that memorable night in the cellar.

So, as I said, I returned to Tor-Fret; weather permitting I visited them at least three times a week. A month passed, and during this time I had had three letters from Logan, nice letters, informative letters, letters that I could hand over to my mother and father, letters that left me cold inside, shivering at the bare prospect of the future.

Then one afternoon, as I got off the bus to go up the hill to the house, I saw two men in the bottom field. They were doing surveying of some sort, with long tapes and poles. Further up the road I met a short stubby man with a big head; he had his hands thrust deep in the pockets of his overcoat and was looking across the valley towards where the men were measuring. I said to him, "What are they doing down there?" and he turned to me and answered, "Eh? Oh, we're just seein' how many houses we could plant."

"Houses you could plant?" My voice sounded awe-stricken. "Who said you could build houses here?" I spoke now with a dignity, as if the land were mine.

"Well, that's what will happen when it's sold, an' it's going to be sold, isn't it? I've always had me ear to the ground an' that's put me where I am the-day. . . . Bradley's the name. An' what do they want to hang on to all this for, anyway, you tell me? What good is it to them, eh? And people living on top of each other like rabbits in the towns."

As I looked at this man I knew he wasn't worrying about people living on top of each other like rabbits. His concern would be how cheaply he would get the ground, and how dearly he could sell it again to a builder. I turned from him abruptly and hurried up to the house, to be greeted immediately by the old men who were definitely in a state of nerves. And this included Hollings, and did not exactly exclude Patterson. I found them all in the kitchen. Mr. Bradley had apparently paid a visit to the house and had startled them with his information.

It was Mr. Stanley who turned to me as if I had the power to wipe out their fears, saying, "It isn't true, is it, Kate? Logan wouldn't do this. He wouldn't sell the whole place, not without telling us?"

Before I could speak, Mr. Bernard, his head bobbing like a golliwog, spluttered, "Could, you know. Not entailed, no heirs, nothing. Own boss, own boss. Couldn't blame him."

"But he wouldn't." I looked around them. "He wouldn't do anything behind your backs."

"No." It was Hollings now speaking. "No, madam, I think as you say, he wouldn't do it behind our backs."

"Well, something's moving." Mr. Stanley was speaking again. "There's never smoke without fire. . . . What would we do?" The two brothers now looked at each other, these two men who had been born in this house, and then Mr. Bernard muttered, "Stephen, poor Stephen."

As I look from one to the other of these old men, and at this moment even Patterson came under this heading, for he seemed to have jumped over the boundary of middle age, I felt like a mother responsible to a number of children, and as such I went out of my way to soothe them, and I said, "I'll write to him now and post it on my way down."

"Do, do. Do that, Kate. Yes, you're a better hand at it than any of us." It was Mr. Stanley speaking again, and the others nodded eager agreement. "Yes, that's it. You write."

I left them and went into the room I still called my room, and, sitting down, I wrote to Logan. I cannot remember word for word what I said, but as I wrote I know I became angry, for by now I too felt that there was something afoot. Men didn't come measuring the land for houses unless they knew that that land was available, and not just a strip at the bottom of the road, but this house also, the home that meant so much to so many because it sheltered lives that were running to the end of their courses.

It was on a Tuesday when I posted the letter. I reckoned he would receive it by the Thursday and perhaps I would get a reply by the Saturday. So Friday seemed an empty day, a day of waiting when nothing would happen.

On the Friday morning I went down to Bill Arnold's and did my usual work. It was a nice morning, very cold, but with the sun shining, and when I left Bill's I had a reluctance to return straight home. What I really wanted was to do something to make the time pass quickly until tomorrow and the post arriving. So I went into Rodney's shop and bought some rolls and a cake. The rolls were hot and I broke a bit off one and ate it. And Rodney, seeing me do this, laughed and split another one open and, thickening it with butter, handed it to me. And then he said, "Would you like to come to a weddin', Kate?"

"Oh, Rodney, you are going to be married?"

"Aye, yes, I'm goin' to be married. The sooner the better I think now."

"I'd love to come, Rodney. When is it?"

"Well, not till Easter."

"I hope you'll be very happy, Rodney. You deserve to be."

"Thanks, Kate. And now you must come out of your shell and follow me lead."

"Yes, yes, I must, Rodney. I'll have to see about it."

He saw me to the door of the shop, and I was still smiling when I turned from him. But I had not gone many steps before the smile slid from my face. Why should the news of Rodney's coming marriage make me feel so unhappy? I was glad for him, really glad, but I was sorry for myself for I felt lost and lonely, and I told myself once again as I had done over the last few weeks, that I was a fool. A fool for a second time.

When I came on to the level of the fell path I saw my mother at the door and she waved to me and I waved back. She was enjoying the sunshine. Her face was bright and she looked happier than I had seen her for a long time. In the little hall she helped me off with my coat, and then she nodded towards the sitting-room. It was a motion of her head which she used when she was indicating that my father was up to something. So it was with the expectation of seeing my father and what he was up to that I opened the sitting-room door, and then I stood still.

Logan was standing with his back to the fire and he

was alone in the room. I closed the door behind me and leaned against it for a moment before I said, "I didn't expect . . . When did you come? . . . Why?"

He was smiling broadly, his eyes hard on my face, and it was quite some seconds before he spoke. "One thing at a time, Kate," he said. Then, "You didn't expect me, not after that stinker of a letter you sent me? Don't you think that was enough to catapult any man out of his complacency?" I could not answer, and he went on, "I arrived in Newcastle this morning, but as to why I've really come back, well, it will take a little time to explain that." He took a step nearer to me and held out his hand now, but I found that I couldn't move from the door. It was as if I was glued there. I ignored the outstretched hand and asked in a flat-sounding voice, "Are you selling up then?"

"Well, what do you think?"

I did not know what to make of this reply. I could gauge little from his tone, yet it seemed to confirm what had been in my mind since I saw the men measuring the ground, and so I blurted out in a high indignant voice, "You can't do it, you can't sell the place. If it was empty, yes, but not with all those old people there, and they depending on you. They'll rot in a nursing home. The uncles would die."

"You're very concerned for them, Kate, aren't you?"

His hands were hanging stiffly by his sides now, and as I continued to look at him I found myself being again consumed by anger. I had never known such a force. It became so overpowering that the perspiration began to run down my arms. I found I must not look at him any longer and I turned my face away as I said, "Yes, I'm concerned. Any ordinary person would be. I think it's terrible, scandalous. You talked about Mr. Maurice." He hadn't. "I think this is worse than anything he ever did. I'm sure he'd never have . . ."

He held up his hand and cut in quietly, "Say no more, Kate . . . until I tell you something. . . . Your letter was the first indication I had that I was going to sell Tor-Fret or an inch of the land."

I turned my face slowly towards him. My anger seeping away, I was left feeling drained, weak, and very foolish. My head drooped and I muttered, "I'm sorry, but ... but the men were there measuring, and they said ..."

"That man Bradley would say anything. It was he who was after the land before. Whoever set the rumour about, it didn't originate from me or anything I might have said. ... You think I'm the kind of man to throw aside my responsibilities, Kate?"

"No. No, I didn't ... I don't ... I'm sorry. But it was seeing the men there, and them actually measuring. And they had been up to the uncles and everybody was upset. ... I'm sorry."

Now I looked at him with eyes clear of anger and saw that here was The Big Fellow, or nearly so, he looked so much better. I said somewhat sheepishly now, "How are you feeling?"

"I just don't know at the moment, Kate." The corner of his mouth was lifted. "I'll be able to tell you better in a little while. You see, I was coming home on Monday in any case. I had intended to stay away until ... until my affairs were put in order. ..." I knew that he was not referring to his business because his partner was quite competent to carry on for the time being, but was referring to the proceedings which would annul his marriage. "I wanted to play fair but the strain has been so great that I ... I ..." He spread his hands towards me. "I just had to come and see you, tell you what I felt." He stopped speaking and moved nearer to me until there was only the breadth of a hand between us. "Have I got to tell you, Kate?"

Had he got to tell me? Use words when his eyes were pouring love into my body, sending my senses swirling, and filling the void of loneliness with trust and security and tenderness? Had he got to tell me?

I shook my head vigorously, I was gasping like a runner. I could not speak, not one word, and then we were enfolded again as on that night on the fell path. So close did he hold me, and so tightly did I press my arms about him that our bodies seemed to merge one into the other. When eventually my lips withdrew from his I dropped my head on to his shoulder, and with his mouth moving in my hair now he said, "Oh, Kate, I've been lonely for the sight of you. At times I felt like a boy again, crying for my mother. Does this sound silly? It may do. But, Kate, I need you in so many ways, as wife and . . . and mistress . . . and mother. Does this frighten you? Tell me, Kate, does this frighten you?"

I lifted my face and looked into his eyes as I said, "Nothing that you could demand of me could frighten me, Logan."

"Not even being mistress of the House of Men?"

"Not even that. Nor of the tongues that will surely wag. Nothing will frighten me as long as the master of Tor-Fret stays by my side."

"He'll stay by your side, Kate, never fear. He'll never want to leave your side, that will be the trouble. You don't know what you've taken on, my Kate. The Big Fellow of Tor-Fret is no angel, as indeed you know, and if I know anything about him I should say he's the kind of fellow whose demands will wear you down. What have you got to say to that?"

"So be it." I said. "So be it."

And my heart and every vein in my body echoed joyously: "So be it . . . so be it."

CATHERINE COOKSON NOVELS
in CORGI

THE PRICES SHOWN BELOW WERE CORRECT AT THE TIME OF GOING TO PRESS (DECEMBER '79).

☐ 10916 9	THE GIRL	£1.00
☐ 11202 X	THE TIDE OF LIFE	£1.25
☐ 10450 7	THE GAMBLING MAN	95p
☐ 11204 6	FANNY MCBRIDE	95p
☐ 11261 5	THE INVISIBLE CORD	£1.25
☐ 11087 6	THE MALLEN LITTER	£1.00
☐ 11086 8	THE MALLEN GIRL	£1.00
☐ 11085 X	THE MALLEN STREAK	£1.00
☐ 09894 9	ROONEY	80p
☐ 09596 6	PURE AS THE LILY	£1.25
☐ 09373 4	OUR KATE	95p
☐ 09318 1	FEATHERS IN THE FIRE	£1.00
☐ 11203 8	THE DWELLING PLACE	£1.25
☐ 11260 7	THE INVITATION	95p
☐ 11365 4	THE NICE BLOKE	£1.00
☐ 08849 8	THE GLASS VIRGIN	£1.00
☐ 11366 2	THE BLIND MILLER	£1.25
☐ 08653 3	THE MENAGERIE	85p
☐ 11367 0	COLOUR BLIND	£1.25
☐ 08561 8	THE UNBAITED TRAP	85p
☐ 11335 2	KATIE MULHOLLAND	£1.50
☐ 08493 X	THE LONG CORRIDOR	95p
☐ 08444 1	MAGGIE ROWAN	£1.00

All these books are available at your bookshop or newsagent, or can be ordered direct from the publisher. Just tick the titles you want and fill in the form below.